ViSIoNS

AND OTHER STORIES

VISIONS

AND OTHER STORIES

BY
MICHAEL FILLERUP

SIGNATURE BOOKS
SALT LAKE CITY
1990
· · · · ·

to Rebecca

"Family Plantation Day" first appeared in *Sunstone* 14 (April 1990): 26-35.

"The Renovation of Marsha Fletcher" first appeared in *Dialogue: A Journal of Mormon Thought* 16 (Summer 1983): 79-99.

"The Bowhunter" first appeared in *Dialogue: A Journal of Mormon Thought* 21 (Winter 1988): 151-68.

"A Game of Inches" first appeared in *Sunstone* 12 (Sept. 1988): 23-28.

"Hozhoogoo Nanina Doo" first appeared in *Dialogue: A Journal of Mormon Thought* 18 (Winter 1985): 153-82.

"Visions" first appeared in *Sunstone* 11 (May 1987): 12-19.

"The Orchard" first appeared in *New Times* 17 (8-14 Jan. 1986): 40-48.

Cover Photograph: John Snyder©

Cover Design: Randall Smith Associates

94   93   92   91   90   6   5   4   3   2   1

LIBRARY OF CONGRESS CATALOGING-IN-PUBLICATION DATA
Fillerup, Michael, 1953–
     Visions and other stories / Michael Fillerup.
       p. cm.
     ISBN 0–941214–91–5
     I. Title.
     PS3556.I429V57   1990
     813'.54–dc20   89–24175
                                                                    CIP

CONTENTS

Here

There

HERe

Family Plantation Day

. . . .

Last Saturday Floyd Fairbanks drove a rented John Deere tractor across the ward garden, through the picket fence, across Brother Guillermo's weed field, through another fence, across the dirt highway, and into the irrigation canal. We watched, cave-mouthed, shaking our heads and rubbing our eyes like cartoon caricatures. No one could believe it. "Floyd?" the rest of the ward whispered with facial spasms as the story circulated up and down the pews the next day, a step ahead of the sacrament. "Floyd *Fairbanks?*"

Why, Floyd was the rock, the pillar, the foundation of steel and concrete. Whenever the sign-up sheet went around for hospital visits or a day at the Bishop's Storehouse, Floyd's bold signature always topped the list. Sustaining vote? His big freckled paw was the first to go up. Big, handsome, affluent at thirty-five, he was a scholar (summa cum laude BYU; M.B.A. from Stanford), an athlete (all-state football, 1968-70), an Eagle Scout, a returned missionary. His beautiful wife could sing, dance, and decipher the complexities of an IBM interface. Tall, blond, blue-eyed, with her hair in a Sunday bun, she looked like Miss Sweden. Her cheese fondue was the best in the valley. She and Floyd lived in a four-bedroom house ten miles out of town. Did I say house? Hacienda. A jacuzzi in the master bathroom. They were the couple with the proverbial everything.

But "everything" makes us—you, me, the rank-and-file—pause,

look, and prod. It is a counter-doctrinal concept: just as no mortal is perfect, so no man or woman has "everything."

Floyd and Charlene Fairbanks had no children.

After ten years of trying, they had resigned themselves. Condolences were brushed aside with little homilies pilfered from the Richard Evans quote book: "Far worse things have happened to far better people . . . " True, true. After all, we're not talking death, dismemberment, starvation, torture in the Nicaraguan jungles. We're not, after all, talking hard-core tragedy. Pity fades fast. Plus it's hard to shed too many tears for someone who looks like a movie star and drives a cherry red Mercedes. These two-income families . . .

So what got into Floyd? Who knows? Not I. But saying this I feel a fib. The polygraph goes haywire. Mad jags. My nose grows an inch. My ears stretch and droop. You see, I notice things. I look, I observe. What else can you do during sacrament meeting when you're refereeing four kids? Actually, the children do very well. Janet has agreed to put Nancy Drew aside until after the sacrament. Katie likewise holds her coloring book and crayons in check. At five, Susan's behavior is still negotiable— Quiet Book, Etch-A-Sketch, and three sugarless mints if she makes it through the bread and water without leaving her seat. The boy, the three-year-old, I stuff with Cheerios and cheese squares, silently urging the deacons to put it into overdrive. Hustle buns, boys!

Jenene is there, of course, my alter-ego other-bookend, issuing silent first and second warnings that keep the kids in line, remarkably effective since instituting Lee Canter's Assertive Discipline for Parents. (She is my superior in execution; Dad's the soft touch, the marshmallow man.)

As the bread and water make the rounds, my eyes wander, take a brief bird flight from Gethsemane. Am I looking for foibles, cracks in the dike? Or simply trying to hasten the clock by becoming oblivious to it? Whatever, I look, I listen, I see and hear things I maybe ought not: the Bartlett boy, ten, a Blazer A, the way he scratches his teenage sister's back, up and down and all around—innocent affection, surely, but why the very adult expression on her face, that slow eye-closing ecstasy? Or Bruce Saunders, how he and Carolyn wage eye wars over who will drag the twins into the foyer this week. Or Sally Rogers, who just last month delivered number six in seven years without trying, whispering to Sister Simmons: "I can't *believe* it! I feel so stupid." (Sally, you of all people should know better! The doctor's wife!)

Or Floyd. Four or five years ago I'm talking about, when I was new to the ward and all I knew of Brother Fairbanks was a month of accumulated hearsay, a comment here, a brush encounter there. Not much in other words. But it took no Sherlock Holmes to infer the obvious: no kids. However, this is not the type of observation I'm referring to.

It was fast and testimony meeting. Bill Paxton had just blessed his twin girls – Bill the proud poppa holding up his two pop-eyed dittos. Later, Bishop Marler introduced a new couple, Brother and Sister Harmon from Bountiful. "And from what I understand," Bishop Marler said, "Bonnie is going to be a mother soon. February? Of course, in our ward, it's only news when one of our young brides *isn't* expecting!"

The hearty chuckles, the girlish titters. The pinched smiles and eyes of the elderly.

Floyd was on my left, his big block of a body hunched forward, head dipped like a buffalo's. Staring at his giant hands, tugging at the stingy red hairs around his knuckles, nodding, mumbling to himself. A dour look.

Not Charlene. In her colorful Easter dress, she looked positively euphoric, sunshine in her soul. I concluded the obvious: Charlene was basking in the light of future motherhood while Floyd, the father-to-be, was suffering premature withdrawal pangs: demotion to number two, forfeiting the final lock on his life, staggered sleep, scheduled sex – in fact, all bodily pleasures realigned to fit the whims of this mystery newcomer. The spontaneity that is the fuel of romance, kaput! A veteran Dad, I could empathize. My intentions were good when I leaned his way and whispered, "Is your wife expecting too?"

The tugging ceased. A smile moved across his lips like a zipper. He did not look at me; his eyes were on his hands. "Nope,"

· · · · ·

he said, shaking his pompadoured head. "We're one of the exceptions."

Gambled and lost! I tried to console him. It wasn't hard—or should not have been. Fatherhood. The stories I could tell! Why, our little Katie had had us up the night before with the twenty-four hour bug, coughing, crying, throwing up. Jenene and I were suffering the day-after consequences—rash rings around the eyes, the waterlogged look, the body aching everywhere. I felt like a punching bag. I leaned Floyd's way again and whispered the same pearls of wisdom Jenene's mother had once passed on to us after tiring of our six-month lamentation over "trying" to make a baby: "Enjoy it while you can."

Floyd began nodding again, moving his lips. The smile returned, this time for good, though a little sinister I thought but rationalized that orthodontia can sometimes determine a happy or sad countenance. Then he clutched a handful of reddish hair just above his wrist and ripped it from his skin. I felt a nudge on my other side. "Bread, Dad," Janet said, passing me the silver tray.

It takes no Sherlock Holmes.

I could empathize, yes, but only to a point, for I am a father, a parent, a partaker of the fullness so to speak. The married childless have no special programs in the church, no satellite broadcasts, no dinners or roadshows strictly for their kind. They occupy an unacknowledged limbo. And it is a state I sometimes covet. All parents occasionally do. Check: except for Bill Paxton.

I cannot imagine Bill prior to his kids. They cling to him like little marsupials. Bill is one of these new and improved fathers of the 1980s who plays the "greatest calling" of life admonition to the hilt; who is so infatuated with this adventure called parenthood that his family has become Siamese. In his household everything is a family undertaking: prayer and scripture study at 5:30 a.m., followed by a family jog around the block (the baby in a Gerrycarrier, bobbing along on Bill's back). Camping, hiking, church, meals, movies—everything is a family happening. Only their modesty rules out communal showers.

So when the stake president gave our ward the dubious assignment to "do something" with the two weedy acres behind the old Spanish branch, and Bishop Marler, espousing grand visions of fresh watermelon and tomatoes as big as basketballs to supplement summer feasts and fall fiestas, instructed the elders' quorum to plant a ward garden, it was no surprise when Bill suggested we make it a family event.

"Sure," he argued in his nasal twang, his Adam's apple bobbing enthusiastically. "A family affair. Wives, kids. They could help weed and plant–a great learning experience. With a picnic lunch after!"

By the time he'd finished he was talking homemade root beer and roto-tiller inservice for the Primary kids. Crew-cut hair bristling with excitement, electrified by the idea of it, he turned to me and Roy Brown, his faithful counselors, for support. We nodded, half-convinced of the efficacy of the project and thoroughly convinced that there would be no talking Bill out of it, so why oppose? Floyd gripped and released his thigh-thick neck. He exhaled slowly, deeply, conspicuously. Quorum secretary, he would not speak unless spoken to. Democratic Bill prompted him. "Floyd?"

"I don't know," he said, his shoulders rolling like a giant wave about to break. "I'd just as soon start early and get the job over with. Too many cooks in the kitchen, you know."

He argued impressively. Starting at sunup, we could till, plant, irrigate, and be out of there by noon. "Bring the wives and kids and we end up with a giant babysitting party."

Nodding, Bill thanked Floyd for his input. "Those were excellent points. . . . Dave? How do you feel?"

"Either way," I said. "I see pros and cons to both."

"Roy?"

Roy Brown shrugged. "Up to you, Bill."

Bill started in on the virtues of family togetherness and his homemade root beer. Floyd pointed out that with an "Elders Only" project we would finish early enough for the husbands to spend the entire afternoon with their families, to do as they pleased–"work or play!" But even in his subdued fervor, his blue eyes blazing, I detected a timbre of futility in Floyd's voice, as if he knew, from the outset, his vote would be registered but ig-nored. He was trying to kill the sacred cow.

Bill acknowledged Floyd's foresight and logic, offering the usual strokes, noting Floyd's diligence when involved in such projects, but the final verdict was family. Floyd lowered his head. Bill's bird-like hand lighted on Floyd's monstrous shoulder. "I know!" he said, finger up, the light clicking on. "We'll call it 'Family Plantation Day'!"

Only Floyd and Steve Tryon and his wife were present when we pulled up by the old Spanish Branch. So much for our seven sharp kickoff. Floyd, in a pea green jump suit, was waist deep in weeds, swinging his hoe like Goliath mowing down the flimsy ranks of Israel. Susan and Benjamin scrambled out of the station wagon and immediately lost themselves in the joys of desert dirt. (Our older two, Janet and Katie, had reached the age of sleep-overs and peer group preference. There went *our* Family Planta-tion Day.) In faded blue jeans and a pink t-shirt, leotard tight, Jenene muffled a yawn and groaned, reprimanding herself for watching a grade B late-night movie. I waved to Floyd who con-tinued hacking down the enemy.

Steve Tryon was genuflecting by the roto-tiller, yanking the cord, teasing the choke, trying everything short of consecrated oil and the laying on of hands to resurrect it from its winter coma. Bridgett Tryon was raking the vanquished into big green mounds as the cracked adobe visage of the Spanish Branch looked on like a peevish old patriarch. Every three or four rakes, Bridgett straightened up and pressed her hand to her lower back, wincing as if she'd just been stabbed there. I could barely make out the design on the front of her t-shirt: a stork with crossed saw and hammer underneath and "Under Construction" printed below that. I estimated three months.

Bridgett waved to Jenene who waved back.

"Duty calls," I said.

"Talk me out of it," Jenene said. "Please . . . "

I whistled the first two bars of "The World Has Need of Willing Men" and handed her a rake.

Steve Tryon gave a hopeful shout as the roto-tiller roared convincingly, stinking up the cool morning air with blue exhaust, but it shortly sputtered and died. Steve kicked the machine, then plopped down in the dirt, looking as if he'd just missed the winning free throw.

"Je-*ne*-ene!" Bridgett straightened and rubbed.

Jenene muttered sourly, "She plays it to the hilt." Smiling, she waved again and marched toward the weed mounds, mumbling and murmuring to herself. She was not in good spirits this morning, and not because of the movie or the prospects of sweating and grunting all day in the one hundred-plus heat. These might be her excuses, later, but I knew the real reason: last night she had asked me, once again, and I had refused.

"Have a good one, Jen," I said, without sarcasm.

She cast me an ambivalent glare. I grabbed a hoe and trudged towards Goliath.

Aside from a bit of bluish-gray lathering the peaks of the Superstitions, the sky was bare, stropped and shaved. Caught behind the minty froth, the sun was like a blind man trying to prod his way out. Once it did, it was going to be another scorcher. Sauna City. By noon we'd all be cornflakes. But for now, cast in cool translucence, compliments of a mild Sonoran southerly, the morning felt fresh, fertile, the dew on the weeds and crabgrass sparkling like diadems. Damp and cool, the shaded earth smelled aphrodisiac.

"Not much of a turnout," I said, joining Floyd.

He paused for a second. "Mormon time?" he grumbled, and resumed his steady hacking. Evidently he was in no better spirits than Jenene.

"Anything in particular you'd like me to do?" I asked.

"Grab a hoe."

He hadn't noticed I was holding one.

I raised my hoe like a weapon and struck the blade to the ground: the severed weeds released a juicy green scent. I took another swipe, another. Weeds were falling left and right.

"Deeper," Floyd grumbled. "You're cutting too shallow."

I should have known.

After what seemed like an hour of intense hacking and chopping, I looked up only to find that I had taken at best a bitsy baby bite out of the infinity of weeds in front of me. A glance at my wrist-watch revealed I had been at it all of ten minutes. I was further humiliated by the massive shadow of Floyd Fairbanks working relentlessly behind me, cutting a swatch twice as wide as mine, and twice as fast. Granted, the shadows had an enlarging effect, but still, the man's arms looked as thick as my thighs. They were swinging to and fro like a giant metronome, chop-chop-chop, never missing a beat. Watching, listening, sensing the stiff fever that was not sun-induced in my arms and shoulders and Floyd's shadow passing back and forth behind me like the Grim Reaper, suddenly I was feeling my age like thirty-nine stones stacked on my shoulders. I could literally feel myself sagging under the weight, growing hunchback.

A beep! beep! spared me from further self-scrutiny. It was Bill Paxton, pulling up in his old Chevy van. The side door rolled open and the Paxton tribe poured out—eight of them, including two sets of twins. They marched out to the field and immediately set to work, hoeing, digging, raking, like little foreordained angels. Becky stepped down from the van—blue-jeaned, freckled, smiling like a June bride though sideways she looked as if she'd swallowed a volleyball for breakfast. She waddled over to join Jenene and Bridgett.

Bill shook my hand vigorously, then offered his to Floyd with such good will and enthusiasm that even Goliath had to momentarily put aside his hoe and reciprocate. As if on cue, the sun broke through the clouds, igniting the weedy field. In seconds the morning turned from cool to warm as the gray shadows of the churchhouse darkened to a midnight pitch. Old Brother Guillermo stepped outside his stucco shack, visoring his eyes as he gazed at us through Coke bottle glasses, wondering what these gringos were up to now? He shook his silver-gray head and trudged back inside, the red chiles by the doorway glowing like petrified fire.

Alvin and Diane Lyon drove up in their Rambler station wagon. Before it had come to a halt, four towheads were leaping out, whooping and hollering like a war party as they charged towards the dirt mounds, brandishing plastic Ninja swords. More families followed. By nine the sun was high and hot, and the grounds teeming with activity–kids in Levis and t-shirts making mini-cities in the sand, the women raking up the last of the weeds the men, led by Floyd, the human propeller, had quickly finished off.

Ben Huber drove up with another roto-tiller–Ben the High Priest, come to add patriarchal ballast. "I thought I'd best make sure you got the job done right," he quipped to Bill. Our quorum president thanked him profusely.

Ben resuscitated the ward roto-tiller, then started up his own, his bullfrog belly jostling as he guided it smoothly up and down the weeded area, its twin blades (which to me looked like a pair of wickedly bent stars) slowly churning up the earth. Working the far side, Bill Paxton gripped the handles of the ward roto-tiller for dear life, his wiry arms shaking as if he were being electrocuted.

Some of the women had begun digging furrows and it looked as if, soon, we could begin planting seeds. The wonders of communal labor! The morning moisture was long gone and the shadows had shrunk to tight dark rings around the scrawny olive trees. Faces were reddening and underarms growing half-moons and full-moons of sweat. Floyd, I noticed, was working further and further away from the general cluster. Pausing to survey the scene, he looked like Brigham Young minus the beard–that same paunchy authority and lion look. Or another image: a feudal lord overseeing his estate. His eyes were on the ladies now. He licked his lips, lizard quick. Twice. Then lowered his blade into the dirt.

I looked across the field at Jenene, apparently in better spirits now, laughing amidst the other Levied ladies. Every time she bent over to rake, her bottom swelled like a denim valentine. When she straightened up, her hair, loosely bound in back with a barrette, reached down past her hips. The sun was selectively picking out the blond streaks. Snatching glimpses of her, I felt like Jacob laboring in the fields for Rachel. My thoughts went

. . . . .

11

back to those days of student poverty when I would sit in my 7:30 class, chin in hand, secretly inhaling the residue of Jenene's wonderful brackish smell—sniffing it like a cocaine addict, her sweet love smell propelling me through the day. As if she had been reading my thoughts, Jenene twisted her head just enough to look my way. I raised my hand and smiled, but she didn't smile back. She was still angry about last night.

Jenene and I married when I was twenty-four and she twenty. Following the normal course of things, obeying the first great commandment, two years later we were parents. I was juggling three jobs, working my way through law school—up at 4:00 a.m., home at midnight, the kid, the baby, a cry in the night, my wife a warm body to come home to after washing the janitorial grit from my hands. We lived a mile from campus in a battered trailer of corrugated metal. The front door had been cut from an old billboard. "Frank's Tavern" it read on the inside. When it worked, the swamp cooler shrieked like a harpy. The summer heat was hellfire—Satan's sweathouse. What little fat Jenene had accumulated melted off her like wax. One other child was born while we lived in that tin can. Like sardines. Wall-to-wall sleeping bags. Tough going, tears at times, but we made it okay.

Our other two, Susan and Benjamin, were born under more convenient circumstances. By then I had started my practice and we lived in a house with three bedrooms. For the first time, Jenene was delivered by her very own gynecologist instead of being treated like leftovers at the county hospital. Susan and Ben have, or will have, all the so called advantages—swimming lessons, piano lessons, violin lessons, Cabbage Patch dolls, a sweet sixteen Camaro, not to mention a full-time Dad. You might say they were born in innocence, free of canned hash and cockroaches, which is good in many ways but not so good in others. The older two know the value of a dollar. That sounds soap box, but you won't see Janet or Katie going around the house leaving lights on. But neither of them plays the violin either.

After our fourth child, Jenene and I decided enough was enough. (Yes, we had hoped—prayed—for a boy, but we would have stopped regardless.) Her parents and mine were letter-of-the-law Mormons, raised on the old school ethic, popping out a kid a year. Birth control was a no-no. Onan would be cursed. Fine. But the women paid for it. Following her seventh in nine years, Jenene's mother suffered a nervous breakdown. Valium Valley for her. My mother–I recall all too vividly those torturous Sabbath mornings ("Sunday Bloody Sunday" she called them). My father the bishop was up and gone before sunrise, leaving the get-ready gauntlet to Mom: brushing hair, washing faces, socks on, shoes on, dresses and coats on, chasing around the kitchen like a short-order cook. Zipping up her dress as she herded the eight of us snarling, quarreling towheads ("Jeff hit me!" "Shut up, Jack!" "You two quit fighting or I'll–") out the door and into the Renault Dauphine. Squeezing us in–crunch, slam! One for the Guiness Book: nine in a Renault. Two in diapers. Always. Filthy. The stench. Mom singing hymns to herself, trying to block out the noise, to keep her cool inside a car that reverberated like a zoo: chirp, shriek, growl, hiss, grunt, snort. Hyena highs. The Sunday nuthouse. Honey in the hair, bubble gum on the seats.

"Wait till your father gets home . . . just you wait . . . " Pale threats. He rarely did before bedtime. By then we, Sunday's hellions, were asleep. Peace . . . peace in the house. Silence so golden. Why disturb it with delayed discipline? Relax, enjoy . . . while you can. Once I was old enough to drive, my mother stayed home Sundays and made it a true day of rest. The bishop's wife! The talk, the gossip. But after the early morning havoc, as soon as the car pulled out of the driveway, she would pull down the blinds and collapse on her bed. From that time on, I think she half-lived for Sunday mornings, when the house was empty and we were gone. Not that she didn't love us in a motherly way; she just needed some time to herself. To recuperate. To heal.

More and more I appreciate what she went through, having stumbled a few feet in her moccasins. Jenene too. But history, we had decided long ago, was not going to repeat itself. The mother's health, the official new-and-improved statement read, physically *and* mentally, was paramount. Our enlightened age!

Four was our limit. We had both agreed.

But the night Connie Walker delivered her fifth Jenene couldn't sleep. Three massages did not help, or a double-dose of codeine-coated cough syrup. Which was partly why, once again, last night, we were up at an untimely hour talking out an old gripe. She had been pushing for something permanent. A once and for all.

"Okay, but how–or better, by whom? Me or you?"

She had logic, reason, and the physician's advice on her side. For me, it's a ten-minute operation in the doctor's office, a quick snip, sixty-five bucks, 99.9 percent reliable. For Jenene? Major surgery. General anesthesia. Five hundred bucks minimum. Blue Cross/Blue Shield won't touch preventatives.

Reason, logic, the physician's advice. It is only semi-settled. The old guilt stirs. Like an amputee who feels the missing limb almost to the point of touching it; sometimes she wakes up at night, she says, and her belly feels so empty, she will get out of bed, trundle into the kitchen, and forage through the refrigerator for apples, jello pudding, leftover lasagna, anything to fill up the void.

I try, futilely, to console her, reminding her of the long summer nights strollering Susan around and around the block until she finally dozed off, and the midnight feedings and cryings and runny noses and itchy eyes, dropping from exhaustion on the living room floor, or lying by the crib all night holding a pacifier in Katie's mouth. Tawdry days, sexless nights. And the waiting and waiting and waiting–with the little hugs and kisses and mini-achievements and miracles stringing you along– until they can walk, talk, wipe themselves. And don't forget the female fringies: bloated brown nipples, bulging blue in the ankles and calves, splattered veins, crab nebulas, pink squiggles like ringworm in the hips and backs of the thighs. That, too, is a factor.

And lately things had been so nice, so conveniently middle class. For the first time since our honeymoon we had been able to go out weekly to dinner and a movie or sneak away to the Grand Canyon for a weekend or take a class together. Give a little to ourselves, each other–was that so terrible?

Then she would start crying. From the beginning we had agreed we would never limit the size of our family just so we could buy a boat, a VCR, a condo in Fountain Hills.

"It isn't fair," she would say.

I wouldn't argue.

"Will you get one?" she asked again last night.

During the silence, her hand softly stroked my chest. Whispering in her little girl's voice I can't refuse: "Please?"

"No."

I can't tell her why because I'm not sure myself. It's not fear that the doctor will miss-snip and permanently impair me. Nor do I have any plans to start a new family or add to my present one. Four is plenty. Quadruple the national average. In my mind, I visualize her logic so graphically: in one corner, the doctor putting away his scissors, patting me on the back, and sending me merrily on my way; in the other, Jenene's bare midriff, the masked surgeon slicing her open like a fish. They say the tube is hair thin or thinner. They tie it in a knot, literally. Fine tweezer, microscopic work.

"Will you think about it?" she asked.

"I do. All the time."

"Well, think harder!" she snarled and wriggled over to the far side of the bed.

George Huber had finished roto-tillering. He picked up the machine like a toy and dropped it a few feet from me. "That'll do 'er," he said in a Hoss Cartwright voice. He exhaled a deep breath and wiped a red kerchief across his sweaty forehead, like a true blue farmer. Bill Paxton trotted over, grabbed George by the hand, and pumped it half a dozen times, thanking him over and over. George shrugged off the kudos. He forked his fingers through his crew-cut hair, bits of sweat spitting from the tips. He pinched Bill's skinny biceps. "We gotta put some meat on this boy!" – winking at me – "So we can get more work out of him!" Then George drew Bill in close and whispered – counsel from the patriarch – "When I first went into the service, I was skinnier 'n a rail, just like you. But I filled right out. Don't worry." George hoisted the roto-tiller to hip-level and started towards his pick-up. "You'll take to seed," he hollered over-shoulder, "you'll take to seed." Bill whispered affectionately. "Old George . . . "

By noon we were digging furrows, the women gravitating to the left and the men to the right, not by priesthood prescription or pre-conceived plan but some sub-cultural magnetism I found interesting (refreshing?) in a liberated, unisex age. It had occurred so naturally and spontaneously that I really hadn't noticed until now. The men were working at graduated speeds: lanky Roy Brown moving the soil quickly and effortlessly while spider-armed Bill pecked at it henyard style. Steve Tryon hoed along at a steady pace. Alvin Lyon was talking Sun Devil football, could they knock off the Trojans again next fall?

"The Trojans?" Steve said. "Piece a cake. They're jinxed out here."

Roy Brown, who worked cat burglar hours running a sweeper around Phoenix parking lots, was complaining about Gloria again. "Always moaning and groaning–'I'm so tired, I'm so tired.'" Spreading his legs and protruding his gut, walking duck-footed along the furrow. "Like *I'm* not, you know? I get home at five a.m. I'm tiiii-red! I'm huuun-greee, if you know what I mean."

"Two in two years." Alvin Lyon shook his blond head. "No willpower, Roy."

Gloria pregnant? Again? I looked across the furrows at Sister Brown, still slender, elastic, twentyish. Next to her was Christy Tanner, young but burgeoning, her arms sagging like a grandmother's. Beside her, methodically hoeing away, was Becky Paxton, the broomstick that swallowed the volleyball. Then Bridgett Tryon, Diane Lyon, and Judy Stapley with a papoose on her back. Working side by side, they looked like figures in one of those conception-to-birth charts, a scrambled version you had to re-arrange in proper sequence, with Gloria Brown at one extreme, Becky Paxton, ready to deliver, and Bridgett Tryon some-where midway.

And then there was Jenene. Where did she fit into the ma-ternity line-up? At the very beginning, of course, in the "pre"-position, but not really. Something about her carriage excluded her from the chart. She was taking a breather now, straddling a furrow, hands on her hips, looking moderately bored, somewhat tired, and very attractive.

I don't actually believe the law school grind aged me faster than bearing four kids has Jenene–she just hides it better. Plus I am four years older, prematurely gray. At thirty-nine, things are happening to me now I never would have fathomed ten or even five years ago. Parts are beginning to wear out. My ignition's bad. I sometimes run out of gas before the finish line.

Jenene is just the opposite. At thirty-five she is getting her second wind. Somehow she has matured without really aging. People can't believe she has a thirteen-year-old daughter. She could easily model swimwear. Of course, that is the romantic in me talking. In the everyday trudge and grudge of life, the familiar becomes commonplace.

But now, watching her shapely figure amidst the expecting mothers, I was seeing her through the eyes of an everyday observer. Even in blue jeans, digging furrows, sweating in the trenches–what was it? Not only her figure and the wonderful little wobbles that accompanied it, but, too, the effortlessness with which she moved about, so unlike the baby-burdened ladies who seemed to trudge around like Atlas, with the planet strapped to their bellies instead of their backs; that, or with diapered toddlers clinging to their jeans, dragging them around like a ball and chain. All of them–even Becky Paxton, Sister Sunshine–were lagging in the heat.

Jenene? Her hair had tumbled free in back. A few loose strands were sloping across her eyes. With a quick flick of her head, she tossed them aside. There was something telling in that gesture, something I had perhaps been sensing for some time but had been unable to pinpoint. Or had been trying to ignore. At that moment she looked so . . . single, so free.

"How about you, Dave?"

Roy Brown, drawing me into the conversation. "When are you getting back into the race?"

"Me?" I said, without thinking, "I'm sterile."

Roy and Alvin and Steve and Bill all laughed. Then I

remembered Floyd. I looked around to see if he was in earshot. Maybe: he was working solo about fifty feet away. If he *had* heard, he wasn't letting on. Nose to the grindstone, shoulder to the wheel. Sweat was dripping steadily off the tip of his nose.

If nothing else, the kids were having a ball. Several little troopers in He-Man or Dallas Cowboy t-shirts had gathered around the big Igloo jug with paper cups. There was a good-sized mud puddle under the spout where it extended beyond the picnic table and the kids – my Benjamin included – were walking around in it barefoot. The Larson's baby girl was sleeping in a portable bassinet while the Lyon twins were wrestling like Jacob and Esau. My Susan had just re-possessed the Hot Wheels from the Aker boy and was pedaling hellfire along the irrigation ditch. Third-born, she had learned early about squatter's rights. She could be possessive, even pushy, but generally she was the cuddly one in our family. When I visit her classroom at school, she comes right up and takes me by the hand, showing me around. She likes that – touching, contact. At night, after her bedtime story, she asks in her meek, heart-breaking voice, "Dad, will you lay down with me for a minute?" If I say no, she kicks, screams, thrashes. My other daughters will become career women. But Susan, when I ask what she wants to be when she grows up, a lawyer maybe, like Dad? she shakes her head soberly.

"Oh? What then?"

"I want to stay home."

"And be a mommy?"

"Uh-huh."

"Like your mom?"

Nodding vigorously (honor in that). "Un-huh."

We – Jenene – must be doing something right.

By now Floyd was out in Nether Land, totally alone, working at a torrid pace. I felt ten degrees hotter just watching him. His furrows ran in perfect, parallel lines all the way to Brother Guillermo's picket fence. I wondered how much further he would go. In his zeal to finish ASAP, would he inadvertently hop the fence (or bash backwards right through it) and begin working his way across Brother Guillermo's weed field and into the sea of alfalfa beyond? No, he had stopped, thank goodness, and was marching back towards us, hoe on his shoulder like a triumphant but worn-out soldier.

It was half-past twelve and we–the men–had just begun clearing out the irrigation ditch. The women were working in pairs, one good sister poking holes in the soil with the rounded end of a hoe, the other squatting down or bending over to drop a few seeds in. Scott Larson, a latecomer, quickly abandoned the irrigation ditch to join his wife, Denise. Together they were showing their two-year-old the finer points of farming: "First you make a little hole in the ground like this . . . then you put two little pink seeds in the hole. . . . " A wonderful learning experience, no doubt, but slow going. As I looked at the acre-and-a-half of furrows, a giant washboard waiting to be planted, and the irrigation ditch only halfway cleared, I wondered if we'd ever finish. When I told Bill this parental instruction was all good and fine, but it was sure dragging things out, he laughed.

Floyd didn't, however. Joining us from the Outer Limits, he looked at me with hopeful eyes, as if he had just found a lost friend. I was touched in an odd way. When his mouth opened, I waited expectantly, as those ancient elders must have when Zaccharias finally broke his silence. But no words came out. He bowed his head and, muttering to himself, walked off.

"Floyd!" I called after him. "What is it?"

"Nothing," he said, shaking his bison head. "Everything's just fine. Cozy fine." He picked up a shovel and buried it deep in the ditch.

The sun hadn't let up a bit. Bridgett Tryon's face was red, swollen, edemic; any second it was going to explode. Shirts and blouses were soaked. Sweaty bangs were plastered to scorched foreheads. The steady, syncopated chink-chink-chinking of shovels was slavishly symphonic.

I looked over at Jenene, who was wrestling a stalk of milkweed, tugging and pulling and twisting and pulling some more until it finally gave and sent her flying back on her rear. As she got up and dusted herself off, my eye caught hers. I smiled and this time she smiled back. The Arizona heat can melt any iceberg.

She even winked—a truce? As she bent over to attack another milkweed, I admired the Levied flex, like a well-shaped peach. Then I noticed someone else was watching, several feet down the ditch, in between shovelfuls. I told myself to take it as a compliment—which it was, after all—but I was glad when Becky Paxton announced that the root beer was ready, come and get it! and Floyd Fairbanks finally put down his shovel and began marching towards the picnic area with the rest of us.

I let Jenene go ahead to take care of the food while I joined the general roundup. Spotting me, Benjamin raced over and wrapped his arms around my thighs, burying his head in my crotch.

"Hey, Superstar!" I said, hoisting him on my hip.

"Lunch, Dad. Go get lunch." He knew the score.

"Okay, we get lunch, Tarzan. Where's Sooz?"

"Ober dare," he said, pointing with his chin.

"How about Mom?"

"Dare."

I toted Benjamin to a scraggly patch of grass where Jenene and Susan were arranging our lunch on a checkered quilt. Other families had done likewise until the grounds looked like a vast quilt of quilts. Ours was right between the Paxtons' and the Larsons'. Floyd, I noted uncomfortably, had pitched his long body directly behind us. No quilt or blanket, he was stretched out sideways, like a sultan on the sand.

Roy Brown said the blessing and instantly the sultry air was rippling with the sounds of cellophane and aluminum foil. Fathers fetched root beer for their families while mothers dished out potato salad. Kids with root beer mustaches sat on blankets clutching fried chicken legs or peanut butter sandwiches, depending on the family fare. I soon found myself caught in a cross-conversation between the Larsons and the Paxtons. Scott was telling Bill and Becky about the Grand Canyon, a tough hike to the bottom. "It'll take you all day."

"And with your kids . . . " Denise shook her head skeptically.

"You're taking your kids?" Scott's face looked dirgeful.

Bill, savoring his root beer like fine wine, shrugged. "It'll be a good growing experience."

"Growing what?" I said. "Blisters, ulcers?"

Everyone nearby laughed—even Floyd. He too had joined our little circle. Brother Guillermo shuffled outside, visoring his eyes, his cracked brown face a miniature of the old adobe churchhouse behind us. Becky Paxton jumped up and signaled him over: "Have some root beer!" Scott Larson, who had served a mission in Ecuador, translated into Spanish. Brother Guillermo just smiled, his mouth hanging crookedly, a broken hinge. Becky dipped a cup into the big stainless steel pot and rushed it over to him.

Floyd had not counted on any lunchtime miracles. He'd brought enough food to feed the five thousand. He had already finished one ham and cheese on rye and was starting on another. Each was neatly packed in a square Tupperware container, custom-made for sandwiches. He also had a bowl-shaped container with a hearty serving of potato salad and a large cube-shaped one that protected a thick wedge of chocolate cake. Jenene looked over at Floyd and smiled. "Where's Charlene?"

"Working." His mouth opened like a pit as he bit into sandwich number two.

"On Saturday?"

Chewing, he nodded. The sun had burned a red stripe on the back of his neck and an arrowhead down the front of his chest. "Somebody's got to pay the rent!"

Jenene laughed at the hackneyed joke. So did Floyd. She fingered the loose hairs from her face and gave her head a tell-tale toss.

I was, for no good reason, jealous.

"More chicken, Sooz?" I said, holding up a drumstick. Grease-streaked cheeks bulging, she nodded. Her gut was as big as her heart. I gave Jenene a little nudge. "More chicken?"

"Sure," she said, and rejoined our circle.

"How you doing there, Ben?" I said. Ben held up his half-eaten drumstick and nodded approvingly.

By 2:00 p.m. the mothers were folding up blankets and wiping

· · · · ·

little faces while the men—most of them—sauntered back to the fields. I stayed behind—ostensibly to help Jenene fold up the quilt and repack the ice chest. Floyd was still eating.

Becky Paxton stood nearby, admiring her husband's valiant return to the furrows. "Bill drank too much root beer," she said maternally. "I hope he's all right."

Jenene smiled. Floyd stood up gruffly, dusted off his rear, and headed out, his body making Lilliputians of the kids as he marched through their play area. Jenene turned to me. "Did you hear that? Bill gets sick if he eats too much."

I said "Oh?" but I really wasn't listening. I was watching Floyd, his massive body dwarfing even the men. I shut the lid on the ice chest. "You win," I said.

"Win?"

"Last night," I said and walked off to join the other men, feeling very peculiar down there, as if it had fallen asleep and would never wake up again.

Rejuvenated by Bill's homemade spirits, we worked double time. In an hour the irrigation ditch was cleared and water was coursing through it. The men were hoeing little mounds in which the women, following closely behind, planted cantaloupe seeds.

I had had enough farming for one day. My hands were blistered raw and my body felt deep fried. My heart was not in it, or my mind. I gazed enviously at the children—wading knee-deep in the irrigation ditch. Benjamin, a giant among the three-year-olds, had stripped down to his underwear. Watching him splashing in the water, I was moved in a way that parents, in rare ruminating moments, when they are not diapering or cooking or obsessed with the stock market or paying the electric bill, sometimes are—a difficult feeling to describe to those who have not experienced it firsthand. Vestigial? Atavistic? The mirror in reverse? Whatever, I saw myself at three years, a little blond boy discovering the secrets of sand, speech, bowel movements; then Ben in my shoes thirty years from now, hoe in hand, a young man looking at his little boy, thinking what I am thinking, feeling as I now feel, and so on and so on. Then I remembered something that had happened years ago in Sunday school class.

Harry Goulding was the teacher—*Brother* Goulding, the Pan Am pilot, perpetually tugging at his tie, clawing his slicked-back hair: "All right, who can tell me what infinity means?"

Bruce Williams, my second-cousin, the class cut-up: "The Boy Scout manual!"

We kids all laughed, of course. Oh, that Bruce! Always so full of it! But this time Bruce wasn't laughing. He was glaring at us, his bushy brows leaping all over his forehead. We were the clowns, his expression said. What's wrong with you people?

"Oh, okay," Brother Goulding said, folding his arms, nodding, waiting for the punch line, the pie in his face again. "And would you like to elaborate on that, Brother Williams?"

"The Boy Scout manual. There's a picture on the cover of a Boy Scout holding a Boy Scout manual with a picture of a Boy Scout holding a Boy Scout manual. . . . "

Why that suddenly impressed me I wasn't sure. But now I was drifting further back, a three-year-old again, sitting in the front row at sacrament meeting, my father the bishop on the stand. My eyes were glued to the chapel floor, watching an army of ants swarm the fuzzy green carcass of a caterpillar and drag it millimeter by millimeter across the linoleum floor. I watched from the opening hymn to the closing prayer: in that time, the ants dragged it half a foot.

But there was more: the sun glaring down on the dolphin-sleekness of my bride, gliding through the blue waters of Torrey Pines; hotel drapes scalloped by the autumn breeze, the smell of rain on pavement as I unwrapped the wrap-around dress, seeing in the flesh, stroking for the first time those little twin mammals with the protruding eyes. Late nights in the loft. Midnight massage. Lightning flash on naked thighs. Drowsy sunshine. Leopard stretch. The gut wrench down-on-all-fours head-over-the-toilet vomit all. City nights. Bleeding neon. Little hairy head squeezing out between bent legs like a carnival freak show. Groans. Giggles. Guffaws. Christmas lights. More wrappings and unwrappings. Soft mornings. Symbiotic warmth.

"Hey, Peterson! You trying to grow something over there?"

Floyd. Goliath. Mr. Clean Jeans.

"Yeah," I said, turning his way. "Truth."

"What?"

"Truth!" I said. "I'm growing truth!" Then I gave my head a shake, spraying sweat everywhere. My answer meant nothing. It was just a silly word, the first that had popped into my head.

Floyd shook his head and worked on. I was a hard case, his tumescent lips were muttering, or a lost case. Something.

What happened next was strange. Jenene, bending over, was moving slowly backwards along a furrow, planting corn seeds. Floyd, also bent forward, hoeing, was moving backwards in the opposite direction. I could have said something—"Jenene! Floyd! Red Alert! May Day!"—anything to prevent the inevitable rear-end collision. But I was curious to see the outcome. When their two backsides smacked like an oversized kiss, it was pure slapstick. Jenene whirled around, obviously flustered but trying to hide it. "Floyd," she said, very businesslike, as if nothing had happened, "aren't you done with that row yet?"

Floyd's response was less amicable. He remained bent over, like a paralyzed hunchback, and threw an arm backwards, pointing roughly in the direction of Roy Brown. "Down *there*!" he barked.

"I already planted there," Jenene said. "Besides, I could do that in two minutes."

"Then don't do it!" Floyd growled. "Anything you can do in two minutes isn't worth doing."

"Don't worry, I won't! You can do it yourself. You can do the whole stupid row yourself for all I care!"

Floyd stood erect, hands on hips. The last straw. He said something and Jenene said something back. Soon they were going at it like husband and wife, like two lovers. They weren't exactly yelling and screaming, but it was a firm, frank exchange, a very private argument that abruptly ended when Bill Paxton's nasal falsetto butted in from across the field: "Floyd! Hey, Floyd!"

Floyd kicked his hoe aside. "Now what does *he* want?"

Bill trotted eagerly towards Floyd, who was waiting for him like a gunslinger at a showdown.

"Floyd," Bill said, out of breath, "do you think you could

run the tractor over the west side? Since we're here and we've got the equipment, we may as well . . . "

Floyd didn't answer. He shouldered past Bill and mounted the John Deere. It roared consumptively as he shoved the throttle into gear. Slowly, like a harnessed beast, it began crawling across the field, bits of gas and dust spitting out of the engine as it gathered momentum, its powerful treads leaving behind ice tray indentations as it advanced towards the west end. I can't say which face was more intimidating, the tiger-toothed grill of the tractor or the stone-cold look of Floyd as he expertly maneuvered the vehicle. He made one complete circle, then a smaller circle inside it, and another inside that, gradually moving towards the center.

With the mounds and furrows planted and water from the ditch irrigating them, the other workers had dropped their hoes and shovels and had clustered around the Igloo jug, sipping ice water and root beer as they watched Floyd do his thing. I watched, too, as I walked over to join the group.

Denise Larson was remarking on the wonders of technology while Roy Brown and Scott argued the Yankees and the Dodgers. Alvin Lyon said something and everyone laughed, myself included, though I had no idea what we were laughing about because my eyes and thoughts were still on Floyd.

He had already plowed the area once and was now spiraling in towards the bullseye for a second time. He was also doing strange things with the stick – shoving it forward, yanking it back, slapping it to one side, then the other. When he plowed across the center patch and made another wide, sweeping turn, as if he were going to go in for a third run, Steve Tryon quietly set down his paper cup and walked out to meet him. He waved his hands back and forth, then sliced his hand across his throat. Enough was enough.

Apparently Floyd didn't agree. Instead of turning back in, he drove the John Deere straight across the field and on through Brother Guillermo's picket fence. The splintered pieces went flying like a house of cards. That's when the others lowered their cups and watched, shaking their heads and rubbing their eyes, thinking, hoping, it was some kind of joke, a prank, a mirage. When Floyd plowed across Brother Guillermo's backyard, the old man ran outside shaking his fist and screaming in Spanish. We all tossed our Dixie cups aside and went running after Brother Fairbanks.

It was twenty minutes—a mile later—before we finally caught up with him. The John Deere had made a crash landing, head-first, into the irrigation canal, its grilled face sinking slowly into the muddy bottom. Floyd sat stoically in the driver's seat like a valiant captain going down with his ship. We all gathered along the upper bank and watched.

"What's he saying?" Jenene whispered. The sudden pressure of her hand on my arm seemed an intrusion, a violation of something I didn't comprehend.

"I don't know," I said, which was basically true. Floyd was very calmly addressing the algae-colored water in jumbled phrases that made no sense at all: "Probably won't get out of bed at all . . . nobody knows because it's under the rocks . . . I'm not going to finish till the paperwork . . . "

Someone—Alvin Lyon, I think—said it must be the heat, but Floyd rambled on a good five minutes before calmly turning towards us and, directing our attention to the flock of gray storm clouds that had appeared out of nowhere, said, "We'd better hurry up and finish planting before it rains."

Jenene and I didn't say anything about Floyd the rest of the afternoon. In fact, I didn't say much period. I must have been acting a little morose because around 6:00 that evening Jenene finally asked what was eating me. When I said, "Nothing," she said, "Well, something's eating me, and I'd rather be the eater, not the eaten. So go put on your shoes."

We went to Cafe Casino for dinner and then to a movie. I don't remember the film, but during it I must have experienced a mood shift. I left Floyd talking to himself as the John Deere sank into the quagmire, and put my arm around Jenene, writing little love notes on her shoulder with my finger. When we got home, I took a quick shower, then laid out my suit and shoes for church the next morning while Jenene prepared for bed. There was something I wanted to tell her, but I wasn't sure what; something I could not explain in good lawyer's logic, and even if I could, it wouldn't have come out right. So I got into bed, thinking to myself another time, when I had my facts straight, when my mind was right.

Jenene and I prefer the mornings and afternoons. At night we are usually too tired. So it took her by surprise when I began making overtures. She tried to laugh it off at first, but soon I was pressing her with an urgency that startled both of us. Gradually she warmed up, softening for several minutes before withdrawing with an abrupt, near comical, "Excuse me," and groped into the bathroom. The light went on. By the time her puzzled face popped out asking if I'd seen her diaphragm, I was standing in the doorway, clutching her arm, pulling her out, down, onto the floor.

The Renovation of
Marsha Fletcher

. . . .

Marsha crumpled the letter into a ball and hurled it across the living room. It caromed off the TV screen and rolled a few feet before settling in the middle of the carpet. Once again she inserted her fingers under the waistband of her jeans and began rubbing, very lightly, as much as she dared, her vanishing abdomen.

"Damn these stitches!" she complained, hoping Robert would hear. It was Saturday, and he'd just finished his mid-morning shower. In their twenty-nine years of marriage, he'd rarely showered, let alone shaved, on Saturday morning. He always waited until late afternoon, just before taking Marsha out to dinner, or Sunday morning before church. For the past six weeks (Marsha had been keeping tabs), he'd showered and shaved every Saturday morning and right around noon had left the house, always with a valid excuse: three times to work overtime, twice to attend the San Diego State game (he'd even shown her his ticket), and once to get a tooth capped (Dr. Bunzel had verified the appointment). Today he was working overtime again.

The doorbell rang.

"Bob!" Marsha shouted down the hall. "Could you get that?" Her husband's electric razor droned monotonously.

Marsha managed to rise using the arm-rest and walked to the front door, limping like an injured athlete. She opened the door and wasn't particularly surprised to see a Mexican standing before

. . . . .

her. This close to the border, she saw a lot of immigrants passing through. Generally they wanted a couple of dollars or a good meal and were willing to work. Although Marsha pitied them (she knew what it was like to go without), she'd always distrusted them, convinced they were the catalyst for San Diego's social problems.

This one was about seventeen, with a mop of thick black hair covering his ears and forehead. His bronze skin, unblemished, shone as if it had been lacquered. He was wearing a baggy white shirt and dingy white pants held up by a piece of twine knotted around his trim waist. His shoulders were broad and his forearms well muscled.

"*No trabajo*," Marsha said automatically.

"*Nada?*"

"*No. Nada.*"

He forced a smile. Marsha noticed that his front teeth were dark and jagged, rotting away. They all looked pathetic with their smudged faces and rotting teeth, but he was so young. He turned quickly and began trudging up the long driveway to the road at the top of the hill.

"Sorry!" Marsha called out after him. "*Lo siento!*"

He didn't seem to hear. Marsha closed the door and returned to the sofa.

Robert's electric razor droned on.

Marsha picked up the pen and pad of paper lying on the arm-rest. Letter writing was about the only thing she'd been permitted to do since her last operation. It was her third day home, and during that time not once had she ventured beyond the oleanders that fenced off their lot from the rest of the neighborhood.

It annoyed her, being cooped up indoors. When her children were growing up, she'd always driven them here and there—to ball games, music lessons, scout meetings, church socials. Now she liked to take long drives alone to the beach. "My therapy," she told Robert, half-jokingly. She loved the winding drive through Via de Dios Canyon and the smell of the salt air. It worked on her like a balm miles before the Pacific came into view. And she loved the sea: from a distance, a vast, silken gown fringed with white lace; up close, a mystery.

She preferred the beach in winter, when the hot dog stands were boarded up and the waters deserted except for a few die-hard surfers. She loved the changing winter moods—sunny skies over blue-green waters one day, a thick fog painting it melancholy gray the next. She loved the relentless hammering of the surf: all day and night the waves rising and crashing down upon the shore, instants of thunder fading into silence, over and over and over.

Marsha stared at the blank pad of paper and then at the row of photographs on the TV. Five individual portraits, her three daughters and two sons, were flanked by family portraits—the two older girls posing with their husbands and children. Marsha focused on Adelle, her youngest, her unmarried daughter, still living alone and sorting packages for United Parcel Service, still taking three showers a day and karate lessons four nights a week, still despising men. Urgent, muscular, reclusive Adelle, who, until the day she moved out, had gotten up at six in the morning to jog with Marsha at the high school track. Adelle. She would be the easiest.

Dearest Adelle,

As I sit here laughing, feeling very warm & secure to be thought of & labored over, it occurred to me that Sarah in the Bible must have felt just like I feel: "Am I, at 47 yrs., to have pleasure?" When I feel 1,000 yrs. old, feeling sorry for myself, convinced pleasure will never come again, there you are, reducing me to a joyful teenager.

Marsha paused. Not informative enough. Adelle liked facts. Hated "emotional drivel." Or so she said.

Dr. Norman, while taking out the stitches from the first surgery, went on and on how I wrecked his back for life.

"Pretty Boy" hates stripping veins because you have to keep turning the "cadaver," as he calls it, and this is hell.

The worst part was the waiting room. One lady came out in a crouch clutching her breast with tears streaming down her face. She sat down to get enough strength to leave & said she'd had a radical mastectomy & Dr. Norman just popped the swollen scar tissue by squeezing as hard as he could with his hands. The lady started sobbing hysterically & was saying things like, "My husband looks at me like I'm some kind of freak . . . he's afraid of me . . . he won't touch me. . . . " I knew it was more than the scar. Men are all alike—you give them pleasure & your body suffers as a result. Then they despise you because of it.

Your Grandma Christiansen had a radical mast. & I know the hell she went through. Back then the surgeons were all butchers. Spot a lump and hack the whole thing off, that was their motto. Did I ever tell you what the surgeon who did the job on Grandma said? "What's the big deal, lady? You're 55!" If I'd been there I'd have kicked him where it hurts. Then, "What's the big deal, Doc? You're 39!" Of course, today's doctors think they're all superhumanitarians. They smile so proud of themselves & their wonderful profession as they tell about all the options modern science has for diseased females: extended radical (very rare), halsted radical (also rare), modified radical (most reasonable, they say), simple or total (controversial) & the good old lumpectomy (the one Grandma probably could have gotten away with!!!). Some even prescribe radiation or chemotherapy, so if the cancer in your breast doesn't kill you, the radiation & chemicals will. The plastic surgeons are even worse. They brag about how they can fix you all up afterwards—"much much better than new!" They miss the whole point.

Marsha turned suddenly, drew the drape aside, and looked out across the driveway. She thought she'd heard someone drive up but could see no one except the Johnsons' girl riding by on

her pinto pony, which seemed to sag from the child's weight.
Her own children had never been overweight. She'd never un-
derstood the inferiority complexes that had nagged them through
high school; they had been—still were—so beautiful. Adelle might
be stocky but not obese.

With all the operations I've been having they're liable to
put me in the surgeon general's hall of fame. In case you've
got nothing more exciting to record in your journal, here's
the latest run down: Three months ago, strip the veins. Last
week, the tummy tuck. Next week, the tooth & mouth job—
the worst of the lot. Then I'll be all fixed up. Just call me the
$6 million housewife!
    Thanks for the letter. That part about how you put down
your boss when he started coming on to you, I couldn't stop
laughing!!!! But for heaven's sake, don't worry about ME! I
may look like death warmed over for the time being, but
underneath I'm fit as a fiddle. I'll snap back. I always do.
Write again when you have time.
                XOXOXOXOXOXOXOXOXOXOXO
                            Mom

The electric razor was silent. Just some metallic clicks as the
cabinet door opened and closed and opened again. The sound of
water. He always rewashed his face after shaving. It was part of
his ritual.
    For a moment Marsha pictured his naked body, big, broad,
the shoulders rounded like a bear's, slumping forward from bulk,
his chest carpeted with grizzled hairs. His muscles had softened
as he'd worked his way up from baggage boy to supervisor. But
his forty-eight years had compensated in other areas: the bright,
metallic streaks in his hair gave him the look of a British aristo-
crat, and the wrinkles and tiny pouches under his faded blue eyes
made him look more seasoned than old; vintage stuff. Marsha
recalled an old TV commercial in which a graying man in a black

tuxedo hands red roses to his slender, smiling, middle-aged wife: "You're not getting older, you're getting better. . . . "

This was true, for Robert. But what about *her*? Rippled blue legs and lumpy landscape. If the body was indeed a temple, then women had permitted desecration. Sister Harper, her buttocks swaying like the Liberty Bell, conducting the monthly homemaking lesson. Fat and happy. Too fat and happy. Or worse, poor Sister Watson who at thirty-two with a scholar's mind and a grandmother's body was too intelligent to be fat. Or happy. Just used. No, Marsha didn't despise them. Pitied them, yes. Almost as much as they pitied her.

Marsha snatched the pen from the arm-rest and scribbled a hasty postscript on the outside of the envelope: "Woman is the nigger of the world."

She looked at the portraits on the TV set. Sherril, Cozette, Adelle, Gary, Stephen. Stephen would be next. What to do with Stephen? Eighteen, sharing an apartment in Billings, Montana, working seven-to-seven in a warehouse shelving brake shoes for four dollars an hour. Her wayward son. Not prodigal. Not even a black sheep. Just missing. Gone.

From the beginning his teachers had pressured him: "You're sure not like Sherril!" "Why can't you read like Gary? That Gary, he was a reader!"

Sherril the valedictorian, Cozette the artist, Gary the all-league linebacker, Stephen the . . . pothead? And Adelle? The karate expert? The man-hater?

Marsha glanced around as if someone had lifted the lid off her mind and were peeking down at the image inside: Stephen's fifth grade teacher, a crew-cut drill sergeant type, warning her to get Stephen involved in sports "or he may have a problem with his masculinity." It was absurd, of course. The man was absurd. And yet Stephen's ex-wife had never responded to him. She'd admitted this to Marsha, hushed. Marsha had read Stephen some very convincing passages from Janov's *Primal Scream*. But Stephen had moved out after a two-week R & R at home. As far as she knew, he hadn't gone out with a woman since the divorce.

Dearest Stephen,

We're doing some research into small towns for future use. Chula Vista is getting so large, & we find ourselves jumping & flinching every time we drive into town, dodging all the maniacs on wheels. It could only get worse, so we may not want to retire here when your dad is 65. We have this U.S. catalog that lists acreage way out in the boondocks for each state. So far, the most alluring is Colorado. Your own trout stream, hunting, fishing, etc. in Delta, Colo.

She stopped. She wanted to say: your dad didn't mean what he said about you being a parasite. Just because we got married when we were your age and his father dumped him on the spot, he seems to think all birds have to leave the nest at the same time, but you know he really does love you, deep-down, even if he doesn't act like it at times . . . justifying, qualifying, apologizing, lying. And Stephen would know. Maybe not consciously, but he would know.

Someday I may get your dad in a 4-season climate wilderness. He's a little turned on by this catalog. I know it's hard for him, because I was raised in Utah until I was 17 & storms really excite me. Dad has always lived in Calif. & storms make him feel like the sky is falling.

The bathroom door opened and Robert's voice echoed down the hall: "Did you call me, Marsh?"

"No, I didn't say anything."

"I thought you said something."

"No."

She watched his bear-like body, the towel wrapped around his waist, cross the hall and disappear into the bedroom. She hobbled into the kitchen, opened the refrigerator, and studied the shelves: a ten-pound horn of cheese, a bottle of bran, fresh fruits and vegetables, a jar of brewer's yeast, and on a separate shelf a row of small bottles—cod liver oil, B-complex, vitamin E, rose hips. Marsha had always distrusted doctors, even before her operations. "Proper diet and preventative care," she'd always preached to her children, heaping vitamins on their breakfast plates.

She took two of the B-complex tablets and poured herself a glass of carrot juice. As she alternately popped the vitamins and sipped the juice, her eyes wandered out the window, beyond the redwood deck, and down into the Chula Vista Valley, spread out like a multi-colored fan. Split-levels with roofs of Spanish tile studded the hillsides, their backyard swimming pools gleaming like inlaid turquoise. In between, the precise rows of orange and avocado groves stood like green regiments. A narrow highway bisected the base of the valley, with either side furrowed dark or grass green. At the far end of the panorama, smooth, humped hills, like the flanks of palomino ponies, walled the valley, a soft contrast to the harsh brush and stubbled buttes immediately surrounding their home. Except for a small spotting of clouds and the bright, throbbing sun, the sky was immaculate blue. A perfectly unbothered blue, thought Marsha, setting her empty glass on the sink. She began scratching her abdomen, softly at first, then with increasing intensity.

"Marsha! Have you seen my blue socks?"

She stopped. Slowly removing her hand from her jeans, she clasped the refrigerator door handle, gently but firmly, with her free hand. "No, I haven't."

"Never mind. I found them."

His dresser drawer slammed shut.

Marsha looked back outside at the Johnsons' orange grove. A man in white with a gunny sack slung over one shoulder was standing halfway up a ladder picking oranges. Was it the wetback? She hoped so. He'd looked hungry. She thought about him, his pure black hair and hard muscles, his face the color of the distant hills. What would his fine hair feel like? His soft face? It seemed so long since she'd truly embraced a child. Or a man. She realized she was no longer looking out over the valley but instead at her own vague reflection, pale and hollow, a premature grandmother.

Marsha gulped down another glass of carrot juice and returned to the living room. She glanced at the portrait of Cozette, standing beside her husband, an angular, boyish-looking young man of twenty-three with carefully sculptured hair, wearing a bright blue suit. Jerry's mouth was small, lamblike, with thin, unkissable lips. Painfully religious, born into it, the son of a bishop who later became a stake president, he was a product of the unbroken Mormon mold: baptized at eight, Eagle Scout, two-year mission, temple marriage. Thoroughly saturated, with the if-ye-love-me-keep-my-commandments ideal the church stood for. As devout as she had tried to be her first few years with Robert.

Cozette. Tall and slender, like Marsha, with long blonde hair. She could have been a model. Or better, an artist. She was only twelve credits shy of her B.A. in art when she was "blessed with little Christopher" and had dropped out of school.

Robert emerged from the hall fully dressed, flicking some lint from the sleeve of his navy-blue sport coat as he headed into the kitchen. She could smell his cologne. As he yanked open the refrigerator and began rummaging through the shelves, Marsha stiffened. She felt pale, faint.

Dearest Cozette,

I'm going into the slaughter-house again next week. This time for my teeth. If I didn't explain, they are going to uncover the entire bone & take an impression. In one week they take out the stitches, in one more week they uncover the bone again & insert an appliance over the entire bone. They sew you up leaving 4 protruding steel pillars exposed, welded to the bone appliance. The teeth will snap onto the pillars, & this remains fixed when I eat. This will prevent further bone loss since friction will be eliminated. The Dr. showed me how it works & it's as effective as implants onto the bone in eliminating movement. The Dr. said the first couple of weeks I'd be sorry I did it, but after the mouth heals, it will really be worth the initial discomfort.

"Bob?"

He peered around the corner, two big surprised eyes. "Marsh?" he said, overly concerned.

For a moment she recognized a bit of the old boyishness and she almost laughed. Marrying him she had hoped for a mind and spirit to match his strong body. These were the sins of her youth: Faith. Hope. Shortsightedness. Naivete. Idealism. Still, in twenty-nine years he had matured. In some ways. Which was far more than she could say for his father, Oroville Fletcher, the granite-jawed retired building contractor who still gulped his morning cup of Yuban but carried a temple recommend in his wallet. Cocky, bald, muscle-bound, the king chauvinist who used to whip off fifty one-armed push-ups for his astonished little grandchildren. Always giving them gifts but always demanding. *Thank you Grandpa Fletcher thank you Grandpa Fletcher thank you Grandpa*. Refusing to tend them as infants. Even for an hour. Instead he sat watching TV while his corpulent wife tottered about the house cleaning. Occasionally slapping her around. For burning the roast, for over-starching his shirts. For the hell of it. Disciplining, *training* her. Because it was his right, he felt, by virtue of his sex or whatever.

Robert had at least matured beyond a caveman conception of women. Which was quite remarkable, considering his upbringing.

Marsha set the pen and pad of paper gently on the arm-rest and smiled at her husband, still peering around the corner. "Could you get me that medicine in the bedroom?"

"Sure, Marsh."

"It's on the dresser."

Marsha's eyes followed him down the hall until he disappeared into the bedroom.

You know, when you consider the pain & expense when you allow tooth decay until you can afford it, it makes you wonder why somebody didn't warn you when you were too young to realize. I remember pledging $500 to the church building fund while my teeth needed work. What a dumb generation we were.

"Here you go!" Robert held out the bottle of medicine. "How are the stitches?"

"Okay." Marsha unscrewed the cap and peered into the bottle as if she were looking down a well. "Thanks."

"Well, I guess I'll be seeing you." Robert raised his big flat palm in an awkward farewell. "Need anything at the store?"

"No."

"Well, we'll see you then." He bent down and kissed her forehead.

"Remember when we were first married?" she said. "Every time you'd leave for work I'd come to the door."

"And put your arms around me," Robert said. "I remember."

"When do you think you'll be home?"

"Probably around four. Maybe five."

In spite of herself, she snapped at him: "That's what I like about you, Robert—you're so decisive!"

"Five," he said flatly.

Marsha shook her head, exasperated. "I'm sorry, Bob."

"Sorry about what?"

"I don't know. Everything. Hawaii."

"Hawaii?"

"I was awful in Hawaii. Here we'd gone and saved all that money."

"It was the rain, Marsh. We didn't expect it to rain the whole time."

"But I bitched. I bitched at *you*, not the rain. When we were walking along Waikiki, I bitched because you were walking so slow."

She noticed him sneak a glance at his watch.

"Look, Marsha, forget about Hawaii, okay? It was the menopause. That's what Dr. Norman said."

"Do you think I should have taken that estrogen?"

"Jeez, I don't know."

Marsha folded her arms and literally shivered. "The thought of putting all that junk into my body . . . when you know sooner or later it's going to crop up in the form of cancer. . . . "

Robert shrugged. "I don't know. From all I've read and heard, it seems if cancer's going to get you, it's going to get you. If not through hormone shots, then some other way—the water, the air, preservatives, diet drinks. But if your number's up, one way or another, it's going to get you. And there's not much you can do about it."

"Get *me*?"

"You. Us. The whole damn world. You know what I mean."

"It's not fair."

"Who ever said anything about being fair?"

Robert glanced at his watch again, openly this time. "Look, I'd better get going." He kissed her lightly on the cheek.

After his car pulled out of the driveway, Marsha got up and opened the drapes to the picture window. Briefly she scanned the landscape. To her left, in the Johnsons' orange grove, she noticed the same white figure she'd seen earlier, still picking fruit. Again, she wondered if it were the Mexican boy—or rather, the young man. No, he was just a boy. Like Stephen. Had Thelma Johnson fed the boy? It was just like her to hire wetbacks dirt-cheap, fifty cents an hour, and not even feed them a decent meal. He'd probably been working all day without a break. Probably starving. Tell us about it in church, Thelma. Tell us about it Sunday when you bear your testimony.

Marsha eased down on the sofa and angrily picked up the pen and pad of paper.

By the way, your letter about Stephen was absolutely perfect. With all the PIGS daddy works with who brag about kicking their kids out into the street, every bit of pressure for going the extra mile is needed to counteract the poison influence. Your dad needs generosity pumped into his veins every day.

Marsha wondered if she should give the details. How Stephen had suddenly showed up on the doorstep one morning, long stringy hair covering the collar of his Levi jacket, eighteen, broke, and already paying alimony; how Robert had answered her plea with a flat, emotionless "No"; the argument, she and Robert yelling in the bedroom while Stephen sat like a marionette in the kitchen, waiting to see who would pull his strings this time; Robert fuming as he stormed out, shouting over his shoulder: "Two weeks! That's it. Two weeks."

Stephen was talking for the first time in years. He talked about teachers doing jobs on him way back in grade school. His face got red. It really is shocking how little a parent knows of what a child is feeling.

Marsha glared at the paper wadded in a ball in the middle of the floor. Sherril's letter, received that morning. Angrily she resumed her letter to Cozette, the letter Jerry would certainly read— he read all of Cozette's mail and she read all of his. They shared everything.

My only advice which is sound but totally against church doctrine, is not to get pregnant again. It's your body, Cozette. If you really don't want a hanging leaky bladder etc. not to mention the outside hanging parts (every pregnancy takes its toll), then assert yourself. After all, no one else is sacrificing *their* beautiful body. Sorry, Jerry, but think about it: you really *like* your body intact, don't you? Nothing personal, Jerry. You are No. 1 husband & father in my estimation. It's not your fault that you have a patriarchal hang-up.

Jerry wouldn't like it. "What's she whining about this time? Birth control again? Cozy, what does the church say?" Cozette obeyed him like a child. Hopeless. Cozette wouldn't listen, just as Sherrill hadn't—overruled by Brian, conditioned by the joys of motherhood, a "woman's place . . . "

Marsha's hand stopped, but her thoughts continued meandering, stumbling through a labyrinth of memories: Robert, his fullback shoulders swelling his skin-tight t-shirt, standing beside his monster jalopy in the Jefferson High parking lot, laughing at his diploma on graduation day; driving all over L.A. on their wedding night, searching for a motel; Robert fumbling with the luggage, fumbling with her spaghetti straps; a month later, her big dreams–happy marriage, big house, big happy family–crushed: in the tinted window of Angelo's Pizza Parlour, Robert sharing a booth with a chesty redhead, laughing as he inserted a thick-crusted wedge into her mouth. No confession, no remorse. Marsha, already pregnant, taking it like a good old broad, taking it as her mother had taken it, twenty years, hiding the pain and hurt and humiliation. All through Robert's lean years: bread and cheese in basement apartments, the children–one two three, bam! bam! bam! The episiotomies hadn't even healed. A two-year break, then four five, bam! bam! The blue worms growing on her legs, thicker, bluer, the muscles in her belly sagging further and further, once good supple healthy robust flesh turned to flaccid dough. Which she hid from the world, public and private, dressing and undressing in the bathroom to spare herself Robert's queasy gaze.

Robert's promotion. The Dream House. The kids all in school. Measuring day after tedious day with soap operas and game shows. Mechanically taking the sacrament, then not, then sleeping in Sundays while the kids, the youngest eight and the oldest sixteen, diligently attended their Sabbath meetings. Robert, the workaholic, up at 5:30 and home at 10:00. Too much time to think, to read, to remember–her youth, her childhood. Growing up in Salt Lake City, so piously and genealogically insulated from the coarse scheming world, when everything was directly or peripherally church-sanctioned and everyone believed as she had, and the fragrances, colors, moods, and seasons were not much different than when her grandmother was a little girl standing on the porch of her pioneer home, watching the bright lights of Saltair. Spring hay rides and wienie roasts up Big Cottonwood Canyon, with the boys in Levis and crew-cuts flirting in their awkward adolescent self-conscious Mormon way. Back when she, as a young woman, a female, had felt at least equal to the young men, those gawky Aaronic Priesthood holders going about their Sabbath business in a sort of jovial stupor. But moving to California at seventeen and a year later marrying Robert, she'd suddenly been relegated to the office of "wife"—*the* wife, house-wife, later euphemized to "homemaker" though still and always *the wife*, a title which had blackballed her, first for life, then three years later, following the sealing ceremony in the Los Angeles Temple, for time and all eternity. While he'd been designated the husband, the head, the poppa, the patriarch. And from that point on she was no longer on par but always supine, on or off the delivery table, legs spread, feet in the stirrups, a sacrificial lamb.

Too much time to remember, to relive. To fantasize about being a physician or attorney or professor. Being not body-bullied. Being woman. Beautiful intelligent unapologizing uncompromising woman.

Robert's first and last confession of what she knew was nei-ther his first nor last affair—"Never again . . . I swear it!"—sent Marsha driving recklessly down the highway, heading nowhere. An hour later, parked on the surf-eaten cliffs of San Elijo, gazing down at the sunset reflections on the sea. Watching the surfers in black penguin suits paddling in to shore and the couples, young and old, strolling along hand in hand against the fiery western sky. Darkness smothering the last flicker of light. Then all night in her car listening to the monotonous surf, watching the stars ride each wave to a peak then tumble into the madhouse of white water. Listening to each turbulence simmer to a hush; a brief, redeeming moment to recuperate, to poke your head above the rage and steal a bite of air. Then another breaker. Silence. Another. The inexorable cycle.

Recovering. Surviving.

Night classes at Chula Vista CC. Intro. to Literature. The tall, bushy-haired instructor lecturing in his mellow voice. Slouched in a chair in front of the class, hands buried in his pockets, or sitting cross-legged on the table.

Sitting in back, hiding behind the black woman who borrowed her pen every week, she was anonymous, she'd thought, until her midterm conference, a personal conference in a cramped, windowless room walled on three sides by shelves of books.

"You obviously agree with Browning's attitude towards male egoism."

She smiled, nodding self-consciously, glancing down at her hands, cupped on the notebook lying flat across her thighs. Feeling foolish—foolish for being so nervous. A woman ten, maybe fifteen years older than this man, yet behaving like a schoolgirl.

"Tennyson's *Princess* might give you a little different perspective on Victorian attitudes towards the male-female syndrome. You might read a few selections and try a comparison-contrast theme."

He leaned back in his swivel chair, tapping the eraser-end of his pencil lightly against her paper as his eyes pondered a paragraph, never looking up, absorbing it, indifferent, it seemed, to her presence.

She leaned forward, peering stealthily at her theme, as if cheating on an exam. His lips separated, his bushy beard quivering slightly as he whispered through the passage. He was nodding. Smiling and nodding. He flipped quickly through the remaining pages.

"Very good. Excellent." He penciled an A- on the paper and circled it.

"Thank you," she said, accepting the paper from him as if it were a gift.

"Thank *you*," he said. "It's not often I stumble across a theme I actually enjoy reading." The far corners of his eyes wrinkled when he smiled.

As she stood up and reached for the doorknob, he called her back. Yes, it was rather late. Yes, maybe it would be a good idea if he walked her to her car. Yes, she would have a cup of coffee with him, no harm in that.

But it had been a sensuous experience for her, sitting in a secluded little booth having a cup of coffee with another man. A man who had joined her not out of obligation or dull habit but because he was attracted to her, physically, intellectually—at one point she thought even spiritually. They chatted for an hour—literature, movies, overpopulation, women's liberation. During a lull, he casually reached across the table to take her hand, but she jerked it away, avoiding his eyes, which had been cross-examining her, not without sympathy: You are married but are you happy? Why are you so dissatisfied, an attractive woman like you? What would make you happy, Marsha Fletcher? Don't worry, I know. I know. I know what you're feeling. I know what you're suffering.

When he said it out loud, she suspected it was a line. But it was exactly the line she wanted—*needed*—to hear.

His apartment had been far more materialistic than she'd anticipated: a stepdown living room with a tiny bar tucked away in one corner, the adjoining walls lined with shelves of wine; a stereo with monstrous speakers and a garden of indoor plants; in the bedroom a huge TV screen, a digital alarm clock enumerating each green second, a water bed.

As he stood at the bar preparing their drinks, she became uneasy. What was she doing here? And why? He looked over at her and grinned. She hated that grin. Cocksure.

She sat on the sofa and tried to relax. But already she could feel what was coming: the unhurried warmth of his initial touch, his careful, artistic consideration as he proceeded down the length of her body. But after that, nothing—except his long lean fingers curiously exploring the rippled ridges of her doughy belly, and their mutual frustration. He would shrug, exonerating himself: "Uptight, Mrs. Fletcher. Too uptight." She would be left feeling humiliated, bitter, guilty about her sin against not only the God she was feuding with but her self. Ultimately admitting to herself, *I've been had*. As she watched him casually stirring the drinks, his pianist's fingers suddenly turned to icicles. What did this bearded child know about her anyway? Nothing. And what did he really want? A midnight discussion of Swinburne's love poems? Ha! The same thing they all wanted. No, she was not going to be easy. Another feather in his cap.

She stood up. "I have to go."

Before he could even protest, she rushed out the door, leaving him dumbfounded, holding two glasses in his dim-lit bachelor's den.

When she arrived home, Robert was waiting up, angry, ready to pounce, to interrogate. But she beat him to it: "Yes, I was out with another man. I'm ready to tell Bishop Myers about mine any time you're ready to tell him about yours. Good night!" Sobbing, she fled into the master bedroom and locked the door.

Thus ended her first and last fling.

Marsha picked her pen off the floor. Everything seemed quiet. Unbearably quiet. She listened to the afternoon silence that had become both enemy and ally ever since Adelle had moved out: the refrigerator humming, the Johnson girl calling to her pony, a jet purring across the sky. Silence.

> This drug hangover is mentally lowering. I may have to go to the new Golfland we have & vent my frustrations on the video games. You get to kill 6 gunslingers if you are fast enough, & I intend to cheat, rather than holstering my gun between each fight.

Marsha sat the pen crosswise on the pad and slouched down as if her body had suddenly collapsed. She remained limp until the little door on the grandfather clock popped open and the tiny wooden bird slid forward, cuckooing five times. Then five ominous tolls of the gong.

> It's a good thing I have class next week. I'm taking real estate principles & income tax. Don't ask me why. Aunt Toots is getting married—again! I hope she is happy. She deserves it.
> XOXOXO
> Mom
> P.S. XOXOXOXO for beautiful Laura. No one is hungry right after they wake up. Wait an hour & give her fresh air and exercise just before. It stimulates the appetite.

Marsha hastily tore the scribbled pages from the note-pad and hurried into the kitchen to locate another envelope and seal the letter before she changed her mind. Shuffling through a drawer, she glanced at the kitchen clock: 5:15. Robert should have been home an hour ago. Two hours ago. She could phone his office, but what difference would it make? She looked outside. The sun was bleeding through the clouds on the horizon.

As Marsha watched the twilight settling like deep sleep over the valley, she tried to hate her husband. In the past this would have been easier, when he would heave the boys against the walls for quarreling or scold her for not having them ready for church on time or wake her in the middle of the night to demand his nuptial rights. But over the years he had mellowed. No more yelling, no more violence, no more workaholic. No more kids, of course. That had a lot to do with it. Now he got up at 7:00, put in his eight hours, came home at 5:30, shoveled down dinner, and camped in front of the TV with a science-fiction paperback until 10:30 or 11:00, when they went to bed, and slept. He was mellow now. Perfectly mellow. And generous, too, now that he had some money to spare. She'd first suggested cosmetic surgery as a joke, certain he would veto the idea. But he'd surprised her.

"A complete overhaul? Sure. Why not?"

"Robert, you're not serious! It would cost a mint."

Razor poised in his hand, ready to slide across his lathered face, he mocked: "There goes our trip to Europe! And your Mercedes!" He lowered the razor, smiling. "If that's what you really want . . . " He boldly stroked the razor across his left cheek, whistling, grinning at her inquisitive reflection in the mirror. "Actually, if I'd known that's all there was to it, I'd have had you on the operating table fifteen years ago."

"Ha! The truth comes out!"

"What truth?"

"That you think I looked *that* bad fifteen years ago."

"Not at all, Marsh." Another bold stroke, this time across his right cheek. "It was more like *twenty* years ago!"

He raised his big forearm, shielding his face as Marsha shoved him. She snatched the can of shaving cream and sprayed it in his face. He scooped her up in his arms and toted her, laughing, squirming, into the bedroom where he flung her across the bed and plopped down beside her, pressing his frothy face against hers, the two of them laughing hysterically as he covered her cheeks with lathered kisses.

That had been the first time in what seemed ages they had spontaneously frolicked. For those few precious moments wrestling with him on the bed she'd felt as if she really were falling in love again, as if there never had been a first time. And all of her sexual energy, expressed and repressed, culminated in a burst of passion. But that was as far as he'd gone, the kisses. He'd had to run—the football game, kick-off in twenty minutes.

"But what about Europe?" she asked as he relathered his face.

"Who needs Europe?" He set the razor on the wash basin, turned. "I'd rather pay a mint to make love to a renovated Marsha than look at some crumbling cathedral."

She saw that he intended the statement as a compliment. "You're sweet, Bob. Thanks."

The grandfather clock began sounding the hour, each haunting gong echoing in her head. Marsha wanted to lie down and sleep but knew she was not through. Not yet. She returned to the living room and once again took up the pen and pad of paper. Sherril. Her first, the last. The hardest.

Dearest Sherril,

No, I don't begrudge you another child! You know I've always wanted whatever would make you happy & it seems with Brian you've found happiness. Cozette, too, with Jerry. You both have good faithful (if somewhat chauvinistic) husbands, & in this day and age that's really something.

As for the church, don't hold your breath. For you and Brian the church has worked out. But you're both working together to make it work, & that makes all the difference. Your father & I never quite had that vision. We saw potential. We wanted you kids to have standards, avoid the mistakes we'd made. And the church seemed the best way.

No, I don't apologize for the way I'm living now, & I certainly don't expect you to. True, there was a time when I thought the church filled a major void in my life. When I was growing up in Salt Lake & everything we did was church this or church that, & everyone we met was Brother X or Sister Y. But I'm not sure anymore if it was the church or something else.

Marsha stopped, dissatisfied. She was evading what she really wanted to say.

I was thinking the other day about you kids, how as a mother watching you laughing on the rides at Disneyland or riding your rafts at the beach I always got a bigger kick out of it than you did. So maybe this is the real Fountain of Youth—God bless your children & grandchildren!

Did I tell you about my visiting teachers? Sister Williams is about my age. A big heavy-set woman who looks like a veteran from the handcart company. Stoic, hard-nosed pioneer look. Spiritually tough as nails. Her companion is a sweet young girl about 20 with her faith & figure still intact and a 6-month-old baby. One of their monthly messages was on resisting the ways of the world, & Sister Williams used birth control as an example of how the world's standards differ from ours. I disagreed, of course. It really threw Sister Williams for a loop when Sister Mitchell started asking me about different kinds of b.c. "Well, Sister Mitchell, we'd better be going. We've got another appointment with Sister Quiner." Why some people want to keep you young girls in ignorance is beyond me.

The year before, when Sister Williams had a different companion, they had caught Marsha at a bad time, when things—no, nothing in particular, just "things," the cumulative chore of being female mother wife homemaker—had dog-piled on her. The sisters had caught her at her worst, and she had spilled everything.

"Me. I'm losing me. ME! It's like . . . I . . . I can't explain it."

"Have you prayed, Sister Fletcher?" was their counsel.

Sniffling, she shook her head and promised to try. But later, alone, couldn't—couldn't even try—because her problem seemed so intangibly female that only a woman could begin to understand. For there was no appropriate analogy to it, her cumulative grief. And a man, regardless of the extent of his power, knowledge, and compassion . . .

Believe it or not there are some things even God doesn't understand. Not entirely. Pardon the blasphemy but it's true. So what good does it do to scream out for recognition? Marsha Fletcher crying Job from the confines of her $200,000 home. Who gives a hoot if your breasts are sagging to your knee caps? Vanity, saith the preacher. People are starving in Cambodia, be thankful you've got tits period. Besides, you know how I've always despised public grief—the long countenances of the fasters & billboard martyrs. Don't worry. I'm a tough old bird. It'll take more than a few bloated veins and cellulite sag to put me out to pasture.

She glared at the pad, her usually neat cursive gone haywire, oblivious to the ruled lines. No, it wasn't the church she was squaring off with. This was an inequity not of any system or organization but of life itself, the life cycle. Not political or social or environmental or ecclesiastical, but biological. Established from the foundation of the world, the heavens. As old and everlasting as the priesthood she and her female compatriots were categorically denied.

I'd better sign off now. I've passed on enough happy thoughts for one day.

But she didn't even sign the letter before tearing it from the pad, wadding it into a ball, and hurling it across the room.

She sat there several moments, silent, allowing nothing into her mind but the gray fog of that morning. She was tired, she wanted to lie down, she wanted to sleep. But the image emerged. A blonde this time, a platinum penthouse blonde. A busty divorcee with a phony Texas drawl, squeezing his sagging biceps, handing him a drink, snuggling up cozily beside him on the sofa, purring into his ear: *You ah the most aggressive may-un I have evuh known. . . . You ah moh aggressive than Mistuh Mean Joe Greene, or the entah Dallas Cowboy front lion.*

Marsha turned to the window. The sunless horizon was glossy pink, an infection. A solitary pair of headlights drifted down the highway. At the far end of the Johnsons' orange grove an empty ladder was leaning against a tree.

She stared across the valley, waiting for it to darken. Robert. Twenty-nine years she'd waited for the angel to outgrow the monster. Now that it had she wondered, who was this man she'd fought and loved and slept with over half her life? Robert the only child growing up lonesome in L.A. Inventing invisible brothers and sisters to escort him through grade school. He'd wanted kids until he had them. Then sat on his tail, like his father, giving orders. Then took off. First in spirit, then body.

Now she felt nothing but anger. Resenting him. Resenting the age-old equation he had perpetuated: WOMAN = BODY. A woman's worth depreciating from the first time she unlocks her thighs and lets the world in. Yes, he did have his reasons. "But damn them, Robert! Damn your reasons!"

She whirled around and fled down the hall and into her bedroom. Whipping off her blouse and Levis, then panties and bra, she studied her body, tall and naked in the full-length mirror. Three rows of stitches, chapped with scabs, furrowed her lower abdomen. Her "tummy tuck." These, Dr. Norman had assured her, would heal in a matter of weeks. Further down, the veins—the thick, rippling veins that, like the stretch marks, had grown larger and uglier with each pregnancy—these too were gone. Aside from the suture marks patterned at even intervals like rungs on a ladder along the length of her calves, and the little black nubs she had to avoid in shaving, her legs looked quite attractive, more thirty-five than forty-seven. Her legs had always been her strong point and, for a nostalgic moment, she admired them.

Then she focused on her upper half, where the skin was beginning to sag. Not excessively. Not a grandmother's droop. But noticeably—a doughy sagginess that nothing, not vitamin E or Scandia Slim 'n Trim or scalpels and sutures or fasting and prayer could redeem.

"This," she muttered bitterly, glaring at the stitches and the scars and the invisible scars, recollecting the strippings and the shavings and the drugs, the anesthesia and starving for days at a time. "None of it—not one bit of it for you, Robert. But me. For me and me and no one else."

She studied her breasts for some time before pressing down firmly, two, three, four times, reassuring herself of the lump that she'd let Dr. Norman examine, hoping that for once the odds would be in her favor. They weren't. Dr. Norman clinically reviewed her options: extended radical, halsted radical, modified radical, total . . . But she wasn't listening. She was staring outside at the hazy blue sky, wishing it were an ocean she could dive into, wishing she could swim forever down to its pure black bottom.

"I'd like a second opinion."

"That's only reasonable."

Second opinion ditto the first.

"Let me think about it."

"Of course, Mrs. Fletcher."

"I'd prefer to tell my husband myself."

"Of course."

Staring at her naked self in the mirror, Marsha fingered the lump, pinching it several times—gently, curiously at first, like a scientist, probing. Then she began squeezing, harder and harder, wanting to gouge, to rip. Dr. Carlyle, the young plastic surgeon, had assured her with such beaming optimism that reconstructive surgery could provide her with a "cosmetically attractive breast" – a breast, his eyes said as he showed her some before-after photos, that would be much nicer than that shriveled, sagging sack you've got now.

Then she had lied to herself. She had told herself there were alternatives; there were more important things than breasts, sex, self-esteem, womanhood.

Marsha squeezed the lump harder, harder, until the pain stung her eyes and her naked image melted on the mirror. Quickly, recklessly, she threw on her blouse and Levis and hurried down the hall and into the kitchen, darkened with dusk. Laughing and weeping, she took the car keys from the rack above the counter and headed out the front door, pausing just outside to inhale the chilly night air. She glared up at the half-face of the moon, scarred, pitted, nimbused. She muttered defiantly, "I'm a tough old bird . . . I'm a tough . . . "

Minutes later she was speeding down the Via de Dios Highway, heading towards the sea.

The Bowhunter

. . . .

Jack slowed down, looking for a sign. Seeing none, he sped down the highway, grumbling to himself. Dean could have given more specific directions—or better, first-hand instructions, not this friend-of-a-friend nonsense. It was prime hunting time, and he was going to miss it.

He drove another mile before turning around and heading back. Dean had insisted there was a sign: "Don Haines says Dave Alderman says." Jeez! Jack still couldn't believe it—no, he couldn't *understand* it: five years in Flagstaff and his brother had never been on the peaks.

"Too busy," he had shrugged. "Too many irons in the fire, I guess."

No. Too stuck-in-the-muck. Too house-bound. Too Di-a-na.

Jack looked at the fast fading darkness and wondered if he hadn't made a mistake. The massive zig-zag of the San Francisco peaks was emerging like a row of pyramids, eclipsing half the sky.

He turned onto an unmarked dirt road, his Chevy LUV struggling for traction, slipping and sliding along the muddy ruts, compliments of last night's thunderstorm. Several pickup trucks were parked along the shoulder where clusters of camo-coated hunters huddled around campfires, laughing, chatting, sipping from their mugs. He rolled down the window. The smells of fresh coffee and wood smoke filled his nostrils like sweetened snuff. He should have camped out too—to really do it right. But

. . . . .

55

Carmen was already put out enough. Every excursion was like World War III now. The Great Compromise. A little tit for a helluva lot of tat. For two days of hunting in northern Arizona, he had agreed to tack onto their vacation a week at Carmen's mother's in Provo.

The truck rattled across a cattle guard. A half mile up ahead a grove of aspens waited like an army in crazy green headdress. Tight ranks. Like an ambush, Jack thought.

He pulled over onto a level, grassy area and unloaded his gear: a small day pack, a recurve bow with a seventy-pound draw, and a mounted quiver containing six aluminum arrows tipped with broadheads, razor-sharp. He liked to hunt light.

Fishing two tubes of camo paint from his pack, he squeezed some green goop onto his fingertips and smeared it over his face, throat, and hands. Checking his face in the side mirror, he broke up the ghoulish green with quick, short strokes of black. He had never been much to look at—porcine nose, swollen cheeks, a ponderous brow protruding above bleached blue eyes, the left one frozen in a permanent squint, like a boxer's swollen shut. Not like his younger brother, whose dimpled, baby-bottom cheeks and high-flown hair used to break all the girls' hearts. Tall, blond, slender. Classic California. Jack was six inches shorter and thirty pounds heavier, every ounce rock solid. "Orangutan," they used to call him in high school, as much for the ungainly length of his arms as the red fur coating them. (They had paid for it, though, on the football field, with cracked heads and bloody noses.)

Jack looked at his painted hands and wondered what his old classmates would call him now. Camouflaged from head-to-toe, he looked more like a human salad than a would-be Nimrod.

A muddy trail snaked through a meadow of knee-high grass, rising gradually to where white aspens merged with dark, rain-stained pines. Beyond this, the mountains bulged like giant monuments, their silver peaks rising to sharp pinnacles that scraped the gray underbellies of the clouds. Back in Texas he would have scouted out the territory weeks in advance until he had found a frequented trail or bedding site and then set up his blinds. But this was mule deer country. Muleys were vagabonds, wanderers—nothing like the predictable, habit-manic whitetails back home. You couldn't scout a muley in July and expect to find him in the same spot in September.

Jack started up the trail briskly, with quick, military strides, his legs swishing through the damp grass. Soon his sneakers were soaked and his pants damp to the knees. He really hadn't come prepared for wet weather, but since it was only a day hunt he could manage all right.

He climbed over a barbed wire fence and soon found himself weaving through a dense mingling of aspens and evergreens. He moved quickly but quietly, trying to blend with the sounds and rhythms of the forest. Since taking up bowhunting five years ago, he was always amused by poetic descriptions of the "deep silence" of the woods. There was plenty of racket: squirrels chattering like gossipy old shrews, birds cutting in with machine-gun chitter, and from some invisible center, an inexorable buzzing—bees? yellow jackets?—a sound without a source, growing neither louder nor softer but pervading the entire forest. This was acceptable. This was music. It was human noise that stood out. A snapped twig was like clashing cymbals to a buck.

Jack gazed up at the intersecting branches raftering the slug-gray sky. The clouds were big, sodden sponges waiting to be squeezed. The weatherman's promise for clear skies was not to be. It was going to be another wet, dripping day after all. An ambiguous blessing. Although the moisture helped cushion his footsteps, preventing that brittle cornflake crackle that gave away September hunters, it could also make the stalking miserable, especially if he went a long time without seeing any signs of game. So far he hadn't—no tracks, no droppings, no scraped saplings or snagged bits of fur. Normally the sun was a nuisance—casting shadows, flashing warning signals off of rings and belt buckles—but today Jack would have welcomed a little color. Red and gold flowers were scattered about, but there was something moribund about them. Sapped of their brightness, they looked like popped balloons or scraps of crepe paper, a post-party depression.

He hiked on, carefully straddling fallen timber and easing around boulders barnacled with lichen. As he started up a steep embankment and the muscles began gripping in his thighs, he smiled. He loved a swift, tough climb. Soon sweat was oiling his back and shoulders. The faint spray of moisture on his face as he brushed past giant ferns piqued him like after-shave. But by the time he reached the top of the hill, he was feeling down again, and a little queasy.

Damn virus, he thought, lumbering along. All summer he'd been pestered by it. Since Christmas, really. It was either one long, lingering strain or a series of smaller ones. Either way, it irked him. He never used to get sick. Not even colds. But ever since Anna started kindergarten—"the germ factory," Carmen called it. "She brings home every virus in the book." This last was a bugger Jack couldn't seem to shake. He really should have stayed home and rested, to get over it once and for all. That was Carmen's advice, and Dean's. Fat chance! No way was he going to miss out on his hunt.

He stopped a moment to catch his breath. Skipping breakfast didn't help. He was nothing when his blood sugar dropped. Plus he was a little out of shape. Thank long hours with the Bureau for that. The paperwork! Much more than he'd anticipated. Well, that would change too.

He checked the piece of thread tied to his bow. He was downwind, so he began still-hunting—moving in slow-motion, like a statue trying to sneak from one end of the forest to the other without anyone noticing. Although his body was advancing at a snail's pace, his heart was thumping like an engine at rush hour. Yes. This was what he loved; this was what he had come for: the forest like a maze of surprises and possibilities. He was a time traveler stepping into the past, leaving behind cars, contraptions, videos, taxes, shopping lists, agent I.D. cards, and putting himself on simple terms with the animals—primitive terms. *Their* terms. He shunned the devices of contemporary hunters—compound bows with their array of pulleys and cables; artificial scents, lures, rangefinders, and other gadgets to guarantee a kill. He hunted with a simple recurve bow he had fashioned himself—no sight, no finger release. Why, he didn't even carry a watch or compass anymore. Sensing his way through the woods by instinct, shooting by instinct. Bare bow and bare soul. He had once read that many Indian tribes used to undergo a pre-hunting ritual in which the hunters would literally transform into the animal they were to stalk, a prehuman flux. Likewise, he tried to feel himself into his prey.

And he was proud of his prowess in the wilds. Not bad for a kid from the L.A. suburbs, raised on skateboards and street football. His old classmates were doctors, lawyers, professors who drove El Dorados and BMWs. While they were working weekends to make even bigger bucks to buy even bigger cars, he was sneaking around the woods looking for spoors. Three, even two years ago Jack would have smiled at the thought, but lately he was beginning to wonder. Carmen, his job, the kids, life in general. He used to be so confident about what he had done, where he was going, how he was going to get there.

A soft crackle broke his train of thought. He froze, searching the woods carefully for an ear twitch, a gray hump hiding within the mottled green and brown. He had let his mind wander—suicide for a bowhunter. For every deer you actually saw, four or five had probably slipped by. He reminded himself to focus, concentrate.

He spotted a narrow opening between two pines where the grass was trammeled flat. A game trail. As he picked it up, he was surprised—happily—when several shafts of sunlight seeped through the overgrowth, dropping gold pieces on the forest floor. The damp pine needles sparkled like sunken treasure, an underwater mirage. He felt a surge of anticipation. There were deer out there, somewhere. He could sense it.

Soon he found evidence: a pile of droppings beside a lightning-charred stump. They were dark brown, the size of unshelled peanuts. Elk. He mashed them lightly with his sneaker; the insides were moist. Fresh.

He ducked low and turned sideways to slip between two pines leaning against each other like doomed lovers. He had always wondered how elk, with their high, thick chests and branching antlers, could move so adroitly through such an evergreen obstacle course. Magicians, he had mused. Or spirits drifting right

· · · · ·

through the trees. Then three seasons ago he had watched one in action. Picking his way through the timbered congestion, the bull seemed to know exactly the width and height of his rack and had dipped and twisted it accordingly, squeezing through impossibly narrow openings. A magnificent sixth sense.

As Jack followed the game trail, the forest sounds grew more pronounced, more lively and animated, as if the maestro sun had finally raised his authoritative wand signaling the wilderness symphony to begin. All prior noise had been an ear-grating exercise in finding the right notes. But the hole in the sky soon clamped shut, and the sketchy sunlight bowed to wintry gloom. He was climbing uphill again; he could feel it in his legs and lungs. The peaks were long gone, lost behind the wall of evergreens.

He hiked another mile before stumbling upon a flow of volcanic rock. It curved through a grove of aspens, dividing it in two, then soared quickly up the mountain to become its silver peak. In actuality it had taken a destructive downward course, burying anything in its path. Jack wondered how many millions of years ago the mountain had blown its top and sent its broken pieces tumbling down the hill. Was it capable of a repeat performance? Staring at the huge, lichen-covered blocks, he thought of Pompeii and those jungle-strangled cities of the ancient Mayans. The longer he looked, the more it appeared as though some of the rocks were moving–subtly, stealthily. Like hunters, he thought. Sneaky bastards.

Still feeling queasy, he stopped for a short rest and a little food. He leaned his bow against a rock, removed his pack, and spread a plastic garbage bag on the damp grass. He sat down and began bolting down trail snack. Much better. He'd underestimated his hunger. No wonder he'd been feeling so down and out.

The surrounding branch and bristle reminded him of those line-drawing puzzles he used to do as a kid, where you try to find the little pictures hiding within the big. He noticed two squirrels chasing each other from branch to branch, like fuzzy-tailed trapeze artists. They reminded him of an amorous married couple, playful but forthright, the female intermittently stopping the chase to scold her suitor with jittery head and hand gestures that made Jack think of silent films. He chuckled softly.

From the muddy access road the forest had appeared as a thick buffalo pelt, triple-textured, shrouding all but the very tips of the peaks. Close up, though, it became a wonderland of subtle happenings and soap opera scenarios, a microcosm behind every tree—if you looked for it. On every excursion he made a point of noticing something different, something new. If he didn't, it was his own fault. He was out of touch, too bogged down with peripherals—the daily diaper duty of life. Funny, Carmen felt that way about church. "If you're not spiritually fed, you've only got yourself to blame." Jack disagreed. Sundays were sheer automata. Business as usual. The repetition tortured him.

He had joined half-heartedly—not exactly as a condition of marriage, but close enough. Although he had been attending regularly since then, he had never had what he considered a deeply religious experience. He'd had occasional inklings, Sabbath flutters, but nothing that took him by the shoulders and shook fire and thunder through him. The closest he had ever come was his baptism and confirmation. When Carmen's father had placed his gentle hands on Jack's rusty-haired head, confirming him an official church member, hot and cold tremors had scurried madly through his body, like a cat-and-dog chase. It was a weirdly fluish feeling, wonderfully strange inside and out, as if he had been stuck in the icebox and then tossed into the fire.

But the intensity of that moment—like passion?—had gradually dissipated until now it seemed as if it had never happened, or at best had happened to someone else and he was simply reiterating the story. Now he was a Sunday Mormon. He prayed, fasted once a month, paid his ten percent, attended all his meetings. Generally kept his nose clean. But it was ersatz. Letter-of-the-law nonsense. He was enduring to the end, kowtowing to some stubborn sense of principle and duty.

He took a swig from his canteen and ran a sleeve across his mouth. Cool and spiky going down, the water settled in his stomach with a satisfying, split-second spasm. Well-water. Dean had that over him too.

He had wanted Dean to come along. Why else would he have come all the way to Arizona? Colorado had twice the game and was half the travel time, if a deer was all he wanted. But Dean had hemmed and hawed and hadn't gotten a tag and license. Also, he was taking the kids to the county fair today, his three and Jack's two. That was the excuse anyway. Jack had sent him a bow for Christmas, a nice PSE compound, with instructions and a note: "Read! Buy a bale of hay! Practice! Practice! Practice!" Had he? Probably not. Diapers to change, dishes to wash, laundry to fold. Helping Diana with the household chores was one thing; doing half of them when he was working full-time at the shop and Diana was home all day, . . . it wasn't right.

But that was Dean. The stay-at-home. Momma's boy. While Jack and their father had traipsed off to the tennis courts, Dean was in the kitchen making Rice Crispy cookies with Mom. Still, as brothers they had enjoyed some good times together—ditching school and driving down to Ensenada for a day of deep-sea fishing, hot-wiring Mr. Levy's Cadillac and leaving it up for grabs on Mulholland Drive. A shiver scurried across Jack's massive shoulders. What had once stirred fond memories now left him feeling mildly depressed, though he wasn't sure if it was because he had changed or his brother had. Or the world. Life had changed.

No, it was Dean. He could thank Diane—Di-a-na—for that. He was too nosey now. The little brother playing big. Everybody's keeper. Last night on his redwood deck, a black-light glow above the peaks, purple-on-purple, Dean had asked:

"So how are things with you and Carmen?"

"Fine. Great. Like you say, it gets better and better."

This was a lie. Things had never been worse. Lately Carmen had been acting more and more like Diana. She hadn't always been like that. Jack had married an outdoor girl—a hiker, a skier, a swimmer. What had happened? Kids. Kids had happened. Motherhood had sucked the life and vitality out of her. She wasn't miserable, just hampered. Self-hampered. *Everything* was a hassle. Going to the store, a movie, church. She rolled her eyes wearily: dress the kids, pack the diaper bag, get munchies, bottles; strap the kids in the car seat, stop, unstrap, put them in the stroller. Stop-unstrap-strap-go. It wasn't worth it.

But other women managed – Margie Johnson had seven kids and still got around town like a taxi driver. Deformed foot and all. Jack had encouraged Carmen to go out, make friends, take a college night course. Get out of the house for a while. He'd watch the kids. Do *something* to even the score.

"I don't have friends here," she'd say, dripping with self-pity.

"Whose fault is that?"

"I had friends in Oregon."

Of course. She had loved Klamath Falls, and so had he. The town. But his job as assistant city manager . . . He was a rubber stamp, a paper shuffler. He had stuck it out two years before quitting to join the FBI. His military experience had given him an in. Immediately he was transferred from Klamath Falls. Sorry, the Bureau doesn't stake out utopias.

"We live in Houston now."

"I know. And whose fault is *that*?"

"Listen, I'm going hunting. I'll be back tonight – *sometime* tonight."

He didn't like being so gruff, but it was the only way. Every time he had given her an approximate hour, he'd been held up – a late hit, a late stalk. You can't leave the animal out there bleeding to death just to get home in time for dinner. Still, she'd held him to the deadline. Arms folded, tapping her foot, nodding: "Mmmhmm . . . mmmhmmm." The kids screaming like the end of the world when he trudged inside, dinner dished out on their plates, growing cold. Making the scene as godawful as possible.

"Carmen, you can't hunt on a time clock. It doesn't work that way. You don't under –" He wisely checked himself. Accusations of not understanding were the worst insult to an outdoor girl – formerly outdoor – a magna cum laude graduate who spoke three languages and had been published in the *Modern Language Journal*. She was no dumb blonde. But she didn't – she couldn't. Not this.

"It doesn't work that way," he had said.

This time he wasn't lying. In fact, every trip now he drove further and further from home and hiked deeper and deeper into unfamiliar territory, as if intentionally trying to lose himself inside the forest labyrinth. At nightfall, when he should have been heading home, he would continue his aimless wandering as the full moon stalked him from tree to tree. He would hike until 10:00, 11:00, midnight. Sometimes he would lie down on a bed of soft grass and close his eyes to the bubbling of a brook and the chanting of crickets and imagine himself falling asleep and waking up like Rip Van Winkle, with a beard to his knees. The thought always enticed him, but, ultimately, he would hike back to his truck by moonlight and drive on home, stumbling into bed at 3:00 or 4:00 a.m. Carmen? She was out. Zonked. Slipping in beside her, he always wondered if he hadn't made a mistake.

But that was typical now. More and more he shunned company. He wanted to hunt alone, to be alone. And not just in the woods. At work he volunteered for solo assignments. At church he herded his little family into the chapel at 9:00 sharp and bee-lined to the car right after the last amen. He took the rear exit, avoiding the hand-shaking mob. He boycotted church socials, dinner invites, any gathering of two or more. He was turning into a hermit minus the beard.

"Tonight," he had said. "Sometime."

No, he didn't like that tone. But if he was soft, accommodating, sensitive – like Dean? And where was Dean? Hemmed in, penned in. He had to get a passport to go around the block. It was no way to live.

"I can't make friends *for* you."

"*You're* my friend – my best friend."

When she said that, he felt sorry for her.

"You *are*," she insisted.

Someday she was going to use the past tense.

Jack took a final swig and screwed the cap back on the canteen. His eyes quickly scaled the pines. The clouds had darkened in spots and grown threadbare in others, like faded blue jeans. The sun was a fuzzy blotch, a mole stubbornly trying to burrow its way through. Judging by its position, Jack figured it must be two or three o'clock. If he retraced his steps, he would make it back to the access road before dark—no late stalks tonight: Dean would hit the panic button and send out the National Guard. Stuffing the canteen and trail snack into his pack, Jack surveyed the surrounding aspens as if snipers might be lurking within. A light breeze blew, shaking the lime-green leaves like sequins.

He had felt good heading out, but the queasiness returned to his mid-section and quickly spread throughout his body. Nothing serious—feverish tremors, more irritating than distressing, but they were impeding his usually keen judgement. Weaving between the pines, he came to a fallen oak tree. It was rotten timber: he could see and smell the bat dung caulking the hollow center. Still, instead of going around—a minor inconvenience—he clutched a branch for support and swung his leg up over the side. The branch snapped and sent him reeling to the ground. A stupid, novice mistake. He popped up and brushed the wet pine needles off. His shirt and pants were damp on the elbows and rear. He took his arrows from the bow-quiver and eyed each for damage. All okay. He hiked on, muttering self-reprimands.

The humming noise seemed to be growing louder. Was he nearing its source? Or had it centralized in his brain? Suddenly his head was buzzing fiercely. The whole damn hive must have been unleashed inside. He should have brought along a couple aspirin, just in case. But he was too stubborn. Had to do it *his* way. Because he was Jack W. Robinson, and he could outrun outhunt outhike outbike outlove . . . He didn't need anyone or anything. Just like his old man. A carbon copy. That's what Dean had meant to say last night on the redwood deck. Why else had he ushered him outside so quickly after dinner? To show off Robinson Acres? All that he, Jack, could have had? Floodlights illuminated a lawn as big as a football field; the plastic dome over the swimming pool bulged like a giant blister. Every house in the neighborhood soared into the night sky like a churchhouse. Cathedral row. Was Dean rubbing his nose in it? No. That wasn't like Dean. He'd just wanted to clear the air.

"So how do you like your job?"

"I like it—I do." Jack nodded vigorously.

Dean got right to the point, more or less. "I could really use some help right now. I'm swamped."

Who was convincing whom?

"No thanks," Jack said.

"You're sure? This is no B.S., Jack. I really could use the help."

Did he think Uncle Sam was starving him?

"Thanks. We're fine. I like what I'm doing."

"You're sure?"

"Thanks."

Carmen would be mad—furious! She still made occasional digs about "the refusal." Semi-jokingly. "But Jack had been a swinging single then. . . . "

A small tear appeared in the clouds. Sunlight leaked through, tossing quickglitter on the pines. Jack struggled along. He felt so listless, waterlogged. What was wrong? Every step another layer of mud stuck to his shoes. He was walking on twelve-inch heels, teeter-tottering on orthopedic feet.

He stopped to rest again. As he set down his bow and day pack, he saw a white flicker, a quick fuse, in the collage of green. A gray hump emerged from the shadows like a tiny island in the fog. Another hump, smaller and snow-spotted, followed behind. They were in no danger: it was buck season. Antlered deer only. Besides, he would never have shot a doe with a fawn.

The mother lowered her head and began nibbling the grass, but the little guy noticed him. He was approaching on skinny, nimble legs, herky-jerky. Ten yards shy he stopped. Staring directly at the hunter, a camo-Picasso, he tilted his head this way and that, trying to make sense of the mottled configuration of greens, browns, and blacks, this human plant. He edged closer, five feet. Jack could have reached out and touched him. He was tempted—counting coup, like the Indians. The little fellow stamped his forehoof, jerking and twisting and ducking his angular head like a shadow boxer. Curious. Just full of it. Like Dean's kids.

Jack was thoroughly enjoying the spectacle, but the mother was not. Something was fishy, but she wasn't sure what. Intermittently she raised her nose, sniffing suspiciously. Seeing, smelling nothing, she resumed her cautious nibbling. Ultimately her sixth sense got the best of her. She stamped a hoof and motioned to junior with her head. Reluctantly the little guy obeyed but kept glancing back until they had disappeared into the shadows.

Jack clapped his hands triumphantly, violating the silence and sending a clattering of hooves through the woods. "Dean!" he gasped, looking around, almost expecting to find his brother there. "Dammit, Dean." This was it. To bag a buck was nice, but this was the real trophy. The journey truly was the destination.

Riding a momentary high, he spread the plastic garbage bag and sat down, recalling other deer he had taken. Two years ago, for the first time, he had almost been shut out. He had missed most of the season with special training for the Bureau. It was closing day, 4:00 a.m. Carmen didn't like it.

"Sunday now? What do I tell the kids?"

"The ox is in the mire."

"Whose ox? Whose mire?"

"Yours. Mine. J. Edgar's."

"What next, Jack?"

"I'll be back . . . later."

He had driven to a wooded area an hour away and set up a tree stand. It was just after daylight when an eight-pointer began picking his way through the snow. It was a long shot, fifty-five, sixty yards, but he decided to chance it. He nocked an arrow, drew, anchored, released. The arrow hissed through the frigid air: one, two, three—counting to himself—forever it seemed. Then a quick double-rip, like fabric tearing, and the arrow bounced off an icy crust on the other side and scooted off across the snow. The buck looked around as if he had been struck by a pebble, lowered his antlered head, and continued nosing for grass. Then he folded up his spindly legs, lay down on his side, and calmly closed his eyes.

The rule was to always—*always*—wait a half hour minimum before retrieving your deer, no matter how sure the shot, because even a mortally wounded buck could spring to his feet and put a mile or two between himself and the hunter before dropping for good. But this time Jack had broken the rule, monkeying down the tree and sprinting to the animal. His instincts were correct. The arrow had nicked the heart and pierced cleanly through both lungs. A perfect shot, an instant kill. He skinned and gutted the animal in time to make it home for church at noon.

Another shot, two years earlier, had not been so perfect. Again he had shot from a tree stand, but this time it was autumn and the distance only thirty-five yards. But the broadhead had stuck in the buck's spine. He recalled the nightmare in painful detail: the animal lunging forward, his forehooves desperately pawing the ground as his hind legs collapsed: the grunting and snorting and awful head heaving as he dragged himself miserably through the mud. Then Jack, sliding down the tree like a fireman, leaving half his palms on the bark, racing over and putting another arrow in the contorting animal, in the chest this time, the vitals; the buck's head rearing back, his anguished eyes glaring at his torturer—a split second still-shot—then lunging again, twisting his antlered head as if trying to unscrew it, and the sounds—the awful snorting, choking sounds—the crippled leaps, blood dripping from both nostrils. Another arrow, another lunge. More flailing, grunting, snorting. "My God! Oh, my God!" He was turning him into a pin cushion.

Then the buck knife. Grabbing him by the antlers, sawing across his furry throat—a sloppy job; short, jagged cuts, the skin resistant, rubberized. Finally it gave, but a ghastly cry, blood-choke. "Dammit!" The vein! Get the vein! Not the vocal cords! He tried again, carving a fraction higher. The skin broke and blood gushed out like water from a faucet, smothering his trembling hands, splattering on the brown-and-gold earth.

Jack closed his eyes, bracing his forehead against his fists. That experience had almost made him give up bowhunting. He had sat out one season, a depressing winter. Housebound. Pacing the living room like a caged animal, staring out the perspiring windows at the gloomy Oregon sky, the eternal drizzle. No wonder the women went bonkers.

Three years later he shot and killed a man. It was self-defense, in the line of duty. What bothered him far more than taking a man's life—this man's in particular: he was drug scum, a low-life who dealt cheap stuff to grade school kids, a playground parasite—was how easy it had been. He drew his pistol, he pulled the trigger, a man was dead. That simple. He remembered little about the man except that he wore a mustache. Brown. Wispy. Was he white? Hispanic? Married? Kids? Did he like baseball? Who cared? Who the hell cared?

Jack let his mind go blank. He listened to the squirrels shrieking back and forth and the never-ending buzz and the wind like an invisible presence, a cool hand stroking the back of his neck. He felt his strength dissipating again, a slow fever in his arms and shoulders.

He was on his feet. Grabbing his bow, shouldering his pack, heading out again. He didn't go far before entering an area that looked hauntingly familiar. The pines were sparse, arthritic, their crippled limbs cobwebbed with moss. Fallen trees were gutted, sawdust spilling out their jagged ends. The woods here seemed in a state of transient decay. Jack looked around, trying to get his bearings. No, he had not passed this way before. He decided to follow the downward slope, assuming that would eventually lead him back to the access road.

The woods thickened. Soon the pines were packed so tightly he had to turn sideways to squeeze through. Leaning and fallen trees barricaded every opening and thoroughfare. He crawled under some, over others, sneaking through gaps like a rat in a three-dimensional maze. An hour later, knees and elbows raw and bleeding, forehead lacquered with sweat, he stumbled onto another clearing: no; it was the river of volcanic rock. He was walking in circles.

His eyes followed the igneous flow up the mountain. A white mist spilled over the top, billowing downward like an avalanche in slow-motion. Somehow he had gotten turned around. His built-in homing device had gone haywire.

Then he heard a sound like a rope being swung around and around—a huge rope, huge circles. He looked up and saw an enormous bird—eagle? condor?—beating its enormous wings. It was skirting the tops of the pines like a B-52 bomber. The bird traversed the gap in the sky and plunged down into the descending mist. Jack listened until he could no longer hear the haunting whoosh whooshing of its wings.

Gripping his bow, he started back down the mountain—or at least in the direction he thought was down. The woods looked dull and dark now, varnished without the shine. The aspens shook their leaves like a half-hearted cheering section. He told himself to relax, keep cool—follow the fundamental procedures. The Marines and the FBI had taught him that. But suddenly the forest had become his enemy. The pine trees glared at him like totem poles, every knothole a nefarious eye. He hastened his step to a trot. Soon he was sprinting recklessly through the woods, lowering his shoulder fullback-style and crashing through the branchwork. Limbs reached out like withered arms and clawed his camo clothing, scratched his cheeks, went for his eyes. He couldn't account for his panic; this had never happened to him before. Stumbling, he took a shot on the hip that stung like a bullet. He scrambled to his feet and ran on, busting branches, trampling ferns and flowers, a human tornado.

He covered two congested miles in minutes. Sweat poured down his face and stung his eyes. He licked his salty lips. The sky had turned to soot. The mountain grumbled like a cantankerous old man. He was running out of gas. The nausea hit again, hot and cold tremors. He looked around, blinking, trying to clear his eyes. The trees were swaying like dancers on a crowded floor.

Again he ordered himself to slow down. His legs finally obeyed, but his heart raced on. His free hand was a machete hacking at branches. He began talking aloud—praying. Sort of. Except his voice, his words, seemed foreign to him. It was someone else speaking, uncertain quite what to say. Simple words, naive—like Anna and Jack Jr.'s bedtime prayers: please bless Blankey and Pooh Bear and . . . His words were repetitious but for once they were not mechanical. They were real. Please, God, please.

The mountain grumbled again, a cynical reply. His ankles and knees were growing stiff. Rusty hinges. Hot and cold tremors chased up and down his spine, and a sweat and mucus mix formed in his mouth; he swallowed some, spit out the rest.

He saw a dead oak tree up ahead, its thick, gnarled trunk caught in a tortured pose, as if it had been electrocuted. It reminded him of a painting: Gethsemane.

Then he noticed the buzzing had stopped. Everything had. The forest was utterly still. He recognized that silence. He had heard it two days ago when they had stopped at the Grand Canyon en route to Flagstaff. It was just after sundown. The Japanese tourists had capped their cameras and filed back into the tour bus. Carmen and the kids had also gone back to the car. Standing alone on the overlook, Jack had gazed down into the vast, multi-tiered cavity that looked like a stairwell to the center of the earth. It had appeared fake, painted on. Overhead, a crow was circling the empty expanse, pinching something in its beak—bread for some homeless Elijah? As night filled the void like black water, Jack had listened to the bottomless silence. It was the sound of peace and death and what comes after. It was the earth sighing.

Listening now, he heard voices within the silence, whispers flowing secretly from tree to tree. Children's voices. They grew louder, rising to a glass-breaking pitch. He had heard that sound before also, walking down the corridor at church: "Whenever I hear the song of a bird/ Or look at the blue, blue sky." Then he had peeked through the little window on the door at the rows of young children, Anna and Jack Jr. among them, singing obediently along. But his kids had looked so stiff compared to the others, as if they'd had guns pointed at their backs. Especially Anna with her perpetual side-glancing eyes—big, brown, half spooked. Checking the corners—for what? The boogeyman? Child molesters? Kidnappers in Santa Claus clothing? Had he and Carmen laid it on too thick about not talking to strangers and staying close to Mom and Dad? No. They had been frank but tactful. Carmen was good at that. But little Anna sensed some inherent danger—congenital paranoia?—*out there*! At school, at the store, at the park. Walking on eggshells, like a doe in season. Flinching at everything.

Jack Jr. was worse. It had been near impossible getting him to stay in the nursery. That worried forehead. His mother's high cowlick. But why was he so afraid to play bear trap with his cousins? When Dad and Uncle Dean had lain out on the floor reaching for daring victims, his cousins had charged right in, laughing when they were caught and trapped in a scissors hold. Jack Jr. had played the wallflower, fingers in his mouth, blue eyes bulging. Caution was one thing, but intense paranoia? It was no way for a kid to act. Yet the vibes were there.

> Whenever I feel the rain on my face
> Or the wind as it rushes by
> Whenever I touch a velvet rose
> Or walk by a lilac tree
> I'm glad that I live in this beautiful world . . .

Beautiful, yes. The mountains were beautiful, the forests, the oceans and deserts. The animals, they were beautiful. People? The double-breasted executive, how about him? The one who lived in a castle on Houston's west side with his beautiful wife, caught putting semen into the bottle of his one-year-old daughter to acclimate her to the taste. My God! Sicko-weirdo. The kid didn't have a chance.

Kids. If the perverts didn't get them . . . The man who blistered the buttocks of a two-year-old—a Jack Jr. look-alike—that same mournful look of imminent disaster. A fly forever on the verge of being swatted. He'd had an accident, a little dribble down the leg. So what? Hadn't Mr. Macho ever wet his pants? Whack! Whack! Whack! with a hairbrush. "Don't you never do that again!" Later, sniffling, rubbing his fist back and forth under his runny nose, the boy had crept back into the living room where Mom and Mr. Macho were watching TV. She was trailer trash. Swollen arms, swollen face. Levis that could barely contain her thighs. Her boyfriend was spread out on the sofa, cracked vinyl with the foam rubber stuffing leaking out. Shirt open, beer dribbling down his chest, a tattoo on his upper arm: LIVE TO RIDE, RIDE TO LIVE.

"What did you learn, boy?"

"Ass hurt," the boy said, pointing to it. Miming Mom's vocabulary.

The man lunged and grabbed the boy by the arm, shaking him till his eyeballs did somersaults. "What? What did you say? I'll teach you to talk like that!"

He snatched the nearest thing—a pepper shaker—pried the boy's mouth open, and emptied it. The kid gagged, flailing his spider arms, then went limp. The mother screamed—token protests, but they got her probation. The judge tried to strike a deal to have her ovaries removed, but bleeding hearts had rushed in screaming human rights. Human? Mr. Macho got ten. He'd be on the streets in two.

That was the beautiful world his kids sang about in Sunday school. The real world. Jack's world. This wasn't The Cosby Show. In the world he worked in, love was never spoken. Satan picked your nose and made you eat it. Shat and fed it to you on a cowpie platter. Carmen, Diane—what did they know about it? Dean, he knew something but what he knew he was trying to forget. And Jack? He wanted, however blindly, to believe again.

He continued on, walking now, picking his way through the pines. An hour later when he once again found himself standing at the bottom of the volcanic river, he finally admitted to himself he was lost.

He closed his eyes, half-hoping that when he opened them he would be somewhere else. When he did, everything looked out of focus. Fog coming? Or was he going blind? Scales frosting up his eyes? No. Just the virus playing havoc with him. He removed his pack and began stuffing his mouth with trail snack. The raisin-nut-oatmeal mix had a fecal taste. He spit it out and rinsed his mouth with canteen water.

He hiked on, his queasiness giving way to despair. The buzzing started up again, from nowhere, and the taunting chatter of squirrels. His arms and legs were growing numb. He tried to wriggle his toes, but they had turned to stone. His strength was draining fast. He dropped his bow and fell to his knees, then onto his side. He rolled over onto his back and could feel the pine needles piercing him. I'm a pin cushion, he thought. It comes full circle.

He tried to move, but his body refused. He was staked to the ground. Gazing up at the branch-fractured sky, he admitted something else: he was afraid.

The clouds clamped shut. The thunderheads billowed like smoke from a crematorium. He heard the first faint plinks of rain.

It began as a soft, easy drizzle but quickly thickened until fat beads were splattering all over him. He mustered up enough strength to roll onto his belly and then, with nauseating effort, as if he were carrying the planet Atlas-style on his shoulders, he rose up on his hands and knees and squirmed the shoulder straps free. The pack slid down his back and hit the ground. He tried to unzip it, but his fingers were prosthetics. He finally managed, using his teeth, and removed his plastic poncho. But he couldn't get it on. His hands weren't cooperating.

Clawing the soggy soil, he dragged himself towards a fir tree and huddled underneath, head tucked like a skid row drunk, as the rain hurtled ruthlessly down. He looked up. Though it showed no burns or scars, the tree looked lightning-struck. Skeletal. This whole part of the forest appeared to be cursed, scourged. The rain roared down, thoroughly drenching him. His camo clothing clung to him like an amphibious second skin. His teeth chattered. He hugged himself to stay warm. He was crouching under a roof with no shingles.

My God, what had he done? What had he ever done? The day of his graduation, his father shoveling down the rest of his Taco Loco, too hyped up to truly taste the Mexican chef's handiwork: "We'll go fifty-fifty to start, and when I retire, I'll give you the whole thing! That won't be long—two, maybe three years is all."

Jack had forked a gob of cheese off his enchilada and studied it for the longest time as his father's cavernous smile gradually closed. No. Sorry. He couldn't see himself pushing pencils for the next forty years.

His father smiled, nodding. I'm a veteran, I understand, his pale blue eyes had said, dirgeful. He opened his billfold and dropped a fifty-dollar bill on the table – triple the tab. His paying hand patted Jack on the shoulder, then gripped it like a talon. His eyes were filled with tiny pink fractures. Jack was seeing him, for the first time, totally exposed. His bald head – the one that used to flash like a warrior's helmet whenever he charged the net with his Jack Kramer Special – was wrinkled now, a turnip texture.

"Jeezos peezos, Jack! Take the thing, will you?"

Jack looked down; he couldn't bear to see his father like that: pleading. "I can't, Pop."

"Who then? Who? You tell me!"

Dean? The Momma's boy? Take over the dry-cleaning empire he'd built from scratch? It would fold in a week. Dean didn't have the temperament, the gumption.

"Sleep on it. Will you do that? Think it over?" He was begging. It was pathetic. He was.

"I have, Pop. I'm sorry."

"Dammit all! You know what you're throwing away? To go play army?"

Jack stared at his napkin, spotted with enchilada sauce, like blood. Then he felt a thunk, his father's knuckles on the side of his head. Like old times. Except this time he did not call him knot-head. He didn't need to.

Two days later Jack boarded the plane for Officers Candidate School in Quantico. Did he regret it now? Standing on Dean's redwood deck at twilight, gazing across the fleet of multi-storied rooftops and the golf course receding into the pines like a rolling green ocean. Dammit all, Dean! Dammit! Don't look at me like that – that mopey-dopey-eyed pitying look. I don't care. I honestly don't care about your swimming pool and Cadillac and your clear-as-crystal well water. Just please don't look at me like that. Don't think what you're thinking.

No. He was doing what he wanted. Maybe not what Carmen wanted or what Dean and Diane wanted. But you have to trade a lot to live like the lords and ladies of the mountain. White collar bark and beg. Here, boy! Fetch, boy! Roll over, boy! They needed so much – or thought they did – to be happy in the great American way. Hell, all he needed was a bow and a sleeping bag.

And an umbrella, he thought as the rain splattered down, varnishing fallen logs and lichen-covered rocks. He was lost in a rain forest. He fumbled with his poncho, but his fingers were rubber hooks. Fat and worthless.

Gradually the rain thinned. He stood up, but his legs were sand bags. He stumbled towards a huge log and sat down. It crumbled on contact. He was sitting in it, like a porta-john. The Great White Hunter, stuck! If Dean could see him now! If Carmen!

Pressing down with his palms, he tried to lift himself out, but his arms were empty sleeves. He felt like a total fool. Where was his dunce cap? Dean could do no worse than this.

Thunder cracked the sky. The B-52 dropping its leftovers. The sky was black and boiling. Lightning slashed across it. The devil's pitchfork. Or God's crooked scimiter? The mountain exploded again, and the ground beneath him trembled.

Then a pellet struck him in the head. Another. Handfuls. Hard white bullets were striking the earth and hopping around like Mexican jumping beans, billions of them. Thickening like snow. Christmas in September. What next?

Jack covered his head with his hands and waited it out. Carmen would laugh if she found out – and it would not be a fun laugh. It would be sinister. Just desserts. Quiet, think-no-evil Carmen had summoned the gods on her behalf.

What had happened to Carmen? To him – *them*? Had they become dumb statistics, victims of the life cycle: boy meets girl, they fall in love, get married, have children: they grow old, they die. When he tried, he could still see and smell those premarital summer evenings in the hammock on the porch of the old stone house overlooking the Provo Valley. Crickets, the muddy canal, the tantalizing redolence of fresh-cut grass. Warm nights, clear skies, the electromagnetic manta-ray outline of the Wasatch. The cool aphrodisia of apple blossoms, Utah Lake paved with midnight, the furnaces of Geneva Steel lighting up the sky like Moses' fire by night. Her supple body in cut-offs that rode her thighs like a teddy, frayed hems on golden flesh, back when they were both virgins and permanently in heat, drunk with the mystery of flesh and summer and innuendo. Dangling the carrot. Playing her trump card so expertly: a little necking, purring in his ear: "After you're married in the temple, do you think you'll have to wear your garments *all* the time?" Running a finger down his chest, his belly, to his belt. Always stopping there. The prenuptial tease.

Typical, that once the ring was on the finger. No. She hadn't planned it that way. Who could have foreseen? A universal lament among men. Maybe the Italians had the right idea—or polygamy. Then again . . . one wife was plenty. If they only realized their holding power, what just an occasional surprise, to wake up in the middle of the night to her hand stroking you. Yes. No. Go. It wasn't just the raw thrill of it either, but her, your wife, with you and no one else. A stroke of righteous wickedness once in a while. If they only realized. But maybe it was better they remained stale. On ice. Easier to get out the door.

Jack listened to the last hard pellets rebound off the pines. The clouds had shredded slightly. Jack sucked in the wintry fragrance—like Thor, tightening his magic belt to double his strength—and brought his fist down on the log: it gave way like balsa wood. Again. Again. Again. Smashing a gap around his entrapped buttocks, pressing down with both fists, he managed to lift himself out, but the effort sapped his little remaining energy. Three steps and he was on his knees. Dear God, Father. He knew what he wanted, needed, to say, but the words—he couldn't articulate.

He closed his eyes, thinking, saying nothing. When he opened them, sunlight spotted the ground, a leopard look. The wet pine needles glistened brilliantly, yet little drops continued striking his camo hat. He looked up and saw a blue wedge splitting the grim clouds. Sunshine rain. The devil's beating his wife, he thought. Then he realized the drops were falling from the bearded branches overhead. He laughed, his voice booming through the woods. He felt his strength returning, a helium sensation. But when he tried to stand, his body crumbled. He lay twisted on his side, gunned down. Alone – so totally alone. As the sun spots dimmed, his spirit seemed to depart with them, leaving his wrecked body behind. Something grabbed him by the throat, his peppered throat, and reached down until he gagged. He was choking. Thrashing on the wet ground, clawing at his collar, he cried out. It let go. But the voice was not his but his son's. Whiney Jack Jr., spindly, fidgety, nervous-in-the-service. And so tense. When he ate, his bowels knotted up and he would be constipated for days. Screaming on the toilet as he tried to push out baseballs. *Always* yelling – he had no other volume. Loud and louder. So intractable, demanding. Just like . . . Dad?

Jack finally plugged his ears – his heart, too? Had he and Carmen grown accustomed to the constant racket, like the yellow jackets buzzing in the netherwoods? No wonder she looked dragged through ten knotholes at the end of the day. Zombie eyes. He ought to tell her, express at least this much. It was so hard. Hey, but that's life. He couldn't help. Yes. Some things. His gruff homecomings. Eight, nine, ten o'clock sometimes. New job, long hours commuting an hour to and from. Sure he was tired, too pooped for anything. But if there were dirty dishes in the sink, he'd look, grunt, mumble something – kids asleep? Grab his dinner from the oven, wrapped in tin foil. Wolf it down. Caliban. While Carmen quickly cleared the table and slipped off to bed to play possum.

The woods grew darker. His eyes climbed the pines. The sky was smothered again. An old woman's wind-ravaged hair. Witch whorls. Lying on his side, he curled up like an embryo and closed his eyes. Dear God, Father.

When he looked again, little geysers were steaming up the forest, as if a great fire had been quenched. He rose to his feet and slowly, comically, like a drunk on a tightrope, began picking his way through the webwork. Eventually he stumbled across a game trail and followed it through a chain of small meadows, encouragingly familiar, that ended in a thick grove of aspens whose sour apple scent was inebriating. Where was he now? The white-trunked trees formed a protective wall around a garden of hanging vines and flowers. Blossoms of all colors spotted the scene like bright wallpaper. Sunlight leaked through the branched rafters. Looking up, he saw deep cuts and slices of blue. Tiny prisms and mini-rainbows sparkled on the grass. Waist-deep in ferns, inhaling the green delirium, he began shivering again, but not from the wetness or the cold. He felt warm and weak but wonderfully so. Light as air. His spirit departing again but this time his body was coming along for the ride.

Then he saw it—them. There were two.

They were standing side by side, identical except one was slightly larger than the other, like a mature father and son. Big and beautifully black, a small tree branching from each head, they stood perfectly still, like statues chiseled from obsidian, staring at him as if they had been expecting him and were maybe a little peeved because he had kept them waiting.

Even if he had had an elk tag, even if he had been within range—fifty yards, fifty feet, ten inches. No. It would have been the height of petty human arrogance, like shooting an arrow at the sun or trying to build a tower to heaven.

Jack returned their stare, waiting, but for what he wasn't sure. He wanted them to stay, linger, approach even.

The exchange was brief. The bigger one, the poppa, lifted his head slightly—a dare? a challenge? an invitation?—waited a moment or two, then turned and strutted off, his miniature following like a shadow. The aspens seemed to momentarily part for them, an Arabian Nights phenomenon.

Then they were gone.

The barbed wire was a giveaway. He followed it up a small rise and down a mile or so to where the forest ended abruptly, a few feet shy of another fence line. By the time he reached the trail, the sky had cleared except for a few clouds bunched up above the peaks. Birds twittered. The aspens blazed flesh-white as the sun made a soft landing on the hilly horizon. It flared briefly, a phoenix-finale, then dropped out of sight, leaving behind only a gassy pink residue. The blue sky darkened. Calm

· · · · ·

waters. A coyote howled. Then silence. Jack paused to listen. It was the sound of twilight, of the wind. It was the sound of the rock he had tossed over the great canyon's rim whistling all the way down to the bowels of the earth. A bird, a falcon falling.

Daddy-Daughter Date

. . . .

It's a hectic life, a hectic world. But it was her turn and I'd been putting her off for weeks. That's easy to do with Kristin – easier than the others.

I have four daughters and each week I take one of them out on a Daddy-Daughter Date – their "D.D.D." That way, once a month they each get a night out alone with the old man.

Theoretically. In practice I'm sporadic. I'll get busy and skip a week or two or three. Realistically, they average a D.D.D. every two or three months. But that ratio is deceptive. Jackie, our oldest, never lets me off the hook. When it's her turn, it's *her* turn: our squeakiest wheel. The youngest two are less adamant although it usually takes some fast talking and a minor bribe to put them off awhile: "How about I'll bring you home a Rainbow-Brite coloring book tonight, and we'll do our D.D.D. next week, okay?" (When I resort to such tactics, Barbara knife-eyes me from the kitchen. My hands go up, my shoulders too. Guilty. But when your back's to the wall . . .)

Kristin, our second-born, has always been the accommodating one: an all-night sleeper from day one; potty-trained at a year-and-a-half. One of those. But because she is the most amenable, she is also the most easily put off. On her night, after the dinner dishes have been cleared and I have covered the table with floor plans, she will sneak up behind me, elf-like, and whisper in a timid little voice that on the one hand melts my heart

. . . . .

but on the other makes me cringe because, once again, of course, it is the very busiest evening of my life and I simply have not got time, not tonight. "Dad?"

And she senses this. I can tell by the apologetic timbre in her voice which is underscored only by the fatal grimace she semi-successfully hides with a dimpled smile and a sigh. And sometimes less than that. Sometimes she will merely remove the PIMA SAVINGS AND LOAN calendar from the kitchen wall and point to the date, swelling her cheeks like little balloons waiting to be popped, her freckled forehead twisted, her blue eyes drooping like a sad clown's.

"Sweetie," I will say, slipping an arm around her tiny waist, exhaling extra deep, extra loud – poor, tired, hard-working Dad – and gesture towards the blueprints spread out like a multi-layered tablecloth and the half dozen others still waiting to be unscrolled. "I'm really swamped tonight."

That's all it takes. She'll smile her pixie smile. "A rain check, Dad?"

"Do you mind?"

A shrug. "Noooo." Then, brightly, her face lighting up like an instant sunrise: "It's okay, Dad!" As if she, at eight-and-a-half, fully comprehends the adult obligations denying me what ought to be the simple joy of a night out on the town with my kid.

Like I said, it's a hectic life. Some things happen so fast if you blink you'll miss the main event. Any good parent will testify. And it's hard, it's tough. In your mind, you post warning signs: do not, Mitchell Kerns, become so yoked to your job and the Great American Get-Ahead Game that one day you finally pull your head out of your briefcase and it hits you: "Hey, what ever happened to that freckled little kid who used to come around with a Cabbage Patch Doll wrapped in a blanket saying, 'Play house, Dad?' " In your mind you know better. You really ought to sit down and read the kid a story or build her a mini-mansion out of Leggos. But being parents, human, caught up in the food-on-the-table, roof-over-the-head racket – well, you've got to make a living, don't you? *Somebody's* got to pay the rent. You can't play ping-pong twenty-four hours a day. We aren't, after all, kids anymore.

Which was one reason – probably the main one – why Barbara and I instituted the D.D.D.: I did not want to be a stranger to my children. I did not want to become the Invisible Man in my own home. I did not, most of all, want to be like my father.

But Barbara the English major accuses me via Shakespeare: "Your words go up, your thoughts remain below." Take the girls ice skating, she says. Sit down and watch *Return to Oz* with us. Put away those floor plans for one night. She says I'm a workaholic; I say I'm a reformed beachcomber, making up for lost time. I cite old evidence: I never held a job, full or part-time, until I met and married Barbara. A silver-spoon kid, sort of. "Just paying my dues, Barb." Twelve years ex post facto.

But D.D.D. Occasionally I'll splurge and take my "date" to Bob's Big Boy for a hamburger and then to a movie, but more often it's a quick trip to the Dairy Queen for soft ice cream or a sundae. Because we live ten miles from town, I usually run a few errands too. One is Jackie's limit. After that, she begins gritting her teeth, seething, murmuring, "This *isn't* a Daddy-Daughter *Date!*" Kristin, on the other hand, will sit patiently licking her ice cream cone while I dash in and out of K-Mart, Safeway, Waldenbooks. ("Just a quickie here, kid." "Okay, Dad.") Sometimes she will trail me, like a faithful little dog.

I knew the night of June 18th was going to be different for several reasons. First, the moment I got home from work and stepped inside the door, Kristin was there, spindly arms folded, waiting. "Dad," she said, "are we going on a D.D.D. tonight?" Neither her tone nor her expression were demanding, yet it was the first time she had ever confronted me directly about her D.D.D., and with a whole English sentence.

June 18th was also the night I had no excuse. For once I was caught up – or as caught up as I could ever hope to be, given my workload and overbooking mentality. Also, Barbara had conveniently drummed up a dozen reasons why "one of us" absolutely had to drive back into town tonight: Jackie absolutely had to be at the church at 6:30 for a cookie baking party; the wedding present Barbara had wrapped and ribboned for Bill Swenson absolutely had to be delivered ("They're leaving tomorrow for the North Rim . . . *early!*"). And of course there were three or four errands that absolutely had to be run if we were to survive until the weekend. Kristin even had a Happy Birthday coupon for a free Baskin-Robbins ice cream cone that absolutely had to be used tonight because it expired, portentously, June 19th.

And there was Jessie Walker.

Back in March, Kristin's second grade class had written "pen pal" letters to some people in the local rest home. When her letter to Jessie Walker went unanswered, Kristin was disappointed and a little hurt, too. I encouraged her to write another letter, which she did, in her struggling D'Nealian hybrid, and even enclosed her school picture. When that one wasn't answered, Kristin was so miffed she began muttering softcore curses against Jessie Walker, her second grade teacher (for putting her up to it), and life in general. Reluctant to see my angel child develop a warped view of the world before her ninth birthday, I told her to write once more and this time we would deliver the letter to Jessie in person. This perked her spirits remarkably.

That was in mid-May.

"Of course we're going on a D.D.D.!" I said. "Right after dinner!"

Her eyes lit up like New Year's Eve. "Thirty-One Flavors?"

"Sure! We'll get you an ice cream so big it'll take you all summer to eat it!"

"Oh, goody! And then can we see Jessie Walker too?"

"Jessie Walker?" I said, as if I had forgotten.

"You know, the letter?"

"The letter?" I looked at Barbara, not for sympathy but understanding, knowing full well I would find neither. There was no connection in her mind, and only a very nebulous one in mine.

"Sure," I said. "Bring your letter. Third time's a charm, right?"

Weather-wise we couldn't have ordered a nicer evening: warm, clear, windless, just the sort of almost-solstice night we mountain people suffer six months of snow for. The sun was working overtime, showering gold dust through the pines and stretching shadows into infinity. The sky was so sharp and clear the peaks looked like paper cut-outs pasted on. The day was closing like a big, lazy yawn.

It was a short drive into town, fifteen minutes down I-17. Jackie the bookworm sat in back reading Judy Blume while Kristin shared the front seat with me. As usual, she had dressed up for the occasion: a pale green dress with little white polka-dots and a wide, white collar. She sat with her scuffed up knees together and her pale little hands cupped between her thighs, as if she were very nervous or excited or cold. Barbara had tied her blond hair in a pony tail. This image of simple innocence was obscured only by a pair of gaudy red and gold ornaments dangling from her ears like fishing lures. Signs of the times, I suppose.

She remained silent—par for Kristin—leaving me the burden of conversation.

"So how do you like your swimming teacher?"

"Fine."

"Are you glad school's out?"

"Yes."

"Do you . . . ?" I was stumped. What next? Nice weather? Favorite TV show? You like the Lakers or the Celtics in the playoffs? It struck me how long it had been, and how removed I had become from her little world of Barbie dolls and fluorescent jump ropes. It was like trying to make small talk with a stranger in a stuck elevator—these mundane questions! But what alternative? "Excuse me, but how do you feel about America's covert military operations in Nicaragua and the secret Iranian arms deal?" Let it ride, Mitch. Let it ride.

We drove down Milton to Santa Fe, left on Leroux, and on up Cherry Hill to the church where we dropped off Jackie. ("Back at nine, kiddo! Save us some chocolate chips!") Then we went up Fort Valley Road to Bill Swenson's place, a tri-level, barn-shaped house at the foot of the mountain.

Bill is an easy-going outdoor type whose garage looks like a sporting goods outlet—kayaks, canoes, rifles, bows, skis, and enough backpacks and camping paraphernalia to outfit a Boy Scout troop. Pushing fifty, he looks thirty-five, despite a bald dome collaged with autumn-colored freckles and a stiff, reddish goatee that gives him the ruminating look of a Russian psychiatrist. He was getting re-married at the Grand Canyon that weekend. His fiancee and her teenaged son and daughter had moved in a week ago. When Kristin and I drove up, they were all sitting in the outdoor loft, chatting idly over dinner as the last shafts of sunlight smeared a deep blush on the peaks. The TV was on, barely audible. Bill immediately beckoned us upstairs. That required a short journey through the garage, up a ski slope of a staircase that had barely passed code, and through the living room. I led, Kristin following warily behind.

I opened the sliding glass door and stepped out onto the loft. Bill stood up, shook my hand, and introduced me. "Mitch, this is Suzanne. Suzanne, Mitch Kerns."

At first glance, she was quite attractive; at second . . . well, her curly blond mop called to mind Harpo Marx. But her eyes were large and cheerful, with hints of green, and she laughed loudly and spontaneously. I liked her immediately. Her two kids—Don, a wiry, buzz-cut basketball star, and Kathy, a dishwater blond who played seven different instruments—were equally amicable. I'd seen their clean-cut faces before, in the SEARS Christmas catalog.

I handed the gift to Suzanne, who thanked me and said I really didn't have to but . . . "we're glad you did!"

"My—*our*—pleasure. Barbara picked it out. My wife."

"That's really nice, Mitch," Bill said. "Really nice."

Suzanne looked around as if she'd misplaced something. She hadn't but I had. "Your little girl," she said, "I think you've lost her."

Yes, indeed! Halfway through the living room! She was staring up at the trophy on the wall—a huge elk's head whose glass-eyed glare, belying its present status, surveyed the roost as if he were still king of the forest. A rack of antlers branched from his head like giant calipers.

I opened the glass door quietly. "Boo!" I said, and Kristin's shoulders gave a little leap. "Come on out. Join the party." She smiled self-consciously and followed me through the doorway.

"This is Kristin," I said.

Bill, whose voice runs like honey, said, "Hi, Kristin. Would you like a drink? A Seven-Up maybe? Would that be all right?"

Kristin looked down at her shiny Sunday shoes and whispered, "Yes."

"Seven-Up it is," Bill said. Then, to me: "How about you, bud? A little chaser maybe?"

He was joking, of course. He knew I didn't drink. I hadn't, in fact, since meeting Barbara and converting to Mormonism fourteen years ago. A fitness nut, Bill didn't indulge either.

"Seven-Up will be fine," I said.

His powerful kayaker's hand gripped my shoulder as he got up. "Two Seven-Ups, coming up! Hey, sit down, Kristin! Make yourself at home!" He winked at me. "You too, bud."

Kristin and I sat down at the round dining table. Kathy began dutifully clearing the dinner dishes. A soft roar went up from the portable TV. "What's the score?" I asked.

"Lakers by two," Don said. "Another nail-biter."

The sky was growing darker. Red and throbbing, the last shred of sun was snagged in the pines like a scarlet bird trying to shake itself free. Bill returned and gave a can of Seven-Up to me and one to Kristin. She struggled briefly with the flip-lid, then looked at me and shrugged. I popped the lid. She took a long swallow, her little Adam's apple bobbing like a float. Suzanne smiled. "She's so cute."

Kristin always elicits this response from strangers. Old hat to me, I usually don't think much of it. But that night, observing her objectively—the freckled nose, the blond pony tail, the cream-smooth skin unmarred except for the scratches on her knees—why, she looked like the sort of perfectly formed creature that might have pranced around Eden in the buff, chasing birds, sniffing wildflowers.

Suzanne looked at her and smiled again. "Oh, Bill, get the ferret!"

"Yeah!" Don and Kathy seconded.

Bill was up and out the sliding glass door. A minute later he returned, cradling a furry little guy that looked like a cross between a cat and a mongoose. "This is Musky," he said, setting him on the table. Musky began sniffing around for dinner scraps. Suzanne picked up a stray strand of spaghetti. Musky instantly went supine, opening his little jaws while Suzanne fed him spaghetti scraps. "Want to hold him, Kristin?" she asked.

"Sure. Sure she does." Bill rubbed Musky's belly and handed him to Kristin. She stroked his fur, tentatively at first. Behind her the final hints of daylight cut a smelting edge around the mountain peaks. Musky looked up at her and gestured with his nozzled face. More, more! his whiskered expression seemed to say. Kristin looked at me and smiled, her dimples like happy parentheses.

I wish I could have captured that moment on film. But a camera wouldn't have done it justice. The feelings, the sounds and smells. It was so quiet, yet full of gentle little noises: a bird twittering and the fading echo of a pick-up truck. A crow hovering in the sky as the mountains disappeared into the night. It was an All-American pastoral, and while part of me—the lingering skeptic from my '60s youth—sensed something artificial and phoney and too-homey-for-its-own good, my parental instincts wanted to freeze that moment forever.

But the spaghetti scraps were gone now, and so was the sun. Stars were quickly seeding the night. I stood up. "We'd better boogie, kid."

Bill and Suzanne thanked us again. As we passed through the living room, Kristin traded eyes with the debunked king of the forest.

"Where to now?" I asked.

Kristin shrugged. "I don't care."

"Jessie Walker?"

"Okay."

I wanted to get that over with, before the ice cream, so we could end the evening on a bright note. I was not looking forward to the visit for several reasons, the main one being my father.

A few years ago at a family get-together I had the gall to ask about him: where was he? What was he up to? Did anyone know? Following a long silence, Stan confessed that he'd heard, somewhere, from the friend of a friend, that he was in a rest home "some place in New Mexico."

"I hope he dies there," my mother said, "all alone."

I had never actually been inside a rest home. I'd read horror stories about dog food entrees and garlic enemas and so forth. But surely these were exaggerations. Also, I'd heard some very good things about our rest home here in town. If young students like Kristin were writing letters to the clients—or are they "patients?"—someone from within must have spearheaded the effort. I assumed, too, that if kids had been asked to write letters, the recipients would be able to read them and write back. They had been screened, in other words.

Perched atop a grassy knoll, "our" rest home was a fairly new structure, four small units, actually, each with an identical homespun exterior: log walls with big, wide windows that greeted you like welcome signs. Little juniper trees dotted the grounds and several hearty lilacs scented the air. The cobbled walkways, spotlessly clean, were lined with red and gold tulips that looked and smelled sweet enough to eat. A red brick chimney protruding from each gingerbread-colored rooftop and the surrounding pines completed the cottage-in-the-woods look.

The interior boasted champagne-colored carpeting, textured white walls, linoleum hallways waxed and polished to a blinding shine. The amicability ended there.

Entering the main unit, we saw two skeletons in wheelchairs. Female, I think. Immediately they exerted what little strength remained in their withered arms and wheeled themselves towards us. Both wore a look of broken hope: Had we come to rescue them? their forlorn eyes seemed to ask. Faded to transparency, the wattled lids flickering with false hope, they stared at us as if trying to recall faces long forgotten.

Another wheelchair rounded the corner: like an ambush. An old Navajo, wearing a black felt cowboy hat, one eye puffed shut, glared at us briefly through his good eye, then wheeled himself

· · · · ·

away. Down the hall, a splintery old woman sat on the edge of her bed jabbering to a bald man with a crabapple chin wheeling himself slowly by. Her calves dangled below the frayed hem of her blue bathrobe like rods of tallow. She had the starved face of a baby bird, and the same innocent glee. She was moving her bare feet flirtingly back and forth, like Rebecca of Sunnybrook Farm, sharing her latest triumph—or trying to—with the bald man: "I ate all my dinner tonight! I ate every bite!"

There was a loud crash! Shattered glass. I saw it: the bald man had swept his arm across her dinner tray, knocking her glass to the floor. A nurse, an Indian girl, strolled over and calmly rolled the old fellow away as the woman's wounded voice chased him down the hall: "You don't have to act like that! Why do you do that? Why can't you just get along?" Turning towards us—sympathetic ears?—"I'm getting out of here! I don't like the people here! I won't be in here very long. I have family, you know. I don't like these people . . . especially the women. They're not . . . *natural*!"

Another woman appeared out of nowhere, giving Kristin a start. She wheeled towards us with damn-the-torpedoes resolve, finally braking a foot short. Her hefty upper body was covered with a striped blouse of rainbow colors. Penny-sized scabs and liver marks spotted her scaly arms, desert dry. She looked diseased—everyone there did. I felt as those ancients of Israel must have, communing with the lepers. I wanted to keep my distance for fear I, too, might be contaminated. Old age? Mortality? Whatever it was they had, I didn't want it.

If Kristin felt threatened or traumatized, she was hiding it well. Although her hands were knotted nervously behind her back, she managed a courtesy smile, even as the woman glared at us like a mad scientist: rippled forehead, frenzied eyes, storm-swept hair springing from her head in all directions. "I'm getting out of here," she vowed. "Been in here four days." She leaned towards us, her blue eyes shifting left-to-right: our little secret.

"This is not a nice place." Left-right-left. "I don't like to say that, but it's true." Her face reared up. "You don't believe me!"

"Yes, I believe you," I said.

She eyed Kristin up and down as if she were something good to eat. Her forehead relaxed. "How many years are you?"

"Eight," Kristin squeaked.

"Eight. That's nice, that's nice." She gave Kristin another head-to-toe. Envious? Recalling a happier chapter from her past?

"Excuse us," I said, and hustled Kristin away.

We walked down the main hall, past more of the living dead. The carpet was clean, spotless—the walls too, and the linoleum. Yet there was a pervading odor—a nauseating mix of urine and feces and antiseptics. And cafeteria food, that steam-cooked stench. The smell of imminent something: Death, waiting in the lunch line. If my hay fever-impeded nostrils were offended by the scent, Kristin's ultra-sensitive nose must have been on the rack. If so, she was hiding that well also.

We wandered around until we stumbled upon the staff lounge, a cramped cubicle stinking of old yogurt and cigarettes. A nurse looked up from her *National Enquirer*. "Jessica Walker? Room 205."

We walked back to the main hall, but Kristin balked outside the open double doors. Our sneak preview had been plenty. She did not want to go in there, and neither did I. But we had come this far.

"Ah, come on," I coaxed. "Be tough! Be brave!"

She was. I was not.

A gallery of vacant, homeless eyes followed us like dimmed spotlights as we slalomed through the obstacle course of wheelchairs separating us from room 205. We entered cautiously. Two beds were divided by a flimsy curtain. In one, a woman was sleeping—or dead. A skeleton with white hair. The other was empty: a tumble of sheets and blankets. Beside it, in a wheelchair, sat the hefty woman we had spoken to in the hall.

"Excuse me," I said. "Are you Jessie Walker?"

Her chin went up, a vestigial pride. "Jessica Ann Walker! I am!"

I introduced myself and—reluctantly, I'll admit—offered my hand, reading the bony braille in her grip. A sad tale, maybe

- - - - -

91

even tragic. "This is Kristin," I said. "She has something for you." Kristin held the letter out to her.

"Thank you!" she said, grasping it firmly but tenderly, as if it were a slice of bread and she were starving; looking at us that way, pale eyes full of hunger and gratitude. "Thank you," she said, her voice quavering. "Thank—" Rattling the envelope, her face scarecrow seamed: "You're kind. You're both so very kind." She spoke in little sobs and belches.

"Where are you from?" I asked.

"Buckeye! Buckeye, Arizona!" Her eyes bugged briefly, then clenched shut. Painfully, as if she had been stabbed from behind. Her voice broke, staccato sobs. "They didn't ask me or anything. They just sent me up here. . . . " She sucked in a deep breath and wheezed through her nose. Kristin's weight shifted from one Sunday shoe to the other.

I've never been very demonstrative physically, especially towards strangers. A handshake, a guarded hug, was always the rule in my family. Formal affection. However, with quiet effort I put my hand on Jessie Walker's arm—droopy, dry skin. A shaved hound dog's. I was perplexed, confused. Nothing made any sense. Why, for instance, had they sent her all the way up north? If Buckeye didn't have a rest home, surely Phoenix . . . ? And who were "they" anyway, to wield that kind of life and death authority?

"How long have you been here?" I asked.

"Twelve . . . twelve days."

Twelve? What had happened to four?

"My Daddy . . . my Dad—" She broke down again. Her nose began dripping. She wiped it with her scabby forearm and thanked us again for coming. Then her veiny hands went to her wheels, a brief struggle. "Move your foot," she said to me, rather gruffly. I complied. She wheeled over to her dresser, opened the top drawer, and removed a box of Pepsodent. She tapped the tube out of the box. "Here," she said, handing it to Kristin. "You take this. It's yours. You use it to clean your teeth." She made a brushing motion with her forefingers. Kristin nodded. "You have a toothbrush? My Daddy used a toothbrush for—" Her head dropped;

her fists went to her eyes. Godawful sucking sounds, emphysemic. I patted her saggy shoulder.

"You'll be okay," I said. "You're going to be all right. We'll come," and here I paused. She dropped her hands and looked up at me with pleading eyes. "We'll come again and visit you," I said.

"Thank you," she said, reclenching her fists, shaking them. "Thank you. You're kind. So kind."

I shook her hand, fully intending to return, yet knowing I probably would not, knowing that once Kristin and I had escaped her pathetic gaze, I would find enough convenient reasons not to.

"You're kind. So kind."

I shook my head. Sorry. You've got the wrong fellow.

Then Kristin stepped forward and offered her hand, a gutsy gesture. "Nice meeting you," she squeaked.

We left, dodging wheelchairs. The skinny woman in the ragged bathrobe was sitting on her bed. I waved; she smiled and waved back. Like the Tournament of Roses Queen on a hunger strike.

I shoved open the front door and we re-entered the tranquil night of purple skies and pine tree silhouettes. Insects were orbiting the street lights and the spicy odors from Ramona's Cantina were overwhelming even the scent of sun-fried pine needles. Two slender-thighed college girls pedaled by on ten-speeds.

We got in the car. Although it was still warm inside, I rolled up my window, sealing out the night sounds of the city. I knew, as a parent, a father, I should say something, and I wanted to very badly—I wanted to be like Gregory Peck in *To Kill a Mockingbird* and say something simple yet profound and memorable, something that would put the experience into perspective and that years from now Kristin would recite back to me over Pepsi and pizza. With a laugh, a smile.

But my head was not together just then—my thoughts weren't. They were nervous night bugs on a hot tin timeline skittering between my past and future, searching for a friendly resting place. There were none. Only this recollection: my mother in the kitchen with the telephone receiver clamped between her chin and collarbone, jotting a note with one hand and stirring the lentil stew with the other, Stan and Derek wrestling on the living room floor and me sprawled out a few feet from them crying my head off for who knows why as my father—who I remember only as a tall, mustachioed semi-stranger smelling of sardines and chewing tobacco—slouched on the patchwork sofa watching the ball game. Then Mom, cupping her hand over the mouthpiece, hollering at him: "Will you *please* get him out of here for a few minutes!" "Him" being me, though I was a cause of only a fraction of the chaos, albeit a large fraction.

And for once my father surprised all of us: rising in his slow, stiff manner, like the star athlete coming off the bench to win the game in overtime, he winked at Mom and said, "Sure, Mother." Then he walked over to me and held out his mechanic's hand— big as a baseball mitt and permanently creased with grease. "Come on, boy." I was stunned to silence.

We lived in the San Fernando Valley then, when for every housing tract there were still several acres of open fields and orange groves. We had a distant neighbor we really didn't know, Orlando Contreras, who owned several horses. My father walked me down the sloping dirt road towards Orlando's. I remember it being hot, typically August in L.A. The smell of the sun-baked dirt was strong and the weeds, brittle dry, reached up past my waist as we cut across an unfenced field. Little burrs and foxtails clung to my socks and sneakers, an itchy, stickery feeling that almost made me cry, but I held back because I was all alone with my father and afraid, partly, but also proud—or I wanted him to be proud. I didn't want to be a little boob in his presence. Even at that young age I sensed how important that was.

I had no idea where we were going and I was afraid to ask. We finally stopped at Orlando's wire fence. My father began yanking tufts of grass and feeding them to the horses. There were three: a white, a brown, and a great big one he kept calling "Red." He gave a tuft to me. "Go on," he said. "They won't hurt you!" So I did. I fed a tuft to Red and one to the white and then the brown, and then Red again, and so on, feeding them just as fast as my father could hand me more grass, for a good hour it seemed, though it was probably just a few minutes.

There was a culvert nearby, where water poured into a stream. My father knelt down by the mouth and sailed sticks and paper cups and anything else that would float, cheering me on while I stood on the bank bombing his fleet with rocks. "Atta boy! Blow him out of the water!"

By the time we finally left, the moon was up and stars were freckling the sky. Walking home, I knew we'd catch hell from my mother for being so late and holding up supper. My father knew also. Still, halfway up the hill he stopped and put his huge hand on my shoulder and gave it a manly squeeze. Surprise number three. "Hey, buddy," he said, "you're my little buddy, did you know that?"

I nodded obediently, wanting very much to believe him. At that moment, perhaps I did.

"You know something, buddy? There isn't anywhere in the world I'd rather be right now than here with you. No one I'd rather be with. You know that?" Then he gave my shoulder an extra hard squeeze. I was three, almost four. A month later he was gone.

I removed my hand from the ignition and looked at Kristin. She was sitting in her familiar pose, shoulders hunched shyly, hands cupped between her thighs, that cold and nervous look. The tube of Pepsodent was resting on her lap. What to say? This is where you go, Kristin, when the money runs out. When the love runs dry. This is where you go, Kristin, when you're old and no one cares anymore.

"Kristin? Do you see now why Jessica didn't answer your letters?"

She looked down at her cupped hands. "Yes."

I patted her skinny thigh.

"How about some ice cream?"

Very cautiously, as if it were a bomb waiting to go off, she placed the tube of Pepsodent on the dash. "Okay," she said.

The Baskin-Robbins people had turned the air-conditioning

on high. We entered with a shiver. I led Kristin up to the counter where enticing flavors of all colors and descriptions awaited us.

"What looks good, sweetie?"

Kristin rose on her tiptoes and peered through the plexiglass counter at the multi-colored cartons.

"Pineapple sherbet?" I asked, testing her.

She shrugged. "Okay."

She hated pineapple.

"A single scoop of Mocha Fudge," I told the counter girl. "Make it a double."

We sat at a small table in silence while Kristin slowly, reluctantly licked her ice cream cone. I too had lost my appetite but had a convenient excuse to abstain: I'm allergic to dairy products. She knew that. Again I made the mistake of trying to make small talk. "Pretty night."

She nodded.

"How do you like swimming lessons?"

"Fine."

I finally wised up and kept my mouth shut. The ice cream was melting faster than she was licking it. Mud-colored rivulets were crawling over the edge of her sugar cone and trickling down her hand. One Sunday shoe intermittently rubbed atop the other. Seconds passed like hours.

"Dad?" she said apologetically. "I can't finish the rest."

"That's okay," I said, rising, taking the half-eaten cone. "That's fine. You did just fine."

The sky was cluttered with stars, a fool's gold glitter. A single dark puff hovered above the lumber mill like a little storm cloud. We drove under the bridge where Milton became Santa Fe. A passing train sent earthquake tremors overhead.

"Eight forty-five," I said. "I guess we'd better pick up Jackie, don't you think?"

Kristin didn't answer. I clicked on the radio and searched for the Laker-Celtic game. All I got was spit and crackle.

"Dad?"

"Yes, sweetie?" I said, working the knob.

"What happens to your body when you die?"

"It's resurrected," I answered—I won't say thoughtlessly but automatically: one of the benefits of prescribing to a formal faith. "Then you go and live with Heavenly Father."

"I know *that*," she said, a trace of irritation in her voice. "But what happens to your *body* . . . *before* you're resurrected?"

I had no delicate answer to her question.

"It decomposes," I said.

"Decomposes?" Her freckled forehead arched uncomfortably.

I fiddled with the knob. Suddenly it became very important for me to locate that game. I'm not a basketball fan, either. I never have been. Maybe I was subconsciously linking the L.A. Lakers with my southern California past. If so, it was a weak connection.

"It rots," I said.

"Rots?"

"Yes. It's buried in the ground and it rots."

"Like old food?"

"Like food. Yes." There was an unfamiliar edge to my voice that should have put an end to the conversation.

"Dad?"

"Dammit all!" I said, glaring at her. Then checked myself. "I missed my turn, sweetie. I missed my turn." I braked hard and pulled a tight U-ey. Although she was wearing a seat belt, her hands flew to the dash, partly to brace herself but also, I think, to rescue the tube of Pepsodent.

"Sorry, kid," I said, making an easy left onto Leroux. "I'm really really sorry."

This part of town had always intrigued me as a strangely compatible blend of old and new, where neo-1960s shops like Rajun Cajun Foods and Inner Vision Metaphysical Books, catering to the college crowd, mingled with the antique visages of the Orpheum Theater, McGaugh's Bookstand, and the Hotel Monte Vista. The streets were narrow here and, except for early Sunday morning, parking was always nip-and-tuck. Tonight it was exceptionally bad because the intersection at Aspen was blocked off by a fire truck. A large crowd had gathered there, obstructing any passable gaps left by the hook-and-ladder. My initial thoughts

were: "Fire! Parasites! Getting their thrills from a burning building."
But I saw no smoke or flashing red lights. Missing, too, was the
general human hubbub that accompanies true catastrophe. I nosed
my car forward and looked down the intersection: a conglomer-
ation of bodies was twisting and swaying in the street. In the
moon-like glare of two spotlights they looked like giant grunion.
At the far end, gyrating on a raised wooden platform, were the
players, all wearing hair past their shoulders, three of them bearded.
"A street dance," I whispered aloud.
"A what?"
I pulled over – double-parked, actually. How long had it been
since I'd gone to a street dance? Fifteen, sixteen years? B.B., of
course; B.C. Before Barbara, Before Church. I couldn't make out
the song the band was playing, only the electrified wriggles of the
lead guitar and the sassy interventions of a saxophone.
At first I watched solely out of curiosity: long hair, electrocuted hair, pony tails, cowboy hats, sweaty backs, hairy thighs,
peasant shirts, muscle hunks in cut-offs pounding their barefeet
on the pavement like grape stompers: beer bottles, botas, trin-
kets, beads, peace patches on faded jeans. College kids mostly,
cowboy and hippy-types and clean-cut preppies disguised in rags,
all of them twisting, swaying, gyrating in a bizarre harmony of
multi-motion, like an ancient tribal dance. A bearded Arab with
a baby on his back was holding hands with a husky barefoot girl
in blue, her breasts bouncing like a two-beat juggling act. A tall,
leggy blond in short shorts was being escorted by two nasty-
looking German shepherds restrained by a skinny chain. Such a
mad mixture of styles and types! Why, it could have been my
graduating class of '69!
"Come on," I said, and got out of the car for a closer look.
The streets were roped off. Flares burned along the sidewalk
like little red devils. I reached back for Kristin's hand. She clutched
mine like a lifeline as I led her towards the sea of writhing bodies.
We watched from the sidelines. Booze was running in the
gutters. Cops were making their rounds, billie clubs and pistols
holstered. The music stopped momentarily. When it started up
again, I recognized the unmistakable introduction to an old Roll-

ing Stones song. Although the lead singer looked like an imitation Willie Nelson with his suspendered blue jeans, headband, and pleated pony tail, he had plagiarized the rough and raw voice of Mick Jagger. And that was it. I gave Kristin's arm a tug. "Come on, kid! Let's boogie!"

She resisted, but I gently pulled her out into the sweaty, muggy mob and, feeding an old fantasy, led her through an ad hoc combo of the Lindy and the Jerk. She shyly followed my lead, stiff as a nun, while I shook my arms and rear and what little hair I had, like a Watusi on the war path, just clowning around really, trying to loosen her up. But then a circle began forming—the college kids joining arms, shoulder-to-shoulder. They began dancing around and around, kicking one leg out, then the other, swaying this way and that, forward and back, Zorba the Greek style. An arm went around my shoulder, a hairy arm. The Arab's. Then mine went around Kristin's shoulder and another closed the circle on her other side. We were going around and around, kicking and swaying, Kristin looking lost and confused, as if she were trapped on a merry-go-round and couldn't get off, not really dancing but semi-staggering to the beat, half-smiling, trying to play along like the good sport she always was.

Then someone began circulating a long-necked bottle. One by one the dancers took a swig. The bearded Arab took a long swallow and passed the bottle to me. Mick Jagger's voice was a jagged edge ripping through the silken night: "I can't get no . . . I can't get no . . . "

I don't recall what was going through my mind as I tilted my head back and raised the bottle to my lips—a notion of guilt, I'm sure, but a vague notion. I didn't actually swallow more than a few drops, most of it dribbling down my chin and onto my shirt. But this time Kristin was unable to hide her feelings behind a dimpled smile. She twisted free and backed away from me as if in the stark glare of the twin spotlights I had suddenly grown fangs and face hair.

"Come on, kid," I said, motioning her back.

She took another step back. I shook the bottle angrily, drops of cherry-colored fluid scattering from the mouth. "You don't know anything about it!" I yelled in the gruff voice of my father. "You don't know!"

But I could no longer read her expression because of the sudden blur in my eyes. I blinked hard to clear them, but all I could discern was her little voice and her little hand tugging at my shirt sleeve. "It's okay, Dad," she said. "O-*kay*."

A Game of Inches

. . . .

Lighting the wood stove, trying to, I'm thinking of my high school football coach, Stan Friedman. No particular incident, just the recurring image of that dark Semitic bear stalking our helmeted ranks in blue gym shorts and white t-shirt, shoulders hunched from surplus muscle, forearms curved like clubs, clutching his clipboard like a Neanderthal looking for someone to strike with it.

After the third futile match, I congratulate myself for having suppressed all four-letter expletives. It's been five days since our Sunday school lesson, "Tame Thy Tongue," and I'm still batting a thousand. I'm not doing as well in the aftermath of Carla's Family Home Evening lesson on building positive attitudes. I'm having trouble convincing myself that today is not going to be one of "Murphy's Days": a million things to do, no time to do them, and everything imaginable going wrong.

Plus a rotten night's sleep. Davy waking up at 2:00 a.m. screaming bloody murder. Another nuclear nightmare, no thanks to the "Six O'Clock News." Sure we teach him about resurrection, but how can we refute those atomic mushrooms, the twilight tragedies of the world. Ethiopians, char-broiled skeletons with bloated bellies, giant two-legged spiders limping towards oblivion. Emaciated exodus.

"What's wrong with those people, Dad?"

"They're starving, son."

. . . . .

"How come, Dad?"

Greed, selfishness, politics, ignorance, apathy, megalomania. "Lots of reasons."

"Are we going to starve?"

"Not tonight . . . no."

"Do we have a year's supply, Dad?"

"We're working on it, son. Almost."

Innocently laying guilt trips on me.

Last night, after I'd calmed him down: "Dad, would you die to save the world?"

I pause for an uncomfortably long time. "Jesus already has."

"I know, but would you?"

"I suppose—to save the world."

He throws his little arms around me. "Don't, Dad. Please."

Whatever happened to Sesame Street and the Electric Company? He never describes his nightmares in detail, but they are frequent and very real. At five-and-a-half he's stressed out. Like his old man, he grinds his teeth in his sleep: I can hear the tormented gnashing as he twists and squirms in bed. Every night is a wrestling match with the Angel of Death. Eventually he wakes up shrieking. I hurry to the rescue and find him tangled up in his electric blanket like an animal caught in a net. Usually some soft talk and a glass of milk sedate him.

"It's okay, son. It was only a bad dream."

Sometimes, like last night, he'll ask me to say a prayer.

Kneeling by his bed, half comatose, I'll mumble the words that now seem as fixed and automatic as the sacrament prayer: "Father in Heaven . . . bless Davy so he'll get a good night's sleep . . . so he'll think happy thoughts and dream nice dreams . . . so he'll know that You're looking after him and there's no need to fear. . . . "

"Dad?"

"Yes?"

"Will you say another?"

He needs more of my time, but I have very little to spare now. It's taken me three years to get this job at the university, and I'm struggling. I mustn't blow it. We can't afford another move, financially or emotionally. Six in four years . . . No wonder the kid has problems. No roots, Carla said. No security. That's why we left the reservation, to give them roots. A neighborhood. Permanent friends. I'm still second guessing. Maybe we didn't have the Golden Arches or a movie theater or a real house with a microwave and VCR, but at least we had time. I won't go into that. Leave nostalgia to the nostalgiacs.

Now I'm gone before they're up. Three nights a week, when I'm not teaching classes or at a church meeting, I make it home for a late dinner. I see the kids maybe an hour before bedtime. They want to play–"Dance wif me, Dad, dance!" "Swing me, Dad! Swing me!" But Dad's been up since 5:00. He's too beat to swing and dance but does anyway, cautioning himself that if he doesn't he'll regret it twenty years from now.

Not much time for home teaching. Going the extra mile. Four-generation sheets. Friendshipping. Save the world, feed the hungry. But but but. That old song. Somehow I don't think God is the type who'll sit around patiently patronizing excuses. On Judgement Day we'll be scantroned by a "did you/didn't you" device. No. That's the skeptic in me talking. He's been slinking out of the shadows more regularly, showing his scratchy face.

David–all the kids–need more time but they've got to eat too. House payments, car payments, food, fuel. The Great American Lament. Someone's got to bring home the bacon–more bread than bacon lately. So far we've always managed on my paycheck. That's going on fifteen years. Carla's been free to raise the kids, manage the home. But we're running counter-culture. Even our church friends tell us its only a matter of time. Economics, the final word. Get a baby-sitter, get a job. Carla could teach; she's certified. The temptation is strong. But we've still got the two-year-old, our blue-eyed prodigy, child of our young old age. We don't want him raised by Mary Moppet Day Care.

Money. Bread. Mammon. Every time it looks like we might get a little ahead, a little breathing room, something comes up. Last year Carol's braces; this year a leaky roof.

We bought our log home last spring, a thirteen-year-old artifact, and discovered the leaks during our first big thunderstorm in July. Rain hammered the asphalt shingles, played a hard percussion on the skylights which swelled like giant bubbles ready to burst. As water trickled down the slanted beams, I ran around the living room like a sun-blinded outfielder trying to catch the drips in a frying pan. At night, in bed, gazing up at the thick pine beams as rain pelleted the roof, I felt as Noah must have his first night afloat in the ark.

That was four months ago, monsoon season in the mountains. Striking lucky match number five, I'm thinking of Stan Friedman again, something he said during pre-game pep talks: *Boys, remember . . . football is a game of inches*. I don't know why this particular quote comes to mind—he had dozens hand-lettered on cardboard strips taped throughout the locker room—unless I'm subconsciously stretching a comparison between the minutia factor in football and my inability to get a fire started.

Coach Friedman also said that football is the game of life, his being a relatively short one, dying five years ago, gang-tackled in mid-life by a stroke and cardiac combo. High blood pressure. Too many championships slipping through his fingers in the closing seconds, one of those slips being mine. I wonder now if his death was a matter of inches and seconds. *If* the paramedics had arrived a few moments earlier . . . *if* so and so had known CPR.

The kindling has caught fire, a mounting flame. Soon the Fisher stove will be giving off laggard heat. I light it first thing when I get up so at least the kitchen will be warm when Carla and the kids wake up (my small sacrifice to the cause). Otherwise the house would be an ice box. No snow yet, but Old Man Winter's definitely here. I can hear him howling, shaking the pines, banging on the door, seeping through the cracks—all my unfinished caulking! I hate getting up now, hate leaving Carla's soft body warmth. Do I have a choice? Like the bumper sticker says: "I owe, I owe/ It's off to work I go." Or from a more authoritative source: "By the sweat of thy brow thou shalt labor all thy days."

The kids survive in electric blankets.

This morning I'm groggy and grouchy—lazy, too. I pour myself a bowl of Granola Crunch and pull a chair up close to the stove, barely feeling the stingy heat. The logs snap and crackle as the flames go through their slow preliminaries. Gradually they will tighten and intensify, reducing the wood to red-white coals that will begin to exude true warmth about the time I slip out the back door.

It's my day to take the car. Three days a week I bundle up in wool cap, wool sweater, knickers, gloves, the works, and pedal into town on my Schwinn mountain bike, empathizing with Mr. Amundsen as the wind burns my face and slices through my woolen armor. No matter what or how much I put on my hands and feet, after two miles my toes and fingertips are ice cubes. I neither beg nor deserve pity: my pioneer forefathers trekked west with frozen legs falling off. To feel at least this small portion of that suffering . . . It keeps me humble (and healthy, they say, though I wonder sometimes, thawing out in the shower at the end of a sub-zero ride, if I'm not bucking for premature arthritis). But today I have the car. I won't deny a certain pleasure in this luxury–more like relief–not to face the cold grind for a day. Mornings like this, on bike-back, I usually grit my teeth from start to finish. (That's ten miles into town and another three to the university.)

Pulling out of the driveway, cinders crunching underneath, the full moon in the mist like an underwater light half-trapped in crab shadows, I try to mentally undermine Mr. Murphy's odds: a razor nick, feckless matches, bloodshot eyes I can handle. But language proficiency scores, two thousand of them, due on the department chairman's desk by 5:00 p.m., with a complete written summary, including recommendations for student placement and follow-up testing? It wouldn't be half bad if Dr. Fisher hadn't casually dumped it on me three days ago. "Oh, Jim, by the way." My penalty for entering the faculty smoker's lounge.

The annual writing contest is a different story. Sometime today I have to type the last four pages of my article and get it in the mail.

The last day again. Always the postmark, the deadline. Every year I resolve to enter but somehow the clock runs out on me, or vice versa. I try (with diminishing success) to reassure myself it

. . . . .

isn't fear of failure or procrastination but time – no time. Having the car today should help but won't. Errands, chores – they come with the vehicle. Picayune expedients. Today, Carla's miscellaneous shopping list, hastily scribbled on a scrap of paper: weatherstripping at Angel's, a dozen eggs (X-large), two dozen stamps (not the generic kind, please!!!!). Another of her infamous scavenger hunts. The inconvenience of zig-zagging back and forth across town for three items makes me wonder why some genius on-the-make hasn't designed a store where they sell stamps, eggs, and weatherstripping under one roof. Maybe in the Millennium.

As I cross the first cattle guard, it occurs to me that here it is, Friday, and once again I have failed in my Sabbath resolution to be a better person during the week. Every Sunday as the sacrament is circulating, noble, humanitarian thoughts surge through me like new blood. I privately vow to go out of my way to make the world a better, happier place, to do my part, to impact lives.

To date I've done nothing to substantially augment the moans and groans of this planet, but I've done just as little to alleviate them. Every week I fill my sights with good intentions only to lapse into the same old patterns. The spirit is willing, the flesh is fired up, but the dog's got to be fed, the car washed, the papers graded, the firewood split. Noble desires lost in the daily shuffle. "Spiritual fossilization" Brother Sanders calls it. Somehow the malady is a little more palatable once we put a label on it. But I'm as weary of excuses as my superiors must be. I used to look back on my missionary experience to buoy me up, but now that, too, has become a concession.

Crossing the highway underpass, I'm momentarily caught in an open-ended echo chamber: the traffic overhead rumbles like preliminary thunder, a grumbling voice from on high. Voluminous, powerful, like the sea. Full of premonitions. I make a sharp left and cross the second cattle guard. The heater is blowing hot air as I join the parade of headlights, smeared and sticky in the gray light.

As the powdered darkness begins to fade, my thoughts drift like an open boat, destination nowhere. The highway steepens, a sharp incline. The forest is a dark blur, the meadow to my right a blond-on-brown patchwork, an autumn quilt. Frosted, it appears to have grown old overnight. The ponderosa pines lay black lace on the horizon. As the last few stars run out of fuel, pink streamers stretch across the pre-dawn sky. Not candy-colored. More like glorified bandages; the fading aftermath of a hot sky war.

The skeptic in me wonders if in ten years my children will be hiking through forests of burned matchsticks. Or hiking at all. And my grandchildren, scorched red deserts, like the Indian lands on the other side of the mountain. I don't think about it often, rarely dwell on it—who can afford to add stress to stress? I'm not worried for my lifetime but my children's. Not hopelessness but helplessness, knowing that one itchy finger could detonate an early Armageddon, counsels me to ignore the thing. (Deep down I believe God would intervene. If Abraham bargained to save Sodom and Gomorrah for the sake of a righteous ten, why not the world? Plus God, too, is something of a showman, and I can't see him allowing some trigger-happy camel scratcher to up-stage his premier production.)

A diesel truck blows its horn and bellows, advancing on me like a mechanical monster aiming to take a bite out of my rear end. An angry arm pokes out the window, waving me out of the fast lane. He is justified: my tiny Honda Civic, an eggshell amidst mastodons, rolling along as aimlessly as my thoughts: Diane Greenbaum, the new graduate assistant, the one with hair like a French poodle that's just come in out of the rain. Hairy armpits, hairy legs, Levi skirt to mid-thigh; the slogan on her t-shirt: YOU CAN'T HUG WITH NUCLEAR ARMS. Barging into my office like a nightmare from the 1960s, my youth, a deja vu except I'm wearing the suit and tie now. She has organized a campus anti-nuke campaign. Will I march with the others—will I march with "them?" Professors X, Y, and Z—distinguished men, literary men, humanists—they're all participating.

I invent a reasonable excuse for Diane. To myself, I rationalize: I've got papers to grade, tests to score, hospital visits. I'll be lucky to get home by 9:00 as it is. Who's got time to march? I've got a wife, kids, a family, for crying out loud!

The inner rebuttal—reflected in Ms. Greenbaum's stern green

eyes—so does everyone, professor. I'm embarrassed, ashamed—confused mostly—by my reply. Too busy to march for peace? Or an innate skepticism of marches, protests, playing for the press. What is all this hoopla but misdirected energy? Fanfare. Benevolent socializing. Bandwagon sensibility. Especially a peace march. At best, a necessary futility.

Or is this my rationalization for apathy? Diane Greenbaum, dressed like a bag lady and smelling like the men's locker room, but full of commitment, fervor, zeal. Correct or not, well-groomed or not, she had a cause she was willing to fight for, pound on doors, insult her superiors. Which is precisely what she did, insulted me, took a shot: "I should have known . . . from a *Mormon!*"

A Mormon! Spoken with such contempt, derision. Mormon. I considered briefly *my* causes: to spread the gospel of peace, truth, salvation. To save the world. Sure! When it's a major effort for me to drag myself out of bed in the morning—to leave my warm wife and face another day.

I didn't march yesterday. I graded papers in my office.

I'm driving ultra slow this morning, delaying what? Entering town, I watch the sun climbing out of the pines like a sunburned god. I marvel as it slowly peels the shadows from the mountains. A blue mist circles the peaks like the rings of Saturn. I marvel, but only momentarily: proficiency scores. Writing contest. Errands. Chores.

And the boy.

At Sunday school teacher-training last week, the theme, "Reach Out for the One." They showed *Cipher in the Snow*. I can never watch that film without weeping a little within—guilt and despair, for the ciphers in my life, the cipher in myself. Oh yes, Sister Lundquist—*President* Lundquist—zeroing in on me: "Are there any children in your class who might be . . . "

Derek.

This year I'm doing double duty. Second counselor in the elder's quorum, I also teach the ten-year-old boys. Oh, they all have needs, sure. But Spencer, Eric, Ryan, Reed—they live on Cherry Hill, a stone's throw from the churchhouse. They are

. . . .

sound and happy fellows, basking in that lap-dog conviviality of pre-adolescence. Video games and Mars candy bars. They are in good, nurturing hands: doting, bread-and-jam mothers; honorable fathers. Doctors, lawyers, professors. They are on their way: Eagle Scout, Duty to God, mission, temple marriage. Anything I do is gravy.

But Derek. He lived with his mother and sister—an obese girl with squinting piglet eyes who wore costumes to church: knee-high boots with pink fur lining and sleeveless sundresses that exposed in vaunting fashion her massive arms and shoulders patched with button-sized moles and freckles. A recent convert, the mother was short, dumpy, divorced. (Some members said retarded—"mentally handicapped" is the current phrase.) She smelled bad. Body odor. And something else. Urine? I don't know. She dressed in rags. A Goodwill wardrobe.

Derek was a quiet boy with soft blond hair and a vacant look. *Persona non grata.* Disappearing in the woodwork. A victim. I've seen the permanent bruises he tries to cover up on his forearms; the scar like a whip-welt on his cheek. Semi-literate, he stumbled through the simplest scriptures and shook his head when asked to pray in class. The few times he had spoken, his voice was a whisper, soft, apologetic, wind in the grass. During my lessons his eyes drifted off. Where his thoughts were wandering I didn't know. But he wasn't with me. His face had the smooth, uncast features and displaced look of a mongoloid. A sad case. *He* needed time. Masculine companionship. Someone to take him fishing, hiking, to the ball game. A dad.

But so did my own kids. They were growing up without me. The little guy, the two-year-old, what's his name? He's learned another dozen words I'm told. Before I know it he'll be driving, heading off to college. Brother Peterson, get thine own house in order.

But I'd promised myself to touch base with Derek some time this week. *Some* time.

Gaining the summit, the green blur flashing by, I refuse to commit though I've already committed. Another broken resolution? Sacramental good intentions? Play it by ear.

. . . . .

I switch on the radio. 5:58 the D.J. says. Stay tuned for the 6:00 a.m. news. More rioting in South Africa. Shiite hijackers. AIDS in elementary schools. Arms control talks. Catholics and Protestants in Northern Ireland, booby trap deaths in Lebanon, primitive villagers expunged in Afghanistan, big league ball players sniffing coke. More clichés. Painful human clichés. I switch off the radio as I pass the city limits sign.

By the time I reach the university, frost is smoking in the sunlight. A blue mist hovers above the pines. The aspens and cottonwoods desperately cling to a few token leaves.

I enter the main office and my day is ruined by a memo in my pigeonhole: emergency faculty meeting at 8:00 sharp. So much for my productive morning. Dr. Fisher is notoriously long-winded. The Faulkner expert has yet to keep a meeting under three hours.

This one drags on until noon. Before it is over, Dr. Fisher has assigned me to write a summary of all department course offerings—mule work for the rookie—due in his office by 5:00. In addition to the language proficiency report? His silence is a reprieve of sorts.

I skip lunch and plow into it. Outside a naked branch is tapping on my window like a secret warning, Morse Code, trying to remind me of more urgent business. But I'm quickly lost in the task at hand; arms control and apartheid are fading echoes in the seashell of my mind. The tapping persists all afternoon. I ignore it and other promptings.

At 3:45 I drop the ten-page report on the secretary's desk. "Hope you can decipher this," I say with a smile, the best I can manufacture considering the time and task. Friday, an hour before quitting time, she manufactures her best also.

Decision time. Errands. Article. Test scores. Test scores can wait. Hopefully my semi-brilliant summary will keep Fisher and other wolves from the door. But eggs, weather-stripping, stamps—don't come home without them. No town trips till Monday—we're trying to conserve on gas. It's up to me. Friday driver.

I hustle out to my car. The sky is clear, blue, piqued with an autumn chill, the fallen leaves clicking as they dance across the pavement. At the post office I bump into Steve Boyak, an old friend from the reservation. He's moving—no, has moved—to town. Marital problems, he and Doris. He's seeing a therapist. "Too angry—I feel too much anger inside." His ten-year-old boy still dirties his pants. The seventeen-year-old girl is still playing the cello and step-child games.

I listen; we talk. I try to offer consolation. Steve is a godless man with a godlike heart but doesn't know it or won't admit it. I invite him to the football game next weekend. I have no spare money for tickets and no time to go. Steve smiles, the gold in his teeth sparkling. I'll make time; I'll scrounge up the bucks. Break a piggy bank.

At a quarter-to-five I say good-bye. No hope for the article. Wait till next year? I refuse to give up hope. One of these days. Errands.

Driving across town to Angel's, I try to ignore the nagging little voice inside; I argue internally: What will I do, just show up, ta da! Here I am! Big as life! And then what? If I were taking him hiking or fishing, if we had something to *do*. Postpone until a good weekend? There are no good weekends. You haven't even put up the storm windows. You teach that extension course in Page every other Saturday. Now or never, buddy.

I take a hard left on Switzer Canyon Road. They live "somewhere on the west side." The homes here are nice—A-frames and solar complexes nestled in the pines. On the other side of the hill, though, a village of shanties and battered trailers with dirt lawns. Every home a mini junkyard; old refrigerators, engine blocks, car shells, junk.

I park in front of trailer number 86. Wary of dogs, I approach tentatively. A rabbit in a wire cage looks at me as if I were an old friend whose face he can't quite place.

I knock. Derek answers. A moment of surprise, then the vacant look, the passive stupor. I smile though I know I've made a mistake. He mumbles something—always a mumble. The mother appears, short and frumpy. The smell of lard and onions reaches me from the kitchen. I hear the crackling of fried grease. An infant sleeps on the floor. Babysitting to make ends meet. The carpet is ragged but clean. A mildewy odor. On the TV screen He-Man is wrestling Skeletor. Masters of the Universe in black-and-white.

"Hi," she says; her gap-toothed smile. Those poor teeth. "Did you want to visit?" She must recognize me. New home teacher?

"No, I . . . ," I gaze around, the TV, the sleeping child, Derek's vacant blue eyes, the hillbilly environs. "I wanted to know if Derek could go out for an ice cream."

The woman's face is a lamp I've suddenly ignited. And the boy—yes, him too. A shade slower, but his eyes, blue eggs bursting. They are two children gazing at me in wonder and awe and joy; I am Santa Claus bringing an early Christmas. I share their surge of joy and shame.

But now the boy looks puzzled, confused, as if he's just awakened from a dubious dream.

"Go ahead," the mother says, beaming.

We step outside; he looks around—dismayed? Disappointed? He stops. "Isn't there anyone else?"

"No. Just you."

His face is perplexed but etched with an emotion I've never seen on him before. "Why me?" he asks.

"Because—" I search for something simple and sincere. "Because today you're special!"

Oh, it was trite, it was banal, it was soooo typically the thing to say, but it was true. For the moment anyway. Then a startling thing: I put my arm around him—my gads! I never put my arm around anyone but my own kids; the cold Scandinavian in me. But it isn't hard, near spontaneous, and I don't feel like a phoney or a put-on doing it. Walking to the car, I am flying as high as my little friend.

In the car, we get down to brass tacks: communication, conversation, developing a true relationship. It is not the foster dad-son experience you often see on TV movies—that instantaneous bonding of male companionship. He is shy, quiet, diffident in blue jeans and an old gray sweater. (I note the holes in the elbows, the frayed hem.) I ask several conversation starters, trying to find some common ground. His answers are abortingly brief. Paralinguistic.

"So how's school?"

"Okay."

"What's your favorite subject?"

A shrug.

"Do you like baseball?" I have a World Series follow-up in mind.

He shakes his head.

"Football?"

"No."

"Water polo?"

He looks at me with a wrinkled eye. "What's that?"

"Just kidding."

At the Dairy Queen he steals glances at the menu board as if he were doing something wrong. Two girls from the junior high school are giggling loudly. The juke box is deafening. I shout into Derek's ear. "What looks good?"

His face is utter astonishment. "I can have *anything*?"

"Sure," I say, feeling my pockets for change.

He orders a Buster Bar—I order it actually. He points to the full color placard featuring a vanilla ice cream and peanut contrivance coated with milk chocolate.

"You want to eat it here or in the car?"

He points to the door.

In the car he thanks me twice. Another ten minutes of silence and I ask, "You want to run a couple errands with me?"

He nods.

We drive to Angel's in silence. He works on his Buster Bar while I admire the autumn tapestry on the mountains—red and gold arabesques on forest green. At the store he shadows me as I hunt for weather-stripping. He doesn't ask but I explain what it's for anyway.

On the way home, a truck driver pulls up on my left and swears at me for something—driving too slow? Braking prematurely? I don't know. Short fuses at quitting time. Hands clasped meekly on his thighs, gazing at the floor, Derek whispers, "Thanks."

I ask about the rabbit. He answers in complete sentences: it is his, yes; there were two but one died.

Progress, I think to myself. He's opening up.

He tells me, in impressive detail, how he feeds and cares for it. But that is all. Maybe a minute-and-a-half. When he's through, he's through.

So what? So the conversation isn't lively. Is that a requisite for a Buster Bar? Better silence than brown-nosing butter talk.

I slip my hand around his shoulder.

It's 5:30 when I drop him off. I say nothing more about the church—no stipulations, no nice guy coercion.

He thanks me for the fourth time.

I note, in my rear-view mirror, how he stands on the door-step beside the rabbit cage watching me drive away as if he is Cinderella and I'm his fairy godmother.

I pick up a dozen eggs at Safeway and get on the highway heading south. The sundown sky is a peppermint swirl. Cruising along the pavement, the green woods flashing by, I feel as fluid and buoyant as my vehicle. I switch on the radio—habit or latent masochism? More of the same: book burnings, cult heroes, sex in the Southwest, Jesus in ragtime, network religion, contaminated kisses. Local: Diane Greenbaum's anti-nuke march creating some ripples in town, favorable and unfavorable. Threats. Arrests. Follow-ups. America the Beautiful to the rescue. Counting calories as we quarrel over the fat of the land. Physician, heal thyself. This Cabbage Patch Society. The Great American Utopia? A bomb shelter in every basement, two MX missiles in every garage. Cockroach mentality. Survivorhood.

The sun is sluggish going down, a red light glowing in a fog. Martian skies. I switch off the radio before it takes back what little has been gained. I am thinking peace is not the absence of guns but of hate; as long as there are rocks to throw and sticks to swing. . . .

I ease down the off-ramp and take a sharp right, over the cattle guards and up the hill, leaving behind highway, city, test

· · · · ·

114

scores, faculty lounges. Another sharp right and my tires are grinding over the cinder-coated driveway, the nuggety crunch alerting my little two-year-old playing in the sandbox. He freezes like a frightened fawn–that instant of bewilderment: the cat scampers across the porch, a squirrel waves its bushy tail and scurries up a pine, pausing once to scold me with a shriek. The boy's eyes light up like holiday lights. He drops his little hand shovel, the plastic bucket, and toddles towards me on funky Charlie Chaplin feet, a frenzied penguin, his diaper-padded behind swinging comically.

We have this little game. I drop to my knees and hold out both arms while he runs full-speed into me like a linebacker hitting a tackling dummy. On impact, I fall backwards and bench press him into the sky. He spreads his arms and legs: "I'm a bird, Dad! I'm a bird!" He smiles–those dimples belong in Hollywood. I pack him over my shoulder like a sack of flour. He laughs, shouts: "Da-dee! Da-dee-eee!" (Sometimes less dauntlessly; My Papa's Waltz.)

Pausing at the door, I smell enchiladas cooking. I'm a sucker for Mexican food; Carla knows that. Peeking through the window, I see the three girls and my other boy huddled by the wood stove, wearing blankets like Indians (more for fun than warmth), watching Wheel of Fortune. Cindy, the three-year-old, is sucking her forefingers and clutching the rag blanket she refuses to trade in for a newer, silkier model ("It's not a rag!"). Norman Rockwell would have done cartwheels.

I am filled with simple joy. The scene isn't always this idyllic. Some days, bike days, I come home wet and dripping, pooped and pissed. The boy is in bed–a late nap, forewarning trouble. A lousy rotten bad day. Outside the door I hear Carla screaming–is that really my wife? I hear, vaguely, the name of each child enunciated in vain. She is at the stove, stirring a large pot (to boil them in?).

But those days are exceptions. Usually my homecomings are like today, when I feel such a rush of simple peace and happiness it almost frightens me, wondering how long it can possibly last.

Can joy be everlasting? Or is the balance too delicate? Father Lehi's pleasure-pain formula, a little of this, a little of that.

Gripping the doorknob, entering, the shuffle of excited feet, the shouts, "Daddy's home! Daddy's . . . " I'm thinking that life, too, is a game of inches.

THERe

Hozhoogo Nanina Doo

. . . .

Max Hansen dipped his brush into the can and reached to the ceiling, spreading paint thickly and smoothly across the plyboard surface. He paused a moment, listening to a faint tapping sound. Rain? No. A loose strip of metal or maybe a tumbleweed blowing against a window. With his free hand, Max wiped the sweat from his forehead and squinted at his paint-freckled watch: 8:30. He still had to finish the west end of the ceiling where the rollers hadn't reached. Another four or five hours at least. But it was his last night on the reservation (his very last, this time), and he was determined to finish. Even if it took all night. He would finish.

Max dipped the brush again and spread more paint. He hated painting. And this part was the worst, the touching up. Dip and spread, dip and spread. It took forever to cover the bare spots and just as long to drag the ladder around. Slow slow slow.

He had been at it nonstop since dawn. A thousand things had been going through his mind, but at the moment—dipping again, spreading again—he remembered the day he punched the medicine man in the mouth. Poor Ben Notah, the old *shicheii*. The only tooth he had left and I had to go and knock it out. That was a bad one, Father. Even under the circumstances. I knew better. Or should have. It was . . . circumstances. That was the turning point. If I'd controlled it, if I'd stopped it then and there . . . things would be different now, I think. I'd be different.

. . . . .

Weary, woozy, Max stroked the brush directly overhead. Bits of white paint speckled his face, one or two catching him in the eye. Blinking his eye clear, he looked down at the gym floor—row upon row of old linoleum tiles, chipped, cracked, faded to a bleak beige, perpetually coated with dust, some missing, leaving black tar marks and the overall impression of an unfinished puzzle. Cheap, like the rest of the building, a full-sized churchhouse with a chapel, steeple, classrooms, and a "cultural hall." But cheap. Plyboard and cinderblock.

Once again, Max began counting the beams in the ceiling. Counting helped pass the time. How many brush strokes to paint one panel, how many to cover ten feet of trim? Thirty-six beams ribbed the A-framed ceiling. He had barely started beam number thirty-five. Working fast, he could paint one every two to two-and-a-half hours. Faster if I wasn't so damn finicky. I don't know why. This far off the ground who's going to notice? Max looked down at the deteriorating floor. Except me. And You. Thee. Sorry.

Calculating the hours he had spent this week alone, Max felt overwhelmed. The gym had never seemed very big until he had started painting it. Then it had taken on cathedral proportions. He'd be here forever: six, seven, maybe eight more hours. It was Saturday night, but if he had to work on into the Sabbath, well . . . it's for the kingdom, right?

Slipping his free hand under his t-shirt, Max gave his sweat-drenched garments a tug. They tore from his skin like adhesive tape. He ran his hand across his forehead. Painting was bad enough, but monsoon season made it torture. Sticky, sweaty, jungle heat. No air-conditioning, no swamp cooler. Not even cross ventilation. All the window cranks had been broken off—by vandals, mischievous kids, overzealous basketball players. Max had refused to have them replaced until more members—meaning more Navajo members—pitched in with the branch budget. Now in mid-August he was paying for his principles. During the past week, the sweathouse effect had cost him so much in body fluids that his skin seemed to have shrunk to the bone. He no longer looked skinny but skeletal, as if he'd been on a hunger strike. His face, usually summer tan, looked pale, almost gray, and whittled to the bone. His blue eyes looked neutral. Washed out.

Max dipped his brush and slapped it against the ceiling. Five hours, he reassured himself. Five. Then he would lock up the church for the last time and trudge back to his Bureau of Indian Affairs trailer, which he would also lock up for the last time the next morning, and then drive south to Tucson. Away from that thankless classroom in the school that was in no better shape than the chapel. Monday morning he and Melissa would board the 747 to Hawaii for a long-awaited and well deserved second honeymoon. Without kids, without Indians. *Even if we can't afford it. After ten years . . . Alma and the sons of Mosiah invested twice that in the Lamanites, but compare the dividends. When I first came in '73 we had five coming out to priesthood meeting. Now we've got four, all different. They come and they go. Commit and poop out, then commit again.*

Ten years. In that time he had seen dozens of Navajo families join the church; none had remained active. Hundreds of Navajo kids had been baptized and bussed off on the church's Indian Placement Program each year; hundreds more had been bussed back home. Some graduated, then fell away. A few went on to BYU, and fewer still managed a temple marriage. Of these, a handful had forsaken the reservation. The others had returned and, in time, had sought out the peyote meetings, the squaw dances, the bootleggers. *Two steps back for every one forward.* Leaning haphazardly against the trading post, red-eyed, smiling his yellow smile, Natoni Nez once summed it up perfectly: "Brother Max, out here the possible is impossible!" *True pearls of wisdom from a drunken Indian. I don't know. I must be crazy, perched up here on a ladder twenty feet off the ground. The heat's getting to me. Or I'm getting old. Thirty-five and what have I got to show for it?*

Thirty-five. Ten years. No active converts. Except for Sherman Tsosie. Max's first and last counselor, his only active Melchezidek priesthood holder. Portly and pot-bellied, his prickly black hair glistening with grease, he would strut into the chapel every Sunday in a blue leisure suit, sunglasses, and cowboy boots, greeting Max cheerfully, "Ya-tay-ho! Ya-tay-ho!"

The chief. Heart and soul of the branch. Pounding the pulpit in Navajo. Five years ago Max had baptized him and a year later Sherman had taken his family through the Arizona Temple. If anyone was ever ready . . . Then, just before Christmas last year, he left home. Just took off. Went a-whoring. Like the others. I thought I knew him better. I thought I . . .

Max wiped his forehead again – dip, spread, wipe – and added a few more strokes until that section of the beam was thickly and evenly coated. He climbed down the rickety ladder, careful to compensate for the two missing rungs, and moved it a yard or so further along the drop cloth. Uncapping the lid on the five-gallon bucket, he propped it on his thigh and carefully tilted the mouth. Why am I doing this? And why alone? Because no one else would . . . because the project had been dragging on for five years now . . . because it was his last night on the Rez. Fresh paint plopped into the can. Then he heard something else – a vague rumbling outside, then a small explosion, followed moments later by another, like delayed artillery fire. He ignored it and recapped the bucket.

The work had started with a bang, anglos and Navajos working side by side every Wednesday night and all day Saturday. But enthusiasm soon fizzled and the churchhouse sat four years half-finished. Like everything else. And it wasn't even his project. Jeff Peterson, the CPA from Salt Lake. Married to sour-faced Marie, who sat in the back pew scowling every Sunday. Big. Huge. Permanently pregnant. They couldn't wait to leave. Peterson the big plan man. He started the whole thing, called it a vision. Then moved back to Utah and left Max holding the bag. Max and Melissa and Steve Adams. And Sherman. He was there too. They all stuck it out. Peterson's vision became their nightmare. The other anglos said they were burned out and wouldn't lift another finger until more Lamanites helped out, while the Navajos had more urgent business, like hauling wood and water, going to rodeos, or to *yeibicheii* dances . . . or they just didn't show.

Max and his faithful crew of three had managed to complete

the exterior and half the interior before abandoning the project halfway through its second year, just before Max had been called as branch president. He never officially said, "No more!" One Saturday was canceled for a basketball tournament and the next for Tsidii's funeral, then they never started up again. Probably he wanted more Navajos, too. And he pooped out, just didn't care anymore – about anything. And there was Tsidii . . .

So for the next three years the churchhouse had remained a half-painted eccentricity. Then, one hot afternoon last June, Max went to the trading post and checked the mail – a bill from Navajo Communications, a J.C. Penney summer catalog, and a letter from Tucson Public Schools offering him a teaching job. He was stunned. Melissa kissed the letter. Ten years they'd been trying to get out of there and when the ticket finally arrived he was scared to death.

The next Sunday when Max stood to conduct sacrament meeting, he announced solemnly: "We are going to finish painting the church by August 10th. All who wish to help beautify the Lord's house may come on Wednesday nights and Saturday mornings."

But it was summer. Steve Adams, the seminary teacher, was gone, and Sherman Tsosie was AWOL. So Max and Melissa alone had worked like dogs five, sometimes six, nights a week, right up until they had loaded the U-Haul and headed south. For good, they thought. But the painting was not finished. The ceiling. The lousy beams. Thirty-six of them. And a week later, eight days before their flight to Hawaii, fifteen days before his new contract began, Max drove north again to clear up some "paperwork," though the real reason, the one he couldn't explain even to himself, let alone to her, was . . . Forgive the deception, Father. Does the end ever justify the means?

He had arrived a week ago Sunday. Early Monday morning he attacked the ceiling, confident he could paint six beams a day for six days. Six times six and he could be home by Sunday evening as he had promised. But the work dragged, and twelve-hour days stretched to fourteen and fifteen hours. On Friday he ran out of paint and had to drive a hundred miles into Gallup to buy more.

The trip cost him half a day, three beams. Saturday morning when he stepped inside the gym, the south windows tinged with dawn light, a rose quartz reflection, he found himself staring up at nine unpainted beams. Nine times two equals eighteen hours, or two times two-and-a-half equals twenty-four hours, or times . . .

Max glanced at his watch: 9:35. At this rate I'll be here till Monday. Or New Year's. Father, couldn't you maybe help speed things up a bit? I know, I know: faith precedes the miracle. And if I'm so fired up to finish, why am I standing here staring at a ceiling I have no business painting in the first place? He had already moved his family and his furniture, turned in his office keys to his supervisor. He had even given his farewell address at church. That was the toughest. All alone up there, hung out to dry.

He had often wondered how it would feel to stand at the pulpit for the last time, looking down at the familiar faces. But that morning he had faced a congregation of strangers – missionary contacts, one-timers. A helpless, pointless finale. My talk was way over their heads – way over.

He had rambled on toward his real, final message, a scathing condemnation of promiscuity, drunkenness, irresponsibility, slothfulness, wife and child abuse, deceit, jealousy, neglect, lack of commitment – the whole gauntlet of social and moral crimes. But as he looked out over the audience, the men in blue jeans and cowboy hats, the women in drooping skirts and shawls, many of them smelling like campfires, they took on an aura of innocence, became children in his eyes.

"I just want you all to know that I . . . I love each and every one of you." The great cliché! The cop-out! As if you can sincerely love someone you don't know from Adam, Eve, or Jake the Silversmith. But he did. At that moment, he truly did.

Afterwards, moving through the crowd of shy strangers, he felt a warm hand touch the back of his arm. The touch was distinct, apart from the random rubbing of the crowd.

Turning, he saw an old woman, a *saani* in a shiny velveteen blouse and pleated satin skirt, rust red, with a squash blossom necklace as big as a harness bearing down on her sagging breasts. Her face, ridged with wrinkles, was long, flat, caramel colored.

Her silver hair was knotted in back with fresh white yarn. She looked at Max, her eyes stern but sad. He hadn't noticed her during his talk. It was as if she'd come from nowhere. But he knew he'd seen her before.

She greeted him with a hand touch and called him *shiyaazh*, my son. She spoke in Navajo as if he could understand every word. Before he could place her face, someone called his name and he glanced away, only for a moment. When he looked back, she was gone. Vanished. Like a ghost. As if I hadn't actually shaken her hand.

Max could recall only a fragment of what she had said— *hozhoogo nanina doo*. Even with his limited understanding he could decipher it, more or less, but had asked Dennis at the boarding school for verification. "May you go in beauty, harmony, and happiness." Unusual, Dennis said. Not your typical farewell. It echoed the closing lines of the Blessingway ceremony. The words didn't throw me, but why did she say them to me, a stranger, whispering as if she were passing on a secret?

With his fist, Max hammered the lid snugly back on the five-gallon bucket. Brush and can in hand, he climbed back up the ladder, this time planting both feet on the rung above the scarred decal that read: CAUTION: DO NOT STAND ON OR ABOVE THIS POINT. As he painted farther from the wall and nearer to where the twin beams met, he had to climb one or two rungs higher until, painting directly under the apex, he was standing on the very top rung. If I fall and get killed, I'll catch hell from Melissa. In this life or the next, one way or another, I'll catch it from her.

Stretching his arm as far as he could, Max spread more paint. At each ladder setting he could cover about seven feet, stretching three-and-a-half feet either way. It took four settings to reach the apex and another three to the opposite wall. Seven settings, wall to wall, seven times two minus two settings already . . . twelve more times up and down the ladder. Four hours, twelve settings, three settings per hour, seven settings per beam, seventy-two settings per day, 365 days per year times seventy-two times ten years. Max's eyes traveled hopelessly across the ribbed ceiling, down the plywood walls, across the dusty floor. Ten years, and what have I done? Endured to the end, and that's about it.

The end. Bittersweet, like the pre-rain fragrance outside. All week big dark thunderheads had migrated like giant herds from west to east across the sky, blotting out the stark blue. And every afternoon, as if in anticipation, the sun-scalded earth released that same premonitory smell, bittersweet, sexual. But the rain had never come. All week Max had listened hopefully to the distant rumbling of thunder. Stepping outside the hot-house gym, he had watched the rain like a vast gray veil hanging from the dirty clouds, every so often ignited by a streak of lightning. But somehow the rain had evaded the little valley, as if this area alone were being denied. I know it's a wicked and an adulterous generation that asks for a sign, but something, Father.

Max stretched to touch up around one of the eight ceiling lights. Three years now and only four burning. What does it take to replace a light bulb? What doesn't it take? Laziness. Incompetence. Apathy. Passwords out here. It wears on you. It wears. Melissa endured like a spartan, but once she was through, she was through: "You're not going back up there, Max. It's not our chapel anymore. Let the Indians paint it—if they care!" It gets everyone eventually. Some sooner than others.

Elder and Sister Crawford from Wyoming. As broad as he was tall, Elder Crawford always looked as if he had just come in from the fields and had thrown on a suit without showering. Hot or cold out, sweat stippled his crew-cut hair and oozed from his brick-red jowls. His belly curled like a giant lip over his thick leather belt. Max first met him on a Sunday morning as he nervously paced the floor of the tiny trailer where the Sliding Rock Branch met for one hour each week. He was chewing on a toothpick, fretting, stewing, his blue eyes darting between the clock and the lone family that had straggled in, quiet, unconcerned, just before noon for a meeting scheduled to begin at ten.

Later, in the Crawfords' cramped one-bedroom trailer with a bathroom no bigger than a coat closet, Max asked cheerfully, to make conversation, "So how long have you been out?"

"Two months," Crawford answered grimly. "And nine-and-a-half to go!"

Max chuckled amiably. "You're already counting the days."

Crawford fired back humorlessly: "You'd better believe it!"

He caught me totally off guard. Most couple missionaries shoulder it in silence or try to laugh it off. Some even find their niche. Elder Robertson must have fixed half the pickups on the Rez. Driving to work on snowy mornings, I'd see him out chopping wood for old Sister Tsinajinnie. But Crawford was something else.

"In the Missionary Training Center they told us these people were crying to hear the gospel—just crying to hear it! We was all set to come out here and set the mission on fire! But I'll tell you." Crawford shook his bristly head despairingly, snorted, worked some phlegm around in his mouth.

"I'm surprised they said that," Max said, glancing over at Sister Crawford, quietly knitting in the corner. Compared to her husband, she looked frail and timid, a dwarf in below-the-knee skirts as drab as her helmet hair. But of the two, she was the rock.

Max tried to give Elder Crawford some encouragement. "I've only been out here a few years, so I'm no expert. But if I've learned one thing, it's don't try to change them overnight. You'll just get frustrated. It was fifteen years before these people would use a can opener, let alone accept the gospel of Jesus Christ."

Elder Crawford's fat red finger jabbed like a dagger. Max flinched. "That's right!" he growled, his face growing redder by the second. "They're too old-fashioned! I seen some yesterday trying to shear sheep with them rusty old hand shears. Don't they know how to use electric shears?"

"Where do they live?"

"Up to the mesa."

"Maybe they don't have electricity."

Elder Crawford's fat lower lip curled indignantly. His wife looked up from her knitting, then down.

Max continued. "From their perspective, what do we really have to offer? They don't need temporal help. Food, clothing, medical care–Uncle Sam takes care of that with no strings attached."

Elder Crawford nodded and his expression simmered somewhat.

"When they join the church," Max continued matter-of-factly, "they have to forsake squaw dances and ceremonies and Sunday rodeos and picnics and good old Garden de Luxe. All the things that make life enjoyable. And for what? The promise of eternal life? They don't even have a future tense. The peyote church offers them instant visions. We can't guarantee that."

Baring his crooked yellow teeth, Elder Crawford exploded: "That's exactly what I been telling these people! I told this one lady the other day, 'What do you think this church is all about? You expect the church to give you everything without you making no sacrifice! What kind of church don't make you make no sacrifice? You expect us to come out here and wipe your little behinds!' "

Max winced. "You really didn't say that, did you?" he asked, straining to maintain a smile.

"I sure did!" Elder Crawford cocked his head proudly, as if he had just borne testimony alongside Abinadi. Sister Crawford continued knitting.

Why do you send people like Crawford out here? Maybe to open those slit eyes of his. Back home in a good solid Mormon ward on solid Mormon soil, where values and ideals are mutually accepted and love and compassion cut and dry, we get to thinking we're pretty good. Then welcome to the Rez! A brand new ball game with a whole new set of rules.

Elder Crawford continued, musing on his home town: "That's paradise up there. Just paradise. But this here . . . " Mormon purgatory? I promised myself I'd leave before I ever turned into a Crawford. Did I hang on seven years too long?

Max climbed down the ladder, moved it another few feet, and climbed back up. Just the thought of Crawford's burning red cheeks made Max feel ten degrees hotter. He wiped his sweaty forehead. Faint drops sounded for a moment like rain, but then Max realized they were drops of sweat or paint or both splashing on the canvas below. He thought of Christ in Gethsemane, then felt a sense of shame at the triviality of his ordeal. *And what have I learned in ten years—ten times longer than Elder Crawford?*

In ten years he had entered the shacks and hogans countless times, day and night and in all furies of weather, to bless the sick or cast out evil spirits or nullify witchings. Every year he had exhausted his annual leave with the Bureau of Indian Affairs to conduct funerals for the old and weddings for pregnant brides and their reluctant boyfriends. He had visited the elderly, the widowed, the sad, the disfigured, the handicapped, members or not. And he had performed miracles.

No. A miracle had been performed *through* him. He remembered that rainy night. A late knock on his door. Sister Watchman, short, squat, a Pendleton blanket over her shoulders and a scarf around her head, dripping wet, smelling of body odor, wet wool, mutton stew. Her daughter, Coreen, fourteen, dripping beside her. "My mother wants a blessing," she said.

Usually Sister Watchman wanted a couple dollars to visit Curly Floyd the bootlegger. Usually she would have unclasped the turquoise bracelet from her wrist, her only valuable, and silently offered it for pawn.

"Come in," he said. "*Woshdee.*"

They did but stopped on the small linoleum square just inside the door. Their Fed-Mart sneakers were caked with mud.

"What's the problem?" Max asked.

Mother and daughter whispered to one another in Navajo. Then the daughter, to Max: "Cancer!" Motioning shyly to her left breast. "Here. They're going to operate here." She made a slicing movement with her hand. Rain pelted the trailer. Setting a chair in the middle of the living room, Max instructed the daughter to have her mother sit down. He laid his hands on the woman's head and blessed her in the name of Jesus Christ—blessed her to receive the best and wisest medical attention; blessed her with the strength and courage and faith to cope and carry on; blessed her family, her friends, the doctors.

After he finished, Sister Watchman stood up, neither smiling nor frowning, and whispered to Coreen.

"My mother says thank you. She says she'll be well now."

Silently Max watched mother and daughter step out into the rain, too stunned to call them back to clarify the blessing, the stipulations, the no-guarantee clauses. She ignored the fine print, the "if it be thy will," "according to thy faithfulness." She was expecting a miracle, for crying out loud! A miracle! You just don't—well, of course, you can, but . . . well.

"*Hagoshi*," was all she said. It is well.

Sister Watchman returned to her loom and her livestock, and the next time Max saw her, she was alive and well and double-breasted, shooing her sheep along the wash.

He had almost finished another section of a beam when a nagging itch developed in his lower back. Irritated and unable to reach it, he threw his brush into the can, descended the ladder, and walked out into the hot, sticky night.

The full moon gazed down milky yellow, while a handful of stars boiled around it, the remainder blotted out by the congregating thunderheads. On the horizons lights puffed up and faded out, over and over, like a chain reaction of flashbulbs. A muffled rumbling followed, more artillery fire. Watching, listening, Max felt anticipation and apprehension, something longed for yet threatening.

Max stared at the churchhouse. From the foot of the butte, it looked solid and stately, its silver steeple reaching into the heavens. The long A-frame roof, like a transplant from a Swiss chalet, rose boldly out of the horizontal desert and carved a sharp wedge into the night. But he knew its imperfections too well, the gaping fractures climbing the cinderblock walls, the peeling paint, the weeds prying apart the concrete walks, the scabby grass out front. In daylight, naked, the south wing looked more like an Anasazi ruin than a house of worship. It all seemed so futile. A year after it had been slapped on, the brown trim outside was already flaking off. The Rez had no deference for the holy priesthood, let alone Sears Weatherbeater.

He looked across the road at the bonfire outside the Benally hogan. It was big, gold, fluttering like a shredded flag or a maverick sun. A couple of stray dogs were nosing into a tipped trash can. Up on the hill by the water tank, he could hear voices, soft, giggling. A pair of headlights flickered down the road like scavenger eyes. Soaked with sweat, his throat parched, Max closed his eyes and inhaled deeply. A warm wind blew across his weary face, cooling him.

Elder Crawford called it the Land of Desolation, but his head was still in Wyoming, doting on banal Rocky Mountain beauty, snow-capped peaks and pine trees. Yes. It's a harsh, stubborn, mean, bastard land, a desert. But beauty was there. In the bizarre sandstone architectures—vermilion castles, leaning towers, onion domes, minarets, a sombrero tilting on the tip of a wizard's hat. It was in the mesa, barricading the land from the world beyond like the Great Chinese Wall. It was in the colors—greens, yellows, golds, browns, reds, blues—ever changing in the interplay of sun and shadow, every shade and tone imaginable bleeding from the rocks, the sand, the sky. It was in the valleys, vast and empty but for a hogan or windmill, like tiny ships at sea or satellites in outer space. Beautiful, but harsh. Stubborn. Like the people.

He could see that stubbornness in everything, from the tough, stingy sage and rabbit brush which resisted the winds and rain, to the gaping mouths in the sheer, weather-crippled canyon cliffs, to the gnarled rocks and pinnacles, to the juniper trees, whose silvery bark splintered and spiraled around contorted trunks. But it grows on you, if you let it.

Driving the empty reservation roads, he had come to relish the ocean-like stretches of land, so opposite the vertical thrust of pines, of mountains, forever forcing the eye upward, heaven bound. When we vacationed in Tucson or Salt Lake, all the neat little suburban neighborhoods with neat little lawns and neatly marked streets with real gutters and sidewalks and concrete everywhere and everything precisely squeezed together without an inch unpaved unplanted unaccounted for . . . I got claustrophobia. And the long tedious hours they devoted to keeping their yards trimmed and tidy seem presumptuous. Wasted. Are they neurotic and have I seen a new and better light? Or have I just become lazy? Caught the Lamanite disease?

He had come a stripling twenty-five-year-old, fresh out of graduate school, with flashing blue eyes and rosy cheeks into which the creases were daily digging deeper. His face and hands had taken on the parched look of the land, without the color. It wears. The sand in your hair, your food, your bowels. The Dust Bowl blizzards and Sahara summers. The incompetence. The sloth. The hypocrisy and contradictions. The Attakai family, no gas money to drive to church on Sunday but a satellite dish outside their double-wide trailer. Jerry Benally calling at three a.m.: "Go over to the clinic! My brother needs a priesthood blessing!" His brother mashed in a car wreck–Driving While Intoxicated–his second in a month. The Pampers and pop cans and potato chip wrappers littering Sacred Mother Earth.

It wears. The drunks. The panhandlers. The lukewarm Mormons who supplement the sacrament with peyote chips. Or those who are members on the books only; strangers cornering me at the trading post, pumping my arm, asking about my family, my job, the branch. Then: "Can you loan me a couple dollars?" It's insulting, as if a promise to sit through sacrament meeting is worth five bucks to me. As if attendance is *my* hang-up. They show up in the pews for the first time in three years and even bear their testimonies–how they went astray but are back to stay now–then afterwards catch me in my office, shaking my hand again, the alcohol still red in their eyes, giving me a song and dance about how they'd quit drinking and are going straight, have just seen Jesus sunbathing in the wash. "Because I believe! I believe in Je-sus!" Saying the Savior's name not like a Mormon, with meekness and restraint, but that canned commercial hip-hip-hooray fanaticism of a preacher. And inevitably, the request: "So I was wondering if maybe the church could loan me some money." For a truck payment because no Government Assistance check this month– computer foul-up. Or to take his dying mother to the hospital. She was dying the last time he tried to hit me up. I've heard them all. It wears. The land. The people. It gets everyone sooner or later.

Not them, of course. *The* People. They endure. In their own passive stubborn obstinate way. Like the grass, the sagebrush, the canyons.

The light on the horizon still pulsed off and on like a stuttering bulb about to black out under the smothering weight of the clouds. It struggled weakly but valiantly. Silently Max urged it to resist.

As he started back to the church, a huge fork of lightning streaked across the northern sky followed by a bigger, brighter one which plunged earthward like a giant talon. A third streak reached down as if to pluck the steeple right off the churchhouse. Defiantly Max moved away from the building and the butte into an open area where he stood like a solitary pine. He was not afraid. The moon was gone, buried in black clouds. The sky rumbled, then let loose a barrage of cannonballing booms that shook the churchhouse and everything around it. But that was all. No rain.

He headed back inside. The thunder simmered to a faint echo and the lightning to a few dying pulsations on the mesa. Max gripped the ladder with both hands and looked up despairingly. The beams looked like a prehistoric skeleton. He was trapped inside the belly of a whale.

He dragged the ladder a couple feet to the center of the gym, right under the apex. Climbing slowly, cradling the can and brush in one arm, he felt a sour-stomach, acrophobic feeling. His muscles grew limp, his free hand quivering as it moved from rung to rung. Thirty-five times and I still feel like I'm tight-roping across the Grand Canyon. Peterson promised me scaffolds.

Carefully Max crept upwards until he was kneeling on the top. Slowly moving one foot up on the rung, then the other, he raised himself until he was standing erect. He glanced down. The linoleum floor seemed a thousand feet below. Black tar marks glared back at him like Halloween eyes. Slowly, painstakingly, Max touched the brush to the beams, stretching only a foot or two in either direction. Don't let me down now. Not this close. Ten years. It wasn't always like this—I wasn't, was I?

Initially he'd been positive, optimistic. He'd tried to learn all he could about the land and the people. He took night classes in

Navajo language and culture. He picked up local hitchhikers and learned to say no tactfully. At church, in talks and testimonies, he constantly preached unity and the similarities rather than the differences between the anglo and Navajo members, citing the Zion society at the end of the Book of Mormon, in which there were no Lamanites or any manner of -ITES. At socials he entertained the crowd with slapstick skits and John Wayne impersonations. He made few demands on anyone, even at work, indulging the church members, shouldering the burdens of a crippled branch with grin-and-bear-it fortitude. But I let little things get under my skin. The mud. The cockroaches.

Ben Notah, the medicine man. Knocking on my door that tragic afternoon three years ago. I never knew quite what to make of Ben. He was a bona fide medicine man, a great sandpainter, the best. But he didn't look the part, loitering around the trading post in holey sneakers and a World War II trench coat that hung below his knees. A wool skullcap covered his half-bald head. He looked like a troll on welfare.

"Brother Max! *Ya'at'eeh*!" Smiling, his solitary front tooth Skoal-stained, carious, a rotting kernel of corn; extending his hand, plump, crusty, polka-dotted with scabs. "Brother Max, maybe you can help me out? Could I borrow five dollars?"

Before Max could refuse, Ben was making promises: "I'll bring you two sandpaintings tomorrow. The Buffalo-Who-Never-Dies and the Nightway."

"Ben, you still owe me a sandpainting from the last time."

"I'll bring it tomorrow."

"Fine. Then we'll be even-steven."

Ben looked puzzled but smiled. "I'll pay you back tomorrow. I promise. I'm giving a lecture on the Blessingway at the Presbyterian church. I'm getting a hundred dollars. You come too."

I wasn't usually that stupid. Or gullible. But he caught me at a weak moment, right in the middle of scripture study, the Sermon on the Mount. I was fasting, too.

Max opened his wallet and took out a five-dollar bill. "You'll pay me back tomorrow?"

"Honest Injun," Ben said, grinning.

Max never saw the money or the sandpaintings. And when Ben's oily face appeared at the door again, his eyes begging pity he didn't deserve—or didn't need—and stood there alive and well inside that porky booze-abused body while Max's little Tsidii was . . . Max couldn't help himself. His fist plowed square into Ben's face, splitting it from the top of his lip to the tip of his chin. The medicine man sprawled backwards off the steps and into the dirt where he sat up slowly, ribbons of red trickling down his mouth, looking confused, opening his mouth and spitting out his lone tooth, dusting himself off, hobbling out the gate. Max had buried his face in his hands and wept.

Another rumble outside, miming his empty belly. Max sensed the early twitchings of a cramp in his left calf. He closed his eyes and tried to unthink the knot. The day he punched Ben Notah had begun right here. In this gym. This damn gym. He remembered perfectly: chasing downcourt after the speedy guard from Rough Rock, then the loud, dull crash just outside the building. Then silence. The ladder—heavy, wooden, left standing from the previous week's paint project—now lying on his daughter's skull, dented like a tin can. Max had heaved the ladder aside, but her blue eyes and rosebud lips were already frozen. Melissa, walking over from the trailer, hastening her walk, running: "Max! Oh my God, Max!"

Kneeling in the hot noon sun with the bleeding little head in his hands, Max had said, calmly at first, "Go home and get the consecrated oil. It's in the refrigerator, the lower shelf." Melissa, hysterical, screaming until he screamed back. "Dammit, Liz! Shut up and get the oil!" She ran off. The crowd had gathered, mostly athletic young men with glossy black hair and smooth, sinewy limbs but dumbfounded expressions. Max scanned the group hopelessly. "Woodrow!" he called to an elderly spectator who spoke little English. The only Melchizedek priesthood holder in the crowd.

"Come here. *Hago*!"

But Woodrow backed off, shaking his old sandblasted face. I

couldn't blame him. He still hadn't forsaken the old ways. Afraid of the ghost spirit, *chindi*.

The others backed away too, silent, as Max placed his hands on the child's dented skull and, calling her by name, whispered desperately, "In the name of Jesus Christ, I . . . " But he broke down, never finished the prayer. By the time Melissa arrived with the vial of oil, he was covering the child's face with his t-shirt. Bad timing on Ben's part. When he knocked on the door, Max could still smell Tsidii's blood frying on the pavement.

So Ben Notah had lost his last tooth. And the next morning Max woke up with a fist the size of a boxing glove. A veteran at mending barroom cuts and gashes, the doctor at the PHS clinic smiled: "Who got the best of it?"

He did, Max thought, stabbing his brush at the very top of the apex. Just as painstakingly as he had mounted the top rung, he began climbing down. Two shots of penicillin and his hand wrapped up for a week. A Mormon high priest punching out an old medicine man.

That very night the district president, a stocky little Hopi with a goatee, had knocked at his door.

"Brother Hansen, the Lord has called you to serve as president of the Tsegi Branch."

Timing. It was the timing again.

"I don't think I should accept."

"Why not?"

Max hesitated. "You need a Lamanite."

"The Lord has chosen you."

"Are you sure?"

President Seweyestewa paused. "Yes."

He was sustained and set apart the next day.

Max glanced at his paint-freckled watch. Ten o'clock. One-and-a-half beams. Ten settings to go. He'd have to work faster— much faster. He climbed back up the ladder. Strange how he had walked across that parcel of pavement thousands of times over the past three years without thinking of the fallen ladder and his daughter's little head smashed underneath it. Now he wondered how much he had paid for that kind of detachment. Or did I

care that much to begin with? I gave it lip service, too. Fatherhood, my number one calling; family, my greatest joy. Not really.
Not at first. Not until five years ago when our fourth . . .

Tsidii Yazhi, the Navajos called her, "Little Bird," because
her hair was so white and stiff and stuck straight out all over, like
an exotic bird. I could never pronounce it right, always fouling
up the *Ts*, my awful Navajo. Before Tsidii, fatherhood was a
duty, a lot of hassle and . . . adaptation. No. I don't think I
loved her more than the other three. It just took me that long to
finally . . . well, delight in them.

Quickly finishing up the section, he recalled how each morning, as he left for work, she would call out to him, "Wait, Dad!"
and then lug his volunteer fire fighter's coat and helmet to the
door, her face red from the strain, and dump them proudly at his
feet: "Here, Dad!" Fetching his shoes. Announcing the first snowfall. Doing forward rolls across the living room floor. Proudly
greeting him in Navajo: "*Ya'at'eeh, shizhe'e*!" Crying when he left
in the morning, dancing circles around him when he returned at
night. So concerned about him: "Tired Daddy sit down . . . right
here!" Maternal little two-year-old. It really hit me one night
while she was putting her Cathy doll to sleep, just how spontaneous and innocent—pure, how pure she was. And how eventually those cute little arms and legs would grow long and those
pinpoint nipples swell, even her Tsidii hair would grow long and
lay flat.

He wept. Not because she would eventually have matured
and left him, but because, looking at her, the Tsidii-electrocuted
hair, her busy little hands, her unpretentious smile, he realized
for the first time just how deeply he felt for her. All the kids.
Sarah with her studious airs and gangly Mark and Shannon, the
little gymnast. I finally realized, or admitted to myself, yes, they
are my joy, my comfort. And what else matters? Car job money
house? But I wonder now if I don't need the kids more than
they need me. What have I done for them when you get right
down to it? Besides exiling them to an Indian reservation? So
Sarah can't take ballet lessons and Mark still can't swim. They don't
even know who Pac-Man is. No, I won't apologize for that.

· · · · ·

There's more to life than Pac-Man and VCR. They loved hiking the buttes and canyons, and driving up to Tsaile to cut down a Christmas tree. In the spring when the water was running, they'd splash in the wash like little otters. There were powwows and rodeos on weekends, and I took Mark to that Fire Dance. Things they never could have seen or felt in the suburbs. And at least they grew to respect and even love sand and space, seeing thy children in all colors. Not turning their noses up at an outhouse, and the size of a home was no big deal, or a woman scooping out her breast to feed an infant during the sacrament. They didn't cringe at a dirt floor, or pity, and they saw how death can have dignity, even in a pine box lowered by rope into a hand-dug hole. Maybe they didn't realize it at the time, but when we finally packed up and left, they cried all the way to Holbrook. All of them. Melissa too.

Max climbed down the ladder and moved it along the drop cloth. Nine more settings. Three more hours. 10:35. He gazed about the gym at the faded boundary stripes and speckled free-throw lines. Bits of red and green crepe paper clung to the near hoop, remnants of last year's Christmas party.

Mounting the ladder once again, he recalled the district basketball tournament. It had started late. Somehow Tsidii had gotten into one of the five-gallon buckets and dripped paint all over the floor. I had chewed her out, really yelled at her. I wasn't ready to show the increase of love yet. No, I don't begrudge You for taking her away so much as taking her then, on a sour note, my last words, "Shut up! Just shut up and get out!" That, to haunt me till the Resurrection. Timing again. Ten years of bad timing.

"There's more to education than a classroom," he used to tell Melissa. "Think of the cross-cultural experience the kids are getting. They'll learn things here they couldn't learn anywhere else." Then, grinning boyishly, he would point to two dogs mating outside the trading post while a pack of slop-tongued others waited their turn. Experiences. Powwows. Rodeos. Losing a daughter.

He thought Tsidii's death would be the last straw for Melissa, but she had already endured beyond her breaking point. The mud, the wind. Anomie. Isolation. Death came to her as a natural consequence, a fitting culmination. After the initial shock she had resigned herself. But her suffering had stretched out over seven years. Mine . . .

He remembered (climbing down the ladder, dragging it along, climbing up again) midway through their first year, Melissa, a child in each arm, crossing the muddy compound, losing her footing and sliding across the mud. It looked funny at first, like a cartoon stunt. But later, in the trailer: "I've had it with this place, Max! I'm sick and tired of buying milk that's sour because the trading post is too cheap to turn up their refrigerator. I'm sick of the drunks asking me for money every time I go to check the mail and the dead dogs on the road and the starving horses with their ribs sticking out and the old men peeing behind the Chapter House and—"

He promised her they would leave at the end of the year. But with inflation and unemployment, a skidding job market and reservation housing dirt cheap, . . . you get trapped. Financially, emotionally. "One more year" became a standing joke.

One Sunday morning their fourth year, Melissa stormed down the hall: "Where's my slip? No, my *long* slip! Dammit, Shannon! I told you not to play with it. Max, that's it! I'm not going! I'm the only one who does anything around here. I am *not* going! Do you hear me, Max? Do you hear me?"

"Loud and clear."

"I said I'm not going!"

"Don't."

"Sarafina Begay probably won't show up and I'll have to give her Relief Society lesson—again."

But that Sunday the Navajos had poured into the chapel—humble in blue jeans and cowboy boots, a few in mangy suits, old women in velveteen or pleated rags. It was so packed we had to open the dividers and set up chairs in the gym. That Sunday I saw the bud begin to blossom.

And that night, Melissa, in bed, feeling guilty, apologizing.

. . . . .

"I don't know what got into me this morning. I haven't thrown a tantrum like that since high school."

Sitting beside her, reading scriptures: "Forget it. It's just the Rez."

The swamp cooler stirred the musty summer air, and bedsprings had creaked restlessly in the children's room. Guilt pangs. I'd had my share. All those nights coming home late from church meetings, home visits, painting projects . . . when I could have been with Melissa and the kids. Trudging through the door at midnight. Melissa waiting up in front of the TV.

"Kids asleep?"

"Since eight."

"So what's new in the world?"

"Hostages in Iran, Russians in Afghanistan, inflation up to 20 percent . . . same old stuff."

Flopping down on the sofa beside her, looking at bare legs that no longer lit a fire without concentrated effort. Not because she'd gone to pot after four kids. It was me. Fatigue. Burn out.

"Anything exciting happen tonight?"

"Saw Jerry Yazzie at Thriftway. Billy Tso's in jail again."

"Drunk?"

Max shrugged.

"Is he still going to be ordained an elder?"

"Not now. Not if I have anything to say about it."

"That's too bad. He was doing real well there for awhile."

"They all do real well for awhile."

His head fell softly on her lap; she stroked it gently.

"Melissa, you're terrific. It's not every woman who'd put up with all this."

"All this what?"

"All this me." He turned to her with childlike jubilation: "Someday when we've got our own house . . . "

But after their fourth year that line ceased to console her, and by their fifth it was downright irritating, a detonator to quarrels which left the children whimpering in their bedroom. So he had dropped it completely. The line, the promise, everything, until he could finally deliver. And then it was too late. Almost.

Finishing the thirty-fifth beam, he climbed down again. One left. Confidently he re-set the ladder, but climbing back up he was weakened by a sensation that the beams had somehow multiplied, that there were forty, fifty, a hundred maybe. He told himself that was impossible. He dipped his brush and spread. Mountains and valleys. Up and down, up and down. Melissa and me.

There were moments. Summer mornings when her body, like the land, lay deep in shadow, fresh, fertile, the moisture on her brow like the dew on the sagebrush, and the line of her sun-tan a white criss-cross on her sleek back. The phone off the hook, the dog thumping its tail against the front door, the swamp cooler humming down the hall. Slowly she would awaken to his touch; then, as if he'd pressed a magic button, her cool fresh body, ripe from a long night's rest, would awaken, catch fire and envelop him so suddenly that he was always caught a little off guard and could never think through or fully feel what was happening though he always relished it, those intimate moments when together they withdrew from the world.

Now Melissa was in Tucson with the kids. She didn't want him to go back. Maybe she was right. Maybe I should have left it to the Indians. It's their church, their land. I should have listened to Melissa.

Max paused, gazing at the ceiling, at the eight caged lights, the thirty-six oppressing beams. Where's the still, small voice telling me, No no no, noble Max, thou hast done well, my faithful if sometimes begrudging servant? Melissa. Let me see Melissa again. And the kids. Sara, Mark, Shannon. The kids. Tsidii too.

He finished the section in record time—fifteen minutes. Six more settings, one more apex. But the heat and dehydration were getting to him. Halfway down the ladder green and black spots collided before his eyes. He miscalculated the missing second rung and almost fell. Time to end his fast—he'd been going without since dinner last night—take a drink at least. He re-set the ladder and walked down the hall into the men's room. He turned the faucet on cold and waited several moments to see if it would run any cooler, though he knew it wouldn't. A year ago he had disconnected the drinking faucet in the hall saying too many kids played in the water and slopped it on the floor. The real reason was a few adults who made the porcelain trough a spittoon for their chewing tobacco.

Max filled his mouth with water but did not swallow. He swished it around several times and spit it out. The water was warm and bitter, with a rusty, metallic flavor that complemented the putrid smell coming from the ladies' room. He peeked into the lone stall. The toilet hadn't been flushed probably since last Sunday. So what's new?

Pushing down the flusher, he tried to laugh it off, but nausea forced him out. He collapsed against the wall, his hands, face, and neck soaked with a second sweat. His lids clenched shut against his will; the room went black. Bending forward, he dipped his head between his knees and left it there until the darkness cleared and his eyes reopened.

Straightening up slowly, he returned to the gym and climbed back up the ladder, thinking how many times in the last ten years Melissa's old college friends had unknowingly broken her spirit with letters describing their new homes on the hill, then, later, how they were redecorating them, and later still, their new homes higher on the hill. While we bought junk furniture at yard sales and drove our Ford into the ground. Ten years and what did we have? A cradleboard, a couple of sandpaintings. Not that we need a Cadillac—that's the last thing. But it would have been nice—easier for Melissa, I think—if at the end we'd had a little nicer house . . . something besides memories, a headstone.

The world had passed him by. In a decade his younger brothers had graduated from law and medical school and had started thriving practices. His grandmother wrote often reminding him of his choice blessings—beautiful Melissa and the children and his wonderful "mission" among the poor Lamanites. But then, inevitably, the marvelous toys and bicycles and Baby Dior outfits and canopy bed his brothers had sent them, not to mention a new microwave oven, Christmas compliments of his younger brother Robert the attorney.

To Grandma Hansen, "things" are blessings from above, the

temporal reflecting the spiritual. A mixed message. "The humblest hogan can be a temple if thy spirit there abides." Elder Crawford badgering the peyote people: "Look what your crazy religion's gotten you! A shack! A hole in the ground! You'll never get ahead."

Working swiftly, Max touched up another section, descended, dragged the ladder along the drop cloth, and refilled his empty can. He hesitated at the foot of the ladder, then detoured out into the foyer and slowly opened the door to the chapel.

He switched on the light. Large and humid, with a beamed ceiling even higher and more severely slanted than the one he was painting, the chapel seemed like a vast cavern. The plywood walls smelled like fresh paint though it had been two years since they had been refinished. From the base of the pulpit, a framed portrait of the Savior gazed at him solemnly. Max looked away. The quiet room demanded a reverence that was rare those chaotic Sunday mornings he presided over the services. He tiptoed down the aisle, a light film of dust recording his footsteps. He gazed at the familiar old pews of fading varnish, the half-husked covers of the hymn books, the organ no one could play. A few nuggets of sacrament bread had gone stale sitting in the silver trays. Sand and dust coated the window casements. A torn and tattered divider, like a ragged accordion, walled off the chapel from the gym. Cheap, second-rate, abused. Yet Max felt oddly at peace within the room, perhaps because of the many imperfections. The silence was so dense that exterior sounds seemed amplified in contrast—a knock on a door, a passing car, powwow music from a nearby trailer.

Max switched off the light, closed the chapel door, and returned to the gym. Somewhere along the way he had lost his innocence. I came here a man of faith and planted what I thought was a good seed. But the soil, and this ten-year drought—ten times two hundred years—I couldn't get a bud let alone a blossom. Sagebrush and rabbit grass. No roses. Everything withers—everyone. My high school buddies went to Vietnam; I wound up in Indianland. They lost their legs in a jungle on the other side of the world; I lost my marbles closer to home.

As branch president he had started the services at nine a.m. sharp, whether two, three, or a hundred were present. He chastised teachers who shirked their Sunday duties and lowered the boom on members who doubled with the Native American Church. He cut off welfare assistance to inactives and tightened the screws on returning Placement students who ditched church during the summer. He made enemies. Instead of *Hastiin Nez*, "Tall Man," behind his back they called him *Dooldini*, "S.O.B." Twice his tires were slashed and his windshield broken. One morning he found a mangled cat's head on his doorstep; another time, a wad of tin foil with strands of human hair wound around a piece of bone. Still, he played hardball, cried repentance from the pulpit, laid down the law: "As members of the church, fellow citizens, we're all judged by the same standards, regardless of race, creed, color. So I don't want to hear any more of this 'I was witched' business. We're all free agents, accountable for our own actions."

Under Max's stewardship, polygamists, adulterers, fornicators, bootleggers, the unrepentant of every make and variety were called to court and excommunicated.

Max climbed down and moved the ladder along, clear to the other side of the gym. He would work inward, from the wall, towards his grand finale. I went off the deep end, didn't I? Not that they didn't deserve the scolding. But not the venom. Venting myself on them. That day at the trading post when Jimmy Yazzie's pickup stalled and the two women were out there in the snow trying to push-start it, I sat in my Fairmont and watched, thinking, "Dumb dumb dumb. Drive your truck to death, never change the oil, never tune it up. Then you blame it on the dumb white man who made the truck when it konks out on you."

Or Sadie Curly, fifteen, knocking on Max's door at midnight: could she borrow four dollars to buy Pampers for her baby? A baby she shouldn't have had in the first place. Driving around in her boyfriend's sports car. I gave her the money, just like I finally got off my butt and gave Jimmy a jump-start. But the feelings. "Why the hell don't you use cloth diapers—I do! What about your big-shot boyfriend—he gave you the baby, why not the diapers too?" And when I saw the big, old matriarchs taking bows at American Indian Day, I didn't see dignity but obesity. And superstition, fear, futility. And that was my sin, my failure, not theirs.

Max slapped his brush against the ceiling, sending a flurry of white speckles through the air. I don't . . . no, I don't regret for a minute Steve Nakai or Ben Jumbo, the peyote people. Or Jake Bedonie with three wives and so many kids he can't keep their names straight. Or even Clara Tullie who did and didn't understand. But Sherman.

Late one Saturday night, Max noticed a light on in the churchhouse. Walking over, he had seen his first counselor all alone, running the buffer up and down the chapel floor. Wearing sunglasses and those crazy Tony Lama snakeskin cowboy boots, his hair as shiny as black wax, plastered flat on top and bristly on the sides. Those others couldn't have cared less about their membership. They yawned, belched "pass the bottle." But Sherman had come so far, had tasted the fruit. He cared. And I didn't want to convene that court. But I had to. I would have done anything to let that cup pass. The others, no. I grew ogre eyes and turned into Elder Crawford. Still, I could bless them, heal them. You could. The adulterers, the fornicators, the drunks, the polygamists. A terminal woman half in her grave who now passes out in front of the trading post every afternoon, a bottle of T-Bird in each hand— through me You healed her but not my kid. No. I won't go into that. Who am I to question thee? Simple faith. Thinking deep down no instead of yes. A mustard seed and I didn't have it.

Working towards the last apex, Max dipped his brush and stretched far to the right, trying to catch a crack between the ceiling and the beam. A rim of sweat that had been gathering on his forehead suddenly dropped into his eyes, forcing him to clench them shut and wait for the salty sting to pass. Nausea overcame him. The green and black dots reappeared. Hurrying, he stretched an inch too far with the brush. The ladder tilted. He drew back but overcompensated to the other extreme. Two of the four legs left the floor. The wooden skeleton began falling like a tree. Father! No!

Desperately, he heaved his weight and managed to counter the tilt. After rocking to and fro on its four clumsy feet, the ladder finally came to rest. Max steadied the can of paint, laid his brush aside, and tightly closed his eyes, trying to regain his composure as tiny millipede legs ran hot and cold up and down his spine. Not now. Not this close. He picked up the brush and with renewed vigor finished up the section.

Memories crowded in. A summer baptism, afterwards when he grabbed Loren Benally by the nape of the neck and the seat of his pants. The little nerd, stealing my notes during the opening prayer so I had to speak impromptu. It gave Max great pleasure, that hot August night, to heave Loren into the algae-stained baptismal font. But his sister, Christine – when Max and Elder Sprinkle, the young missionary from Idaho, threw her in also. "Crazy squaw!" Max yelled, not for fear of the fourteen-year-old's thrashing feet but another, darker fear. Wearing those short shorts with those glowing brown thighs . . .

Max gave the section a final swipe, then climbed down and moved the ladder under the thirty-sixth apex. For the very last time he climbed back up.

His hands and legs were trembling when he reached the top. Dabbing paint into the wedge, he struggled with more memories: sacrament meeting the next day, towards the end when the entire congregation – even the fidgety comic book kids in back – suddenly hushed as Ronnie T., the cow-punching Cherokee, strolled up to the stand on bowed legs. Halfway through his testimony his bulldog face contracted like a fist and tears streamed down his mud-red cheeks as he began apologizing – to his wife, to his kids, to God, to President Max. Why me? Especially in my state of mind and heart. And for what? Not doing his home teaching? Having a few cross words with his wife? For taking a nip on the sly?

Max on the stand had rubbed his palm across his brow, gazing down, praying for a corner to hide in. After the meeting, he made his confession, one on one, to the Cherokee: "Ron, I'm telling you this confidentially, as a friend. You may think I look holy and happy and spiritually in tune, all dressed up in a suit and tie on Sunday morning with my little family. But the truth is . . . there have been times when Sister Hansen and I have had knock-down-drag-outs right outside the chapel doors. I've had to pray and conduct meetings with my own curses still ringing in my ears. And don't think that's not hard, pasting a smile on your face and shaking hands and trying to look as if all's well in Zion when you feel like a cesspool inside."

Alone in Max's office, the two men knelt together in prayer, then departed, Ron bleary-eyed. Being imperfect, the higher we aspire in love, compassion, morality, and general human decency, the bigger hypocrites we appear. That used to be my rationalization, so I could sleep at night. But I wonder now.

Max wiped his forehead and studied the narrow crack where the two beams joined at the apex. For a moment he was tempted to leave this last little spot bare, unfinished, the way the Navajo did with their rugs and sandpaintings, always leaving a small soul outlet. But that's them, not me. Not *Hastiin Nez. Dooldini. Bilagaana* Blue Eyes.

He dipped the brush deeply into the can and in one swift thrust, like a fencer, sealed the crack. He withdrew the brush and instantly a chain of tiny holes appeared. He thrust again. A third time. A fourth. Sealed. He held the brush in his right hand and the can in his left, both outstretched, high atop the ladder. The brush fell to the floor, hitting the drop cloth with a dull thud.

Climbing down seemed to take forever. For every rung he had climbed up, there seemed to be three going down. The wooden bars were hot irons to his grasping hands. He saw the black and green spots again, then hazy gray light. Then Elder Crawford in a pea green jump suit, his head under the hood of a Chevy pickup. Detaching himself so totally from the land and the people, he had been relegated to full-time missionary vehicle maintenance. Passing through, Max had stopped by to say hello.

"*Ya'at'eeh, hastiin!* I hear you're going home soon."

Elder Crawford didn't answer for some time. He wasn't advertising the fact he had requested an early release. His head remained under the hood: "This is what I sold half my property for—to come out here and check dip sticks."

Later, a week before returning to his Rocky Mountain paradise, he pulled his head out just long enough to confess his failure: "I hate Navajos." Not derisively or vindictively, but sadly.

Max lowered the ladder and set it down against the wall. He rolled up the drop cloth and hammered the lid snugly on the five-gallon bucket. He took the brush into the janitor's closet and tossed it into the sink. He turned on the faucet. As the water struck the brush, milky fluid spiraled down the drain. Fumes from the vats of floor wax and detergents sent nausea and dizziness through him. The close confined walls began tilting. Back to the wall, he sank to the floor. It was my job, my calling. But who was I to judge anyone, least of all these people? Okay, so a lot drink and pray to peyote and rodeo on Sunday and breed like rabbits . . . but the good, the humble, the compassionate.

Delbert John's funeral. Max driving down alone to the hogan to discuss arrangements with the family. There must have been a hundred people crammed in there. Family, friends, neighbors, all ages, bundled up in old coats and blankets. Standing against the wall, trying to appear unobtrusive, Max scanned the crowd for a familiar face but recognized no one. In the middle of the dirt floor an old quilt was spread out with neatly crumpled stacks of ones, fives, tens, and twenties. Next to them was a modest pile of turquoise and silver jewelry and two Ganado red rugs.

One by one, in no particular order, the people stood up and spoke for several minutes, like an all-night fast and testimony meeting in Navajo, the family members giving thanks to those who had come, the others offering condolences and mini-eulogies for the deceased. There were yawns, muted coughs, infant cries, occasional sobs, but mostly silence. Every so often someone sneaked up front and added a few bills to the stacks. Modestly, humbly, almost embarrassed, going up in a crouching walk, the way people do at the movies when they have to pass in front of the projector. But good-sized stacks. There must have been a thousand dollars cash, plus the rugs and jewelry. All that the Friday before the Government Assistance checks came in, when most of them didn't have gas money to get home. No, in that way they have it over us. Death is a community experience—not just casseroles and Hallmark cards. The bell really tolls for everyone out here.

Max ran more water over the brush, reflecting on those somber faces in the crowd. To outsiders—him too, when he'd first come to the Rez—they appeared grim, even hostile. A bitter, grave, humorless people. But that was their facade, like our white man counter, the Ultra-Brite smile. We rarely hang around long enough to see the flip-side. The simple, the happy, the content.

Max recalled the summer evening he drove ten miles down the bumpy dirt road to visit Charley Sam. Just behind the shade-house, in a twenty-foot square of newly placed cinderblocks, twelve kids of all ages were chasing around, laughing, playing tag. No one was excluded. A little boy in sagging Pampers plodded along-side teenaged tomboys in blue jeans.

Brother Sam sauntered outside. "*Ya'at'eeh*, Brother Max!" he greeted cheerfully. Small talk.

"Gotta start workin'," he said.

"Where at?"

"Pin-*yon*."

"That's a long way to commute."

"Yeah. I guess I'll wait for the Fourth of July."

"What's happening on the Fourth?"

"I don't know. Maybe have a family get-together."

Slow and easy.

Tepees and peyote paraphernalia. But you can't deny those twelve kids. Relatives, friends of relatives. And the kids were laughing and happy and Sister Sam didn't chew them out for playing in the dirt, or Brother Sam for climbing all over the pickup. Without guilt, or . . . well, just without. And walking back to the car, remembering how I used to wince every time my kids even breathed on the new Fairmont. No sounds here except kids giggling and the baaing of sheep and just plain flat beautiful solitary land, vast and empty, and so quiet and peaceful with the mesa on fire one minute, deep ocean purple the next. All those colors seeping in and out as if You were backstage with a giant projector showing off. I sensed no bitterness, no frustration in their lives. Not like me, secretly gnashing my teeth, where ambition and aspiration and conscience are guilt, win or lose.

Say, this paintbrush . . . you stick it under the tap and the paint just keeps running. I don't know where it all comes from—all that paint hidden up inside one tiny brush—but it just keeps running and running and running.

When Max started the last phase of clean-up, tugging the steel comb through the bristles, he heard a dainty percussion, like tiny candies striking glass. In the cramped closet, Max listened hopefully. He dropped the brush and comb and stumbled out the door and down the hall into the foyer. Flicking on the light, he saw it, clear, slow, syrupy, crawling like sweat down the double glass doors. He bolted out into the humid night.

Rain was falling but faintly, like clipped hairs. Max looked pleadingly at the starless, blackened sky. Lightning flashed to the north, followed by rumbling growing gradually, culminating in a loud, cannonballing blast. Another flash to the south, followed by more rumbling, more thunder, more lightning, over and over, alternating, lightning and thunder, flash and boom, like opposing armies exchanging heavy fire.

Max smiled. Lightning began running wild on the horizons, roller coastering up and down, a Chinese dragon celebrating the New Year. Max peeled off his t-shirt and dropped his garments to his waist. The faint drops tickling his flesh, he waited for the flood to fall. The thunder boomed and the lightning flashed, but the faint falling hairs thinned rather than thickened.

Max lowered his head with a grin of self-mockery. Within the cannonballing commotion, he heard a weird metallic twang, like a ricocheting bullet, coming from the hill. A savage bolt of lightning reached down and struck within a hundred feet of the churchhouse, skeletonizing everything in sight. Another bolt, just as bright, struck even closer. Then more, one after another, in rapid succession, igniting land and sky as if with white fire, electrifying everything metal.

Max backed against the churchhouse, crouching under the eaves. With each lightning flash, the water tank glowed and shimmered like a UFO; the telephone wires turned into electric eels. The sky was a Fourth of July spectacular in silver and white–dazzling, intimidating–God's almighty signature streaking back and forth across the sky. But dry.

Max hitched up his garments, put on his t-shirt, and was about to head back inside when he saw–or thought he saw–yes, x-rayed in a lightning flash, shawled and stoop-shouldered, an old woman. The elusive *saani* who had wished him peace, beauty, and harmony. He called out, "*Shimasani!*" but his cry was smothered in thunder. In the next strobic flash, she was gone.

Max returned to the janitor's closet and resumed tugging the steel comb through the brush, his hands still shaky from the wild lights, the sticky heat, his hallucination. Or revelation? You keep sending me clues, messengers. Am I too out of touch, or is this a tease? When had he first seen the woman? Like a flash from the wild light show outside, he remembered: his first year, tracting with the missionaries one winter afternoon, beating a snowy path from hogan to hogan. Crossing the frozen wash, Elder Richfield was "moved by the Spirit" to make a detour.

A half mile later they found her, sitting in the bottom of an arroyo, bending forward and back, wincing, whimpering softly. Richfield, the senior companion, spoke to her in Navajo; then to Max.

"She was herding sheep and slipped on a rock. She hurt her leg. Can't walk."

Max and the two young elders rigged up a stretcher Boy Scout-style and hiked her out of the arroyo to their pickup and drove her to the PHS clinic. She said nothing, just sat there wincing, rubbing her pleated skirt up and down her calf. From the clinic she was sent by ambulance to the Indian Hospital in Gallup.

The following Sunday Richfield called him aside. "Remember that old *saani*? Elder Wheeler and I were in town yesterday, so we stopped by the hospital to see how she was doing. Broken leg. She said after her fall she sat there all night waiting to die. Cold, hungry. Coyotes howling. She thought she was a goner."

Then just before dawn, an apparition: a woman with her face, but wearing the buckskin leggings of two centuries ago. "Do not worry, my granddaughter. Two young men will soon come to help you."

The elders. I was the odd-man out.

At the hospital the old woman, leg raised in a cast, looked at Elder Richfield: "I want to be baptized."

Richfield, caught off guard, stammered, "*Hagoshi* . . . that's good that you want to be baptized . . . but the lessons . . . you haven't heard the lessons—"

The woman pointed with her lips to a picture on the wall, *The Last Supper*. "Last night, that man in the middle there, he told me I should be baptized. He told me you would come."

I remember now. Nanibaa Yoe. She was baptized. Then we never saw her again. Not at church. But that simple, unpremeditated faith. Like Sister Watchman. Refuting a tumor in the name of the priesthood! The audacity! But that's the way they are. And it was my own cynicism, coming so puffed up with grand visions, big plans—a ward in two years. A stake in three. Like the other anglos out here on their "mission" among the Lamanites. White Mormondom's burden: save the Indians. But we get jaded, skeptical. Too many failures, contradictions. We lose steam and poop out.

Sucking in a deep breath, Max shook the brush dry, hung it on the rack, and switched off the light. For a moment he considered checking all of the doors, but it was past midnight and who else had been in the churchhouse during the week? So he turned off the lights in the hall and the gym, and, without ceremony or sentimentality, locked up the churchhouse for the last time.

Half the sky was clear and a cool wind was blowing from the south. The sensual, pre-rain fragrance, stronger than ever, perked him up like smelling salts. Still, trudging home, Max felt no more relieved than he had nineteen hours ago, at sunup, or a week or a year or—

As he crossed the trailer compound a big German shepherd darted out with fangs flashing.

"Caesar!" Max yelled, but the animal took a nip at him anyway. "Damn you, Caesar! It's me – Max! Heck! How long does it take? It's only been – " He stopped in mid-sentence, not for fear of the dog but of his own voice, the two painful words. *Ten years, and I still don't know or understand them. They're always surprising me.*

Walking in, he recalled one night leaving the Deswoods' scrap lumber shack, the strange figure peering out from behind a rusty shell of a Chevy, whispering: "Psst! Hey!"

Across the highway disco music was blasting from the trading post and, cast in a sundown silhouette, three men were sitting on a knoll passing around a bottle. The figure wobbled towards Max. Levis and a t-shirt, with oily black bangs and an oily brown face and eyes cracked red and his breath reeking so badly even the mosquitoes stayed away. He almost smacked into Max before stopping, asking in a slow, slurred voice, "I wonder if you can help me?"

"What kind of help?"

"Will you . . . will you pray for me?"

Max, recognizing the subtle ploy, nodded. "I'd be happy to pray for you." He was about to add, "Come to church on Sunday – nine o'clock – and I'll have the whole branch pray for you!" but the man had already bowed his head and closed his eyes, waiting, his face a bizarre blend of drunken remorse.

"Do you want me to pray right now?" Max asked, surprised. He nodded.

Max lowered his head. "What's your name?"

Head bowed, eyes closed, he answered softly, "Chester. Chester Deswood."

"David's brother?"

"*Aoo'.*"

They stood uncomfortably close, their noses almost touching, like two Arabs. Max prayed: "Heavenly Father . . . we ask thee for a special blessing on Chester at this time . . . help him feel better . . . help him eat good foods and take care of himself and obey thy commandments . . . help this illness pass."

When Max finished, Chester extended his hand. But the whole time, even while praying, I kept waiting for him to pop the question. But he never did. He shook my hand and said thank you, thank you very much, his eyes even redder than before. That was all he wanted, a prayer. And returning to my car I kept thinking of all the things I could have said–remember, Chester, that you are a spirit child of God, never forget that; always pray to your Heavenly Father, for he loves you and will listen to you and care for you. I could have done the only thing that makes me worth my salt, out here or anywhere, brought a little comfort to a troubled soul. But even there I fouled up, too busy thinking how to say no no no, *shibeeso adin*. So I muttered a token prayer.

Entering his trailer, Max was overcome by musty, humid heat. He went straight to the refrigerator, took out a bottle of ice water, and tilted it slowly. The moment the icy water touched his lips, the thirst he had been resisting all day suddenly took possession of him. He guzzled recklessly. Half the water dribbled down his chin, soaking his throat and chest; the other half tingled all the way down his gullet and into his shriveled belly. He drank and drank but couldn't get enough. When the two-quart bottle was empty, he broke open an ice tray, crammed the cubes through the narrow mouth of the bottle, and filled it with tap water. Before the cubes could take effect, he was guzzling again. He guzzled until his belly was bloated, ready to burst.

Still thirsty, he went into the bathroom and filled the tub with cold water. He stripped and lowered himself in. The water stung him with an intense sensation of pleasure and pain. His skin contracted and began turning varying shades of pink and blue. He lay there submerged, his long skinny body shivering but sweating too, until the water grew tepid and the numbness wore off. Drying off, he put on his undergarment, took another long drink of water, and turned the swamp cooler on high. It did little more than stir up the fermented air. Max unrolled his sleeping bag directly under the cooler and stretched out on it. He closed his eyes and felt the sticky air on his face and the sweat already prickling in his armpits. He tried to think of Melissa and the kids and the drive home and his new job in sunny Tucson. Instead he saw Sherman Tsosie and Sister Watchman and Chester Deswood and the old woman appearing and vanishing in the crowd and in the rain and in his head. He tried to pray but it came out as it had been coming out all day, all week.

I tried . . . to understand, to feel. But . . . I don't know what they want. I thought I knew what You wanted, once, a long time ago. But that Regional Representative, he came down that spring in suit and tie, shaking everybody's hand. Then had Eddie Roanhorse stand up and tell us his immaculately amazing conversion story. Eddie who I bailed out of the slammer on Friday was proclaiming Jesus Christ on Sunday morning. Again. And Monday the Regional Representative was quoting him at church headquarters.

He came down like the others, asking for numbers numbers numbers. When we were trying to make friends with one or two, real friends, without conditions or stipulations or baptism or priesthood, without pushing or goal-setting and coercing with a handshake and a smile. In boots and blue jeans, shearing sheep and hauling wood and water and eating fry bread with them. To find out who they really are and what makes them tick, and not "them" but Sherman Tsosie and Wilbert Yellowhair and Charley Sam.

But he didn't want to know about that. He wanted to know how many baptisms, how many Melchezidek priesthood holders, how many temple marriages, how many how manys. And: "When can you have a ward here? A stake?" And the clincher: "You anglos are here on a mission to train the Lamanites. It is not good when an anglo holds a leadership position in a Lamanite branch."

He was awakened by a deafening explosion. Sitting up, half-asleep, he listened to the stampede overhead. A white flash filled the trailer and vanished.

He hurried to the kitchen window and drew the curtain aside. Still groggy, he gazed outside several moments before it finally registered: rain. Falling so thickly and swiftly he couldn't distinguish one drop from another except as they riddled the puddles

. . . . .

already formed—puddles growing into ponds and garden furrows into streams and the dirt road into a swamp of chocolate chowder.

Wearing only his garment, he ran outside. In seconds he was drenched. He dropped his garment to his waist and let the rain beat down on his bare flesh. As he inhaled the all-day all-week fecund fragrance that now bore also the tropical smell of the over-soaked soil, he looked up at the falling heavens with a refurbished heart, silently urging the rain to fall harder, faster. He tilted his head back and opened his mouth, catching the hail-hard drops on his tongue. He smiled as they plastered his hair to his skull, stung his nipples, pierced his eyes. He tried to feel every drop pelleting his back, his shoulders, his chest, showering down on him with brutal kindness, as if rinsing off a decade of sweat and frustration. Like the manna-weary Children of Israel begging for meat and then receiving until it poured out their nostrils, so he was getting his rain. He looked down at his toes, squishy on the saturated grass. Out here, out here. We say it's so different, the other side of the moon. But "out here" is everywhere.

He went back inside before he drowned. Toweling himself dry, he felt purged, refreshed, cleansed. He put on a dry garment and lay down on his bag. Ghost-like flashes streaked the kitchen window. The stampede softened to an easy gallop. He closed his eyes, confident he could sleep, but his legs ached and he tossed and turned several minutes before checking his luminous watch: 1:45. He thought of the churchhouse. For the first time, its completion gave him a sense of satisfaction, but only momentarily. There was Elder Crawford again, his confession: selling half his land to check dipsticks because . . . anglo arrogance. Coming here with blossom-as-the-rose expectations. Never thinking until it's too late that maybe our first mission is not to save and exalt the Indians. Maybe it's me, non-drinking non-smoking non-fooling-around temple-married high priest me I worry about. Me, my primary mission, all of us.

Max closed his eyes. The stampede returned. But this time the heavens were scorched red, sundown-stricken. He saw no moon or stars or rain or clouds, only a passionate red fog. Then it began falling. Not rain but fire – hot red coals like stars shooting earthward, thousands of them, approaching but never quite reaching their targets, except directly over the churchhouse where they were showering down thicker than the rain. Max watched incredulously, certain that this time it was indeed the end of the world.

Suddenly, as if all the rain that had fallen previously was lighter fluid and someone had put a match to it, the church went up in flames. All Max could see was the very tip of the steeple, no thicker than a needle, and the flames like frenzied hands reaching angrily for the top. He tried to cry for help, but his tongue was bound. His feet grew cold and numb and the cold shot up his legs and into his chest as he watched the first blackened wall crumble to the ground.

His eyes flew open as he snapped to a sitting position on his sleeping bag. He paused just a moment to orient himself, then rushed outside, his bare feet sinking in the mud. The rain had stopped and the sky was calm, clear, star-cluttered. The moon was fat and full. Everything seemed new, revitalized. Glazed with rain and moonlight, the cars and pickups along the compound looked freshly waxed and polished; the sandstone slabs on the hill shined like tinted glass. Rivulets trickled calmly alongside the muddy road. The churchhouse stood intact, as staunch and solid as the mesas in the distance.

Max mumbled a sincere thank you, but at the same time felt vaguely disappointed though uncertain or unable to admit why. Staring at the chapel, trying to sort his feelings, he saw more an adversary than a friend. There was something about it, had been, these last few years . . . even before the painting project, before Tsidii, Sherman Tsosie, Elder Crawford, Ben Notah . . . not the cheap wood and cracked walls, the eroding floors and scarred pews . . . something else. The way it suddenly and abruptly manifested itself on the otherwise smooth and fluid horizon that ran for miles and miles and miles until – zap! That wedge, that notch, that saw-toothed obtrusion on a sky that often grew so dark and smooth and perfect he couldn't divide it from the mesa, and land

· · · · ·

and sky literally became one eternal round, whole and harmonious, the entire universe domed inside this humble awesome everchanging everlasting patch of sand. And me too. Me, *Hastiin Nez*, *Dooldini*, another, a human obtrusion.

Max's eyes slowly climbed the north face, the chapel side, from the tumbleweed-hidden base on up to the silver steeple, rising like a giant needle ready to pierce some unlucky star. A bitterness burned within him, slowly, like green wood. But the curse on the tip of his tongue became a muted sob. Father, forgive me. And thank you. Again. It is all I have out here.

His gaze grew misty as he looked at the churchhouse for the last time. What he was feeling, he realized, was neither love nor hate, but something approaching reconciliation and regret, yet neither wholly. He waited for his feelings to commit one way or the other. Ten minutes later when they still refused, he decided it was time to go back—to his trailer, to his family, to his new home in sunny, civilized Tucson.

Visions

. . . .

This time, before dousing the light, he triple-checked to make sure he had done everything exactly right, by the book. He had.

He hit the switch. At first all he could see was the pinwheel of fluorescent markings on the timer, set at fifteen seconds. Gradually shapes appeared – boxes, beakers, bottles on the shelf. The red bulb above the sink would have revealed even more, but he had turned it off hoping it might make a difference although he knew it wouldn't.

He waited, nervously fingering another switch, this one a short metal stick protruding from a small metal box on the table. Slowly he drew it back. A cone of light dropped from the Beseler enlarger onto a blank sheet of photo paper on which he focused his total concentration, straining to feel every detail of the invisible image being burned onto the page. The luminous second-hand circled a quarter turn, clicked, and the light vanished.

He picked up the paper by its edges and slipped it into the developer tray, softly tapping his tongs over the surface until it was thoroughly submerged. Gently agitating the tray, he waited. Normally this was the part he most anticipated – the watching, the waiting, the unspoken abracadabra that suddenly turned a blank sheet into a mountain, a deer, a man.

He stiffened at the first sign of an image – a vague gray blur spreading from the center. In seconds a dark fog covered the page. As if surfacing from the bottom of a murky pond, the old

. . . . .

man's face materialized in the solution. Dave dipped his tongs into the tray and pinched a corner of the print but waited until through the watery blur he could see the pollen pouch, the headband, the two decaying teeth in the chanting smile. Then, in one deft movement, like a sleight-of-hand man, he withdrew the print and fed it into the stop bath. But in that fraction of a second, the seemingly scientifically impossible happened—again!

"Damn!" He hurled the tongs aside and kicked a half empty box of A&B Developer across the floor. He felt mad enough to ram his fist through the rotting cinder block wall; instead, he snatched the wet, black print, tore it into quarters, and stuffed them in the trash.

Switching on the light, he plopped down on a stool and gave himself a moment to cool down—another impossibility in that hothouse. Next door the boiler was chugging away like a giant pressure cooker on the verge of blowing up, its unregulated heat seeping through the towels he had stuffed inside the vents. He ran a hand across his sweaty forehead and wiped it dry on his Levis. One by one he reviewed the good prints. Perfect. Flawless. Every one. He shook his head. It made no sense—none! He got up. As if handling a priceless gem, he removed the negative from the enlarger and tucked it inside a protective envelope, which he placed on the table, beside the enlarger. He yanked open the door and stepped out.

The place was empty. Everyone had gone home except Eddie Tom, who was working late again, earning more comp time so he could take a week off for his Fire Dance ceremony. Through the half-open door of the pressroom, Dave could see his anemic profile, seated, shaking a rattle and chanting to the fervent drums of his peyote tapes as sheets of paper ran monotonously through the press. Stiff as a statue. If not for the slight movements of his hands, he could have been mistaken for—well, a wooden Indian.

Dave peered out the window with the spider web crack. Snowing again. Amazing! Crazy! That morning he had walked to the elementary school under sunny skies. Two hours later he was trudging back through a bleak winter scene: leaden clouds, bleached buttes, skeletal trees. Black scribble on white paper.

Since then, things had gone from bad to worse, with the mist so thick now he couldn't see beyond the dirt road. The mesas were gone, the corn fields, the trading post. Even the silver water tower and the gold neon of the Thriftway Store–gone. Invisible in the mist. The elementary school looked like a ship lost in a fog. The Yazzies' hogan was a buoy, and the tepee beside it– who knows? Something out of this world. Like everything else out there tonight.

Staring out the cracked glass, he was startled by an image, a face, vague and ghost-like, staring back at him. It shook him up a moment until he realized the face was his. Nothing to fear– clean-shaven, nothing particularly striking except maybe the deep set of his eyes (which Jenny had labeled "philosophical"). Also, his thinning blond hair, short and springy, which he had been clawing at all day, as he was now, running it through his mind for the thousandth time: that morning, assigned to take pictures of the hogan dedication for the new Indian Resource Center. Hogan? Stucco exterior and louvered windows, shag carpeting, electric baseboard heat. Dry wall all the way. The only thing truly Navajo was the octagonal shape.

And the medicine man. He was real. And for Dave it had been a rare opportunity to photograph him in action. Usually cameras were forbidden at ceremonials. But the superintendent wanted a propaganda slide presentation to impress the feds, and since the school district was footing the bill, what could the old guy say?

The falling snow had thickened, making the window appear as a TV tuned to a dead station. But within the fuzzy picture Dave could visualize the old man perfectly: the velveteen shirt and matching maroon band around his thick, silver hair; the moccasins on his delicate feet and the chunk of turquoise on his wrist; his seamed face, red as a ham and cured by years of sun and wind, desert afflictions. And his hands–big, thick-fingered, dark and oily-looking in the joints and creases, working so slowly yet expertly as he dipped them into the little buckskin pouch and sprinkled corn pollen onto the young woman sitting beside him. Dave had admired the exactitude and concentration with which he had performed the rite, his eyes, buried deep in wrinkles, all but sealed shut, the broken furrows on his forehead twisting and flexing as over and over he repeated his chant.

Dave had shot quickly, fanatically. First the Navajo children and their parents, thirty or so, colorful but somber in traditional attire. Then the medicine man. Three rolls in all. The first two, full-color, had developed perfectly. But when he had unrolled the third, the black-and-white shot exclusively of the medicine man, it looked like a banded snake, with every frame snow-white or jet-black, except one. The last.

Since ten that morning he had been in the darkroom making prints. The color shots he had finished presto by two-thirty, but the black-and-white? He had tried everything to flush the old man out of the dark: new developer, new fixer, dodging and burning, different settings on the timer, every filter on the rack. The stop bath he had changed a dozen times. For paper, matte, gloss, semi-gloss. Nothing worked. There was no explanation for it.

He stared at the snow intensely, as if through sheer will he aimed to make it cease—or better, for the nuzzle of falling pieces to magically rearrange themselves against the foggy background in the perfect similitude of the old man. When after several minutes they didn't, he almost laughed at himself for being unable to laugh—he usually had a good sense of humor about these kinds of things, or thought he had. Hoped. He reminded himself that a week from now, a month maybe, he would relate this all to Jenny and Brian, and they would wake the kids up laughing so hard at his darkroom pantomimes. But now, for the life of him, he couldn't crack a smile. He felt nothing but a gray depression settling in.

The ambience didn't help. Outside, fog and snow. Inside, battered file cabinets holding up plywood partitions. Dried mud, dirt balls mashed to powder on the cracked concrete floor. The secretary's splintered desk consumed half the room. Poor lighting cast everything in half-shadow; the fixtures buzzed like angry bees. All but two windows were boarded up. The building looked condemned. A resurrected warehouse.

What was wrong? Normally it didn't bother him like this. The snow, the dust, the second-hand equipment, the tin trailer he called home, Sunday meetings in the crumbling churchhouse: he had willingly accepted it as part of the experience. An adventure, he had told Jenny. Hardship is a state of mind. As long as you have food in your belly and a roof over your head. And God in your heart. Wherever two or more gather in my name . . . But tonight it was getting him. The gray growing black inside. He could literally feel it, darkening and solidifying. Like rust. Barnacles. He shuddered at the thought. The weather. Sure. And the frustration – who wouldn't be frustrated?

Staring at the snow wasn't going to get him a print, he knew that. He started back for the darkroom but bypassed it and ducked into his "office" – a cramped plywood cubicle just around the corner, at the end of the dark hall. Seated, he leafed through his photography manuals, trying to pinpoint what he was doing wrong. He was tempted to say a prayer but checked himself: why pester God with a routine print? It was almost as absurd as it was embarrassing.

Initially, shooting, he had envisioned a creative piece, a photo montage perhaps, with the wrinkled old face of the medicine man – screened out about 30 percent, for a faded, ghost-like effect – superimposed over the glossy faces of the Navajo children. Title it "Past and Present." Or a radical reticulation, making gorges and arroyos of the old man's wrinkles, his face a replication of the land, merging the old age/timelessness paradox. Sure. Big plans. Like every other no-name photographer on the make. Forever looking for the super-print that would make the cover of *Darkroom Photography* and launch his career out of the two-bit consultancy racket.

Now he would settle for a simple black-and-white print. Then he could go home. Eat. Sleep. Feel human again.

Skimming, he was unable to concentrate. His hands were shaking, his teeth chattering. If the insulation was bad, the circulation was sinful. He gazed up at the weird web of misdirected ceiling pipes that made his cubicle a freezer and the darkroom a sauna. Too much heat or none at all. He tossed the manual aside and stared out the window. The snow had stopped and the mist was thinning. He could see the cottonwoods, black and witch-stricken, like an army of old hags huddling along the wash. The mist had a hallucinating effect. He could have sworn the junipers were shifting left and right and the tamarisk bushes reaching out like brittle tentacles. The scene looked positively Transylvanian. Any moment he expected the wolves to start howling.

He pulled out his portfolio, hoping for inspiration. His first assignment: photos of the impoverished conditions. A rutty dirt road leading to a two-room shack at the foot of a barren butte. Scrap wool corral. Outhouse. Dogs—mangy mutts slinking around like thieves. A pile of tin cans and broken glass. Cheap treasure in the waning sun. Chicken wire over tar paper, curling at the edges like an old manuscript. Inside, cabinets peeling white paint, a birch-like effect. Fire-blackened pots and pans. Nails poking through the ceiling. Windowless walls. An empty Pampers box, jumbo size, overflowing with dirty laundry. The wood stove emitting heat like a blast furnace.

He had seen worse—much worse: in Guatemala, little brown-skinned children wading naked in the sewage canal, playing with the excrement floating by. Still, he was humbled by the campfire stench, the smell of rancid lard and over-fried potatoes, the stains on the warped floorboards. The shyness of the blue-jeaned daughter hiding in the far corner amused him, and the two children sleeping in one another's arms like a couple of bear cubs touched a tender spot. He sensed maternal power in the mother, big and rotund at her loom, and was intrigued by the wiry grandma, in ragged skirt and sneakers, silently rocking an infant in a cradleboard.

But the totems on the grease-stained walls left him thoroughly confused: full-color images of disco-frenzied John Travolta in skin-tight leotards; two Mexican felt rugs, one depicting a sheep-eyed Jesus holding an impaled heart, the other a tepee illuminated by firelight. Also, gourds, rattles, feather fans, a water drum on the wall. And in the far corner, nearly obscured in shadow, a nicely framed photograph of the Salt Lake Temple, aglow with evening lights. Later, driving home, he had asked

Brian—tactfully—what *do* they believe in, anyway? His supervisor shrugged: "Anything. Everything. Whatever works."

Reflecting, Dave tuned in a moment to Eddie's drums and could distinguish, very faintly, above the piercing falsetto of the taped chant and the syncopated pounding of the press, the printer's voice softly keeping time.

Eddie. He had always regarded the printer as a comic figure, a coolie caricature from the old railroad days, with his black bangs chopped straight and high across his oriental eyes. Sitting in the press room from eight-to-five each day, chanting and shaking his rattles; occasionally stepping out for coffee or, less often, to joke with the others: "Have some *gowheeh*, John Wayne." But a loner. Quiet. Different. Dozing off at the Monday morning staff meetings, exhausted from his all-night peyote vigils. Skinny arms folded, skeletal face tilted, nodding asleep.

One morning last fall he had come to work all swollen and puffy eyed, looking as if he had been beaten to a pulp. Face, hands, everything bloated, burning with a savage rash. At first Brian had chewed him out: "Dammit, Eddie! How many times have I told you to keep those bottles capped? Those fumes are deadly. Now get to the clinic, *tsiilgo*!" But when the printer shook his head, softly insisting it wasn't the chemicals, Brian had nodded: "Then you'd better go see your uncle."

Eddie Tom. With the others Dave talked freely: sports, movies, cars, religion too—he wasn't out there just to take pretty pictures—and, despite Brian's occasional digs, he had had some lengthy discussions about church. Most of the staff were college graduates or had worked off of the reservation for several years. Jonathan Yellowhair, he discovered, had been on the Indian Placement Program for five years. But Eddie. Since his arrival in September, Dave had spoken only a handful of words to him. English wasn't the problem. Eddie simply didn't talk much—to anyone. He was in a world of his own. Dave was curious about the rattles and drums and so forth, but he didn't want to be the nosey tourist type. Didn't want to pry. Not like that. With his camera? Several times he had been tempted to sneak a candid shot of Eddie working his rattles alongside the press. Ironic contrast: Modern versus Traditional; Man versus Machine. Always looking for the concept within the image.

Always looking but not always finding. Not in this bunch, anyway. He tossed the prints on his desk and flipped through another manual which only confirmed what he already knew: everything had been done to textbook perfection. Nothing amiss with his technique. The chemicals? He had changed them a dozen times already. Maybe the whole batch was bad. He decided to dip into the brand new supply, just in from Albuquerque.

He got up enthusiastically enough but bypassed the darkroom again and wandered out the office door and down the main hall—just to stretch a bit. Snow was falling but the mist had thinned enough to where he could make out the red and gold neon of the Thriftway Store, halfway up the mesa, glowing like embers in mid-air. Several pairs of headlights were gliding down the highway. Dave attributed his failure to a temporary mental block which was causing him to omit some simple but essential step. He closed his eyes and tried to let his thoughts flow as freely and effortlessly as the headlights on the highway, but his brain remained as fuzzy and confused as the falling snow.

Dave's eyes popped open and searched frantically for the clock. He groaned. Jenny usually waited dinner until six, but it was an hour past that. Better call—he was surprised she hadn't. Or better, go home. Sleep on it. Try again tomorrow, fresh, renewed. Typically he would have, but he sensed that if he left now the project would be lost, irrecoverable. Which was absurd, of course. He had the negative, in hand. A perfect neg.

He returned to the office but stalled several minutes before finally picking up the phone. He dialed slowly. Eddie's wooden figure, framed in the far doorway, had not budged. Dave wondered if paper was even running through the press, or had the printer lapsed into a permanent state of hypnosis. Eddie Tom, totem pole. Good plot for a Twilight Zone script. Maybe he should junk his camera and become a writer. Or a—

"Hello?" Pleasant. Sugar sweet. She should have been an operator.

"Three guesses, no hints."

"Hmmmmm." Impatient. I can humor her but I'd better not get too cutesy.

"Don't tell me–dinner's ready and waiting."

"More like ready and eaten."

Get to the point. She hated this beating around the bush. "Looks like I'm going to have to work late tonight."

"How late?"

"Until I finish."

"How late is that?"

"I don't know. Nine. Ten. Whatever it takes."

"Oh, one of *those* lates."

Yes, one of *those*. "So how was your day?" He gazed out the spider-web crack at the falling snow, bracing himself as she reviewed her daily inventory of domestic drudgery (her term). At her very best, she told him to stick with it, someday he'd knock Anselm Adams flat on his Nikkormat. At her worst, she accused him of caring more about his damn camera "than us." He always denied it–vehemently. God. Family. Photography. In that order. But he wondered how much of that was lip service. If it wasn't, why was he still here? No, don't start that again. Don't start. He had used the family cop-out before. Not this time. This was different. Entirely.

"Is this for work or your own?"

"What's the difference?"

No response.

"Jenny?"

"Cassie wants to talk to you."

"Put her on!"

A meek little voice, a whisper. "Hello, Daddy."

"Hey, kid! How you doing?"

"Fine. Daddy, can you read me a story when you get home?"

"Sure I can."

"Are you coming home now?"

"Not quite yet."

"Why, Dad?"

He winced. "I'll be home just as soon as I can, okay?"

"Okay, Dad."

"Be sure to say your prayers."

"I will."

"Good girl. I love you, kid."

"I love you, Daddy."

"Let me talk to Mommy, okay?"

"Okay. Here, Mommy."

"Dave?"

"Hey, I'm sorry about the delay—"

"It's all right. I understand." She tried. "What about dinner?"

"I'll grab a bite when I get home. Don't wait up." She wouldn't. She never did anymore. He didn't begrudge her. "I love you," he said, trying to put some stuff into it.

"I love *you*," she said, trying her best also.

His re-entry into the darkroom was surprisingly painless. Although the septic smell of the chemicals and the heat got to him, mentally he was sharp, confident, clear-headed. The boiler chugging relentlessly on, he dumped out the old chemicals, broke open the new batch, and started fresh, from scratch: measuring and mixing the solutions, adjusting the enlarger, setting up the trays—the developer, the stop bath, the fixer, the rinse—everything exactly right, according to the book. As meticulous about his ritual as the medicine man had been with his.

He was all set. But when he reached for the negative, it was missing. Gone. He searched frantically, first the darkroom, then his cubicle, turning over every box, every book, every scrap of paper. Nothing! After another foxfire search, he got a grip on himself and determined to go about it logically, starting with the darkroom and systematically retracing his steps. He recombed every inch, slowly, methodically, but no luck. Next he searched areas he hadn't been, or thought he hadn't: Tom Manygoats's cubicle, Jonathan Yellowhair's, Brian's office, the storage room.

It was while he was in the recording room, on hands and knees, combing the floor, that he first noticed the drums—not Eddie Tom's, but distant pulsations of the same varying pitch and rhythm, like an echo of the first. He rushed up front and looked out the window with the spider web crack: the mist was threadbare and the snow had ceased. He could see the elementary school clearly, and the Yazzies' hogan, domed with snow. And to the right of it, surrounded by pick-up trucks, like spokes on a wheel, the tepee.

The campfire within made the cone a giant lampshade; the seated silhouettes wavered like dark flames. Pulling the metal latch, Dave shoved the window open. The singer's impassioned voice, trilling like an auctioneer's, rushed in with the cold air. If not Eddie's chant exactly, it was very close of kin, softer yet more penetrating. As the drumbeat grew faster and higher pitched, Dave felt an uncomfortable quickening inside. Like at the yeibicheii dance in October. Freezing cold, the full moon a slab of ice. Old women in blankets, men in blue jeans, cowboy hats tilted low, huddling around a half-dozen campfires. Sparks swirling into the smoky air—a galaxy of fireflies, or an orange-red rendition of "The Starry Night." Tailgate concessions. Paper plate signs: NAVAJO TACO $2.00, FRY BREAD $.25. Infants in cradleboards, minimummies propped up, asleep. A man lying twisted and unconscious between two cars, his red face and cowboy hat mashed in the sand. Another, staggering into Dave, breathing beer in his face: "Hi-yeah! Can you loan me five dollars?" But not much else happening, he had thought, and was about to leave when a sudden commotion halted him.

It started with the faintest jingling of bells, followed by a shrill whistle, half-human, rising high then low again, spookily falsetto. Instantly the milling and meandering crowd coalesced around the dirt arena as if magnetized, all eyes fastened on the single file figures emerging from the darkness—ash-white creatures in wooden masks antlered with pine sprigs, coyote tails dangling from their breechcloths. Comical, on the one hand, those half-naked, finger-painted beings, some young, most older, middle-aged and showing it, pot-bellied proxies of the gods they were impersonating, yet so totally bizarre—the costumes, the ceremony, the out-of-this-worldness, the way they seemed to grow in stature advancing towards the firelight until, standing directly in it, center stage so to speak, they appeared ten feet tall. Supersomething. Still, any moment Dave had expected some stodgy little white man with a mustache and a beret to step out of the crowd crying, "Cut! Cut!" and a gallery of hidden cameras to appear. That was the southern California skepticism in him. Hollywood and Disneyland.

But the others. Those oily red faces glowing in the light, full of wonder, awe, anticipation, and, yes, a touch of fear—that too—as if Santa Claus were coming to town, or the Navajo version of the Destroying Angel. They watched, as they would continue to watch until dawn, mesmerized.

Throughout it all he had tried to remain detached, objective. The photographer even without his camera. But when the half-naked troupe, immune to the numbing cold, commenced its monotonously vertical two-step earth-pounding dance, repeating over and over the equally monotonous chant, "Ha-ra-ra-*rah*! Ha-ra-ra-*rah*!" like a never-ending snap-count, he was surprised—and a little embarrassed too, as he was now, listening—to find himself tapping his foot in time to the beat.

He yanked the window shut, muffling the drums outside. Returning to the darkroom, he found, lying on the table beside the Beseler, precisely where he thought he had left it, his precious negative. His initial burst of euphoria was soon dampened by a sense of disappointment. Adjusting the knobs, he tried to dismiss the lost-and-found episode as a stupid oversight induced by his panic-stricken state. Defiantly, he flicked on the red bulb and proceeded to do everything step-by-step as he had been taught. A perfect negative, no filters were needed. He killed the light and ran a test strip at five, ten, fifteen, and twenty second exposures. The developed strip showed fifteen seconds was perfect. Confidently, he squared a sheet of photo paper under the enlarger and set the timer at fifteen. He placed his hand by the small metal box, took a deep breath, and broke into a feverish sweat. On contact his finger leaped from the metal switch as if it were electrically charged. He put it right back, however, telling himself this was all so asinine, the knots in his stomach and the trembling in his hands. Why all the adrenal hype? Nervous energy going nowhere. And prayer. Why didn't he just say one? The scriptures said to pray always—over your food, your flocks, your family, your friends. He had prayed over his work before—plenty of times. His Easter morning print. He had sweat blood over that one. Sixteen hours in the darkroom. So why not now? What was he so afraid of? It was all so stupid. The whole damn thing. Winter and he was sweating like a racehorse. Why was he so lucky to be right next to the boiler room? No windows, no ventilation. And the smell! The stench! The chemicals fermenting. Like a still. Souring like milk. Like Junior's breast-fed messies. Sure! Laugh it off. It relieves stress. You'll live longer. Ha! Ha!

He flicked the switch.

An hour later he was smiling as he watched the old man's face form perfectly under the watery blur of the developer. Removing the print with his tongs, he buried it face-up in the stop bath. Sealed! Frozen! But a minute later, transferring it to the fixer . . . "Nooooo!" His tongs caromed off the wall in two pieces. The jet-black print went into the wastebasket in shreds. The negative was next. He tore it from the enlarger, intending to wad it up and put it to rest, once and for all, but stopped.

He switched on the light and held the negative up to it, tenderly. Within the ghoulish image, white-on-black, he could see the old man as he had looked that morning sitting cross-legged in the pseudo-hogan, his eyelids like wattled scales permanently shut. At one point, near the end, he had raised his eyeless face and stared directly at him, the white man with the camera, smiling a carious, two-toothed smile. An infant's gummy grin. Dipping his head, he had begun cackling. Cackling and chanting, delighted, his banded head bobbing up and down, his eyes sealed shut. Laughing at him it had seemed.

"Okay, old man," Dave said, testing the edges of the negative between his thumb and forefinger. "We'll see."

Stepping out of the darkroom at a quarter-to-ten, he looked as if he'd just fought fifteen rounds. Sweat dripped from his face and dark ovals stained his underarms. His eyes were glazed. Snow was falling again. An outside light captured some in a cone so that it appeared to be pouring from the sky into a cornucopia of swirling flakes.

Dave edged open the window with the spider web crack. The snowfall was heavy. The chain-link fence around the schoolyard had turned to white fish scales; the Yazzies' hogan was an igloo. Next door the glow within the tepee was dimming like an oil lamp running out of fuel. He wondered how they did it—staying up all night like that—and why? He could barely sit through sacrament service, let alone an all night ceremony. Sitting, he always got antsy, impatient. Had to move on. Places to go, people to meet, pictures to shoot. Could any of *them* spend the night in a darkroom? Especially this sweatbox. You do what you have to. Wherever the heart is.

What about the old man? Where was he tonight? Right now? Sleeping soundly in his hogan? Or presiding over the dancers in their pine sprig masks and breechcloths? Dave envisioned him standing out in the cold, chanting and cackling as he transmogrified into a snowman. Whatever, he wasn't losing sleep over a cock-eyed *bilagaana* photographer, that's for sure.

Falling slowly and steadily, the snow had a hypnotic effect. It looked warm and inviting, like a great white sleep falling in rhythm to the multi-pulsations of the printing press and the taped drums within, and the real drums without. He wanted to step outside and let it slowly bury him, as it had the old man in his mind. Dave's eyes filled with snow; the fog invaded his body. He told himself to go home and sleep on it, tomorrow's another day. Or junk it altogether. It wouldn't be the first time. Chalk it up to trial and error. The creative process. For every masterpiece, a million fiascoes.

Maybe he should junk the *whole* thing. All of it. Thirteen years and what could he show for it? Nickel and dime jobs to make ends meet, whatever he could scrape up for however long. Three to six months usually, long enough to make a slide presentation or train some staff in the basics. Then, so long, goodbye, nice knowing you. This job, his longest stint yet, would expire in June. Then what? It was no life for a family man. Jenny deserved better. The kids. "A fugitive and a vagabond," his father-in-law had called him. Jokingly at first. Seven years ago, their wedding day. Now he didn't even grin. Somber-sober.

Dave had turned off the lights on his side of the building and was reaching for his coat when he heard the slow clatter of cowboy boots. Turning, he saw Eddie Tom approaching on brittle, wishbone legs. His cadaverous face, glistening with grease and sweat, looked disoriented, as if he had just awakened from a deep sleep. His body appeared to wobble slightly and his hands were shaking as if still working the rattles. For the first time that night, the drums had ceased, outside and in. A lull, welcome but unsettling. Dave felt obliged to speak.

"How's it going, Eddie?"

The stooped little printer protruded his lips and nodded reassuringly, then looked around as if he had misplaced something. "Cup . . . I need a cup."

Dave pointed to the cabinet. Eddie got a styrofoam cup and began pouring himself some coffee but none came out. "No coffee?" He looked thoroughly disheartened.

"Nope. *Adin.*"

The two men stood in silence. Dave wanted to say something, but what? The print maybe? The trouble he was having? Or photography in general, his obsession with it, how certain images, scenes, people grabbed him, kindled ideas, visions in his head. And once kindled, he had to get them down – had to. And if he didn't, couldn't . . . well, he just had to, that's all. To give them substance; to make them real, permanent – immortal? Okay, immortal then. And sometimes it got so bad – the urge, the obsession, the disease – he wanted to close his eyes, go blind to the world for awhile, and receive no more images, no more visions. But he couldn't explain this to Eddie any more than the printer could explain to him his incessant chanting and the drums and rattles all night long.

Sizing up the printer, his grease-stained Levis, his whittled brown face, Dave sensed an unbridgeable gap widening between them. It cut much deeper than complexion or culture. It frightened him, to think how totally different two human beings could be. At the moment he felt as if he were standing on one side of the world and Eddie on the other. The silence was excruciating.

"So what are you working on?" he asked.

· · · · ·

Eddie looked at him as if he had asked in Cantonese. "Title Four brochure. Then the newsletter."

"You going to work all night?"

Eddie smiled. A front tooth was missing. "Just like you, *hastiin*."

Dave gazed around self-consciously. "Well, we'd better get back to work or we really *will* be here all night."

Nodding, Eddie strolled back into the pressroom, but Dave lingered in the reception area. The thought of re-entering the darkroom paralyzed him. The open door was a huge mouth waiting to swallow him. The red bulb within glowed like a bloody moon. Its reflection turned the trays of chemicals into pools of methiolate. Stepping inside, he knew he had made a mistake. His hands trembled as he fiddled with the knobs on the enlarger. The walls pressed in on him. Drums pounded in his brain like the merciless hammers in the aspirin commercial. He felt faint, weak. He gripped the table for support and waited for it to pass, assuring himself it was only hunger and fatigue. He closed his eyes and started to—no. He stepped out.

Returning a half hour later, he tried everything he had before—filters, dodging and burning, different exposure times, new chemicals, new film—but every attempt was a replay of the first. Twenty tries later, he resorted to desperation tactics which would have sent his darkroom mentors reeling: one minute exposures, one second exposures, double doses of developer, skipping the developer altogether and dropping the film directly into the fixer. Any voodoo gimmick he could think of.

Nothing worked.

He broke another pair of tongs in disgust. Hot, sweaty, nauseated, he grabbed the developer tray and dumped it on the floor. Liquid splattered everywhere. He did the same to the fixer and the stop bath, muttering and swearing. Then he went a little crazy. With a sweep of his arm, he sent a whole shelf of bottles and beakers crashing to the floor. He tore up film, kicked cupboards, mashed cartons with the heel of his boot. Bottles shattered, trays cracked. "Damn print! Damn camera! Damn . . . *drums!*"

He was going after the enlarger when the door opened. Wilting with shame and embarrassment, he stooped down admid the wreckage and began picking up the broken pieces.

"So how's it going, Eddie?" Glancing up, laughing self-consciously. "I was just practicing my kung fu kicks."

The printer stared at him, silent, expressionless, a puppet. The seconds ticked off uncomfortably. The puppet spoke. "I used to be Catholic."

Dave stood up, glass crackling under his feet. Why was Eddie breaking his stone-faced silence to tell him this, and why now? He had never looked so wooden, totemic. His eyes didn't even blink; his mouth didn't move. He didn't even appear to be breathing. Just staring, waiting for a response. Dave felt the nausea again—the chemicals, the heat. Finally he replied: "I'm LDS. Mormon."

Eddie nodded. "*Gamalii*. I used to be Mormon too."

"You were baptized?"

"I still am baptized. Catholic, Mormon." He shrugged. "It's all the same."

Dave felt a need, an obligation, to clarify, repudiate, but this was not the time or place.

"Lotta people," Eddie said, peering sternly through tinted lenses, "lotta people don't understand." His needlepoint eyes, chips of obsidian, scanned the destruction as if for the first time. He looked at Dave. "The first time it worked for me, it was the morning after a meeting. My wife, she was bringing in the water. There was a light, like a big spotlight on her. The bucket she was holding, it became a tepee." His dark hands formed a miniature model. With his lips he gestured towards the top where the poles would intersect. "There was a little circle, and then there was a little person. He had brown hair—long brown hair—and blue eyes, and he was wearing a white robe. He came out and put his hand on my wife's head. Then I knew. He blessed her." Eddie scrutinized the enlarger as if he knew something the photographer did not. His tongue flickered, wetting his upper lip "That was right before we got our son," he said. Then left.

Dave stared at the disaster he had created. Bits of light blinked like stars on the shattered glass and splattered chemicals. The press was running again, pounding away, and the drums beating as the impassioned voice of the singer soared to a piercing climax. Dave tried to disregard Eddie's story but, stepping through the wreckage, found himself groping for an explanation, uncertain of precisely what he was trying to explain or justify or repudiate, yet grasping for some way to resolve the whole experience, to answer to it, or for it—the medicine man, the negative, the tales, the superstitions and contradictions. Eddie Tom, his story. Fable. Yarn. All right, *vision*. If he, Dave, could take a picture of it—these feelings, this ambience—record it on film, then he could abstract, reticulate, superimpose; give it clarity, meaning, definition. Sure! When he couldn't even get a print of an old man in moccasins.

Visions! Peyote, pot, mescaline—any fool can induce a vision. No spiritual tuning required.

Dave squatted down and resumed picking up the broken glass. A fragment sliced his thumb. Waiting for the initial sting to pass, he recalled the deeper, sharper pain of a gusty afternoon years ago, kneeling on a grassy hilltop overlooking the Pacific and throwing his voice into the Santa Ana winds. That pain, too, had passed. Gathering up the last fragments, he saw within the twinkling pinpoint reflections of light a mirror of the heavens on a clear desert night. As a boy he had gazed up at those stars confident that if he prayed long enough and hard enough, if he were worthy enough, yes, the veil would part for him also. It bothered him to think how, with his obsession for taking pictures, he had so complacently outgrown that childhood craving to see the Master image.

He trashed the broken trays and set out three new ones, filling each with fresh chemicals. Screwing the cap back on the fixer, squeezing the neck of the bottle as if he meant to strangle it, he realized that it didn't matter whether his failure to produce a decent print was due to his own ineptitude and carelessness or an old man's hex; whether chemical fumes or a witch's curse had inflicted Eddie's bloated red rash, or if his vision was heaven-sent or drug-inspired. It all

. . . .

seemed irrelevant now. Not the point at all. Then what *was* the point?

He stepped out of the darkroom and looked outside. Snow was still falling, quietly burying the town, covering all evidence of tracks, trucks, life. He could barely hear the faint pulsations of the drums, although the press was still going strong. He wandered down the hallway, past the darkroom, and into his cubicle.

He was awakened abruptly by the phone. His back and shoulders felt sore and his neck cramped from the long short sleep contorted in his chair. A photography manual was open on his lap. It took him several moments to get his bearings. Darkroom. Home. Jenny. Jenny! Wondering where he was and what had happened. He bolted up to grab the phone but missed it by a ring.

Silence. No press, no drums. Eddie had turned off all the lights on his end and had left the front door open, the padlock off. The unboarded windows were white, cataracted with ice. Dave shoved open the one with the spider web crack and looked out on an arctic wasteland–bleak white marred by a few black lines, haphazard claw marks. Nothing moved except a flap of the tepee, tugged and twisted by the wind. The stark whiteness of the sky was broken only by a pale circle in the east where the sun was beginning to bore through. Black-on-white, the mesas were half-dead coals.

Dave felt cold and confused. His empty belly groaned but the thought of putting food in it nauseated him. Jenny. Call Jenny. Now. The wind blew cold white powder in his face, numbing his cheeks. He saw movement in the whiteness. Figures, one by one, exiting the tepee, crouching to fit through the small opening, then standing erect. Stretching. Cowboy hats and headbands. Bright red on white snow. One old man crossed himself. Another dropped to his knees and kissed the snow. A third raised his arms to the frozen sun.

Dave yanked the window shut.

In the darkroom he carefully adjusted the enlarger as the boiler next door huffed and puffed like an out-of-shape athlete in

. . . . .

training. He turned off the light and switched on the enlarger. A cone of light dropped the medicine man's image onto the plastic plate. Dave studied it, the sealed eyes, the chanting two-toothed smile. He pictured the old guy lying on a sheepskin by the warmth of a wood stove, sleeping soundly. Unperturbed.

Dave switched off the machine and very carefully removed the negative from the enlarger. Groping for scissors on the table, with two quick snips, one vertically, one horizontally, he released himself.

Ultimatum

It was mid-summer, squaw-dance season, and through the twilight calm a Datsun sedan was slowly zig-zagging up the mesa. The town below shriveled as the car, churning up the sunburned dust, climbed higher and higher above the largess of sagebrush—sagebrush and little else save an occasional hogan or plywood shack or cowboy-hatted horseman rounding up his sheep.

"What kind of mileage do you get?" Howells, sitting on the passenger side, asked Adams. Howells was about thirty-five, heavyset, with wavy hair carefully parted and combed forward, half-hiding a high hairline. A goatee gave his otherwise plump face an acute edge. He was wearing cowboy boots, a bolo tie, and a cowboy shirt with fake pearl buttons. A thick leather belt with a turquoise-and-silver buckle the size of a fist cinched his bullfrog belly.

"Forty," Adams said. "On the highway."

A decade younger, dark-haired and blue-eyed, Adams stared straight ahead, squinting into the billowing dust. Although a half-foot taller than Howells, he was less impressive physically, with sloping shoulders and buttermilk arms. He had dressed conservatively: white shirt, navy blue tie and matching slacks, and black wing-tips, freshly polished.

"Looks like another peyote meeting," Howells said, motioning to the side where, in the proverbial middle of nowhere, a dozen pick-up trucks were parked around a tepee.

Adams glanced left and nodded.

"Norman isn't into that, is he?"

Adams looked tentative. The youthful smoothness of his face was negated by a droopy mustache and a milkiness in his eyes.

"I don't think so . . . no."

"How much farther?"

"Another four or five miles."

Adams braked almost to a stop. Easing up on the clutch, he nursed the car across a foot-deep gully recent rains had carved across the road. He switched on the headlights.

"How long's he been up there with his in-laws?" Howells asked.

"You mean his out-laws?"

Howells laughed, his goatee fluttering up and down.

"A couple months," Adams said.

"That's too bad. He was doing pretty good there for awhile, when he was living in town."

"Yeah. Pretty good."

Adams glanced at Howells who was sitting with his thick arms folded across his chest like a viking chief. Swirls of blond hair coated them like sawdust. In the thickening darkness the conical slopes of talus seemed to drop down the mesa like moon-silvered waterfalls. A red stripe burned faintly on the horizon.

"You hate to do it, but I guess you have to," Howells said.

They drove another mile in silence.

"Did you ever see the movie *Hawaii*?" Adams asked.

"No . . . no, I don't think I have." Howells tilted his wavy-haired head and wrinkled an eye. "No, I'm sure I haven't."

"There's this preacher from New England, Reverend Hale. He goes to Hawaii and tries to convert all the islanders. A real fanatic. A letter-of-the-law man all the way. There's this one young Hawaiian who's studying for the ministry. A good man—sharp, dedicated. But there's a Hawaiian custom: brothers are supposed to marry sisters. That doesn't sit very well with the reverend. He cries sin, incest, and tears the grass shack down. He even hollers at God to take holy vengeance."

Adams sped up suddenly, causing the car to bounce and

rattle like a washing machine gone haywire. The trembling headlights cast a strobic haze over the scattered clumps of sagebrush
and the tiny creatures intermittently darting across the road.

Howells shifted heavily in the bucket-seat. "So what
happened?"

"To the Hawaiian? He quits the church and marries his
sister. Next scene, the flu hits and the Islanders are dropping like
flies."

"The flu?"

"Sure. They had no immunity to it. They never even caught
colds before the *haoles* came."

"*Haoles?*"

"*Bilagaanas*. White men."

Howells chuckled. "They've got us red-flagged in every
language."

"There's this one scene—all the Hawaiians burning up with
fever go running down to the beach and start rolling around in
the water, trying to cool off. One white minister tries to get
them to stop. 'Pneumonia!' he screams. 'They'll catch pneumonia!'
Meanwhile Reverend Hale's standing in the background watching God exact his punishment. He's not smiling, but he isn't
crying either."

Adams gave Howells the once over. "It's sad."

"I'll bet. Sounds like a good movie."

They drove past several juniper trees, hunchbacked figures
hiding in the night.

"I wonder if he really understands."

"Norman?" Howells stroked his goatee thoughtfully. "He
speaks good English, don't he?"

"Very good."

"Not like some of the older people up to the mesa?"

"No, his English is fine."

Howells shrugged. "Well?"

The road grew twice as bumpy as before. Adams eased up on
the accelerator, but the Datsun still joggled as if it were speeding
along a giant washboard. Their voices vibrated as they spoke.

"I wonder how he'll take it."

Howells twisted his head, wrinkled an eye. "Hard to say. We had a guy at work—Gene Bitsui. Pretty good worker till he started drinking again. When he didn't show up for the fifth day in a row, I had to let him go. He seemed to take it okay. But the next morning they found him face down in the wash. Mud up to his ears and a bottle of Garden de Luxe in his hand. You just never know out here."

Adams stared into the yellowish tunnel his headlights were cutting out of the growing darkness. "I don't think Norman would do something like that, do you?"

"No." Howells rolled his hefty shoulders. "Norman wouldn't do that. I don't think so. Not something like that."

As the car climbed higher, deeper blues seeped into the sky, quenching the last red smudge on the horizon. The chiseled ridges and scrub pine silhouettes merged into one, making the mesa a solid black stage beneath the cooling heavens. A star appeared. Glancing into his rear-view mirror, Adams saw the lights of town twinkling like a fallen constellation. One by one the lights vanished as the Datsun rounded a bend. Suddenly something darted out of the sagebrush and into the headlights where it panicked and scampered back the other way. Adams winced at the dull thud, immediately followed by a double-bump. He checked his rear-view mirror. "Did I get him?"

Howells shifted his husky body and looked back. "Looks like it."

"If he'd just kept going."

"I'll tell you, I've seen more dead animals this year than I can ever remember. Dogs, rabbits, coyotes, prairie dogs. The other day I saw a dead cow by a ditch standing on its head."

"On its head?"

"Sure. When they die, I guess their pores close up and all the gas expands inside. Blows them up like a blimp. It looked pretty funny, that big old cow standing on its head like a yoga or something. Kind of sad, too, the way they don't do nothing about it—just leave them there to rot. They won't go near a dead animal, you know. Something about evil spirits. They'll leave a dead dog in the road till it stinks like a sewer. I don't understand it.

Superstitious, I guess. Even the young ones are like that. You'd think they'd know better, but they don't."

The incline suddenly steepened, causing the car to lug. Adams downshifted and the Datsun surged forward, the engine growling and whinnying as it crawled up the hill.

"It's just down here," he said, turning off onto another dirt road, this one so deeply furrowed by tire treads it looked newly plowed.

As the car approached a small cluster of dwellings, several mangy dogs rushed out from under an old pickup, barking and flashing their white fangs in the glare of the headlights.

"Which one's Norman's?" Howells asked.

Adams motioned towards the middle dwelling, a plyboard shack with tar-papered walls. To the left stood a cinderblock building about the size of a two-bedroom house. Carved into the wooden sign nailed above the front door was FRIENDS OF THE RED RIDGE CHURCH. On the far right a mud-roofed hogan bulged out of the earth like a giant bicep. Beyond this was a small shadehouse, and beyond that an outhouse, tilting to the left. Strewn about the dirt frontage were several old tires, pop cans, and broken bottles. A few yards from the woodpile stood a tall pine pole with a basketball hoop fastened to it and a bullet-perforated STOP sign for a backboard. A pair of steer horns had been lashed to a sawhorse for roping practice.

As the two men surveyed the shack, someone peeked briefly out the window, then vanished. Adams switched off the headlights. He and Howells got out of the car. The dogs inched closer, snapping and snarling. When Howells bent down, pretending to pick up a rock, the animals froze, then slowly retreated back under the pickup, every so often emitting a token growl.

"Rez mutts," Howells smirked. "True cowards. My doberman could swallow them whole."

Just shy of the door, Adams paused, inhaling the mixed fragrance of sagebrush and burning firewood. He stepped forward and gave the plywood door three crisp raps. An old woman answered. Thin and frail, she was wearing a blue velveteen blouse and pleated skirt, also blue, which hung within a half foot of her holey sneakers. Her arms and legs were toothpicks, toasted brown, and her skin looked as wrinkled and eroded as the mesa she lived on. A loud, steady sucking sound filled the background—a Coleman lantern, greedily consuming fuel.

"*Ya'at'eeh, shimasani,*" Adams greeted. "Norman *sidash?*"

The old woman's eyes narrowed suspiciously. For a moment it appeared she might close the door on them, but instead she began chattering away in Navajo. Howells looked at Adams, who shrugged helplessly. He turned to the old woman and asked again, "Norman *sidash?*"

"Norman. *Aoo' aoo',*" she said, nodding as she hobbled off.

A few moments later Norman came to the door. Short, solid, compact, with thick black bangs skirting the brows of his slanted eyes, he looked more Eskimo than Navajo.

"*Ya'at'eeh,*" Adams said, offering his hand. Norman placed his palm gently against Adams's and the two exchanged a soft hand-touch. Adams introduced Howells. Grinning like a car salesman, he clasped Norman's hand and gave it a good, firm shake. "Ya-ta-hey, Norman. How's it going?"

Norman looked down, embarrassed. In a voice barely audible he replied, "Okay, I guess." Then, meekly, "Come in. Sit down."

The two guests sat side by side on an old sofa whose cracked vinyl upholstery was partially concealed by a Pendleton blanket. The Coleman lantern, sucking and slurping, burned intensely. Wood chips sprinkled the warped floorboards beneath the stove, which was pouring out a rash of unneeded heat. Its grill was glowing orange, grinning like a jack-o-lantern. Chicken wire caged the two windows and nails poked through the tar-papered ceiling. One plyboard wall was collaged with photographs of family, friends, and young men in uniform. The wall opposite bore a pair of Mexican felt paintings, one of an Indian with full headdress and the other of John F. Kennedy. On a loom constructed from a metal bed frame hung a half-finished yeibicheii rug. The smell of mutton and lard-fried potatoes soured the air.

"Are you going back to school next fall?" Adams asked.

"Still thinking about it."

A little girl sneaked into the room and peeked out from behind the sofa. Glossy black bangs and big dimpled cheeks, she looked like a little Indian doll. Adams's daughter, a blue-eyed blond, could have been mistaken for her albino twin.

"*Ya'at'eeh*, *shi*—buddy!" Adams said.

The girl smiled and looked away.

"Hey, look at that cute little boy!" Howells joked. "You sure are a good looking little boy! How did you ever get so good looking? Not from your father, I'll bet!" He took a stick of chewing gum from his shirt pocket and offered it to her. She shrank away at first, then snatched the gum and ducked behind the sofa.

The girl's mother slipped into the room, almost unnoticed. She was even thinner than the old woman who had answered the door—stick-thin but stiff as iron. She sat down in front of the home-made loom, legs crossed, back straight, and began quietly working on her rug.

"Hello, Priscilla," Adams said.

She glanced over her shoulder and whispered, "Hello."

Adams asked a few more mundane questions—the weather, upcoming rodeos, Norman's job. Then he leaned forward, bracing his forearms on his thighs. "Norman, I've talked to you about this before, you and—"

Just then the little girl poked her head above the sofa and began giggling loudly. Adams smiled at her although right now he felt like anything but smiling.

"Hey, you cute little boy!" Howells teased. "Come here, little boy!"

Half-perturbed, half-grateful for the interruption, Adams waited for the little girl to settle down. He eyed Norman gravely. "So what have you decided?"

The noisy Coleman lantern drowned out Norman's soft reply.

"What? I'm sorry, I didn't hear you."

"We're thinking about it," he said. "When it gets warmer."

What did the weather have to do with it? And when would it ever get warmer than this?

As if he had read Adams's mind, Norman replied, "My grand-mother, she lives at Fish Point. She lives there all alone."

"And you're the only person who can take care of her?"

"No. She herds sheep. She herds them every day."

"I see." Adams said, thoroughly confused. He studied Norman's swarthy face. At that moment his almond eyes looked like the work of a taxidermist. Adams handed him the letter. Howells looked down at his big, ruddy hands, cupped in his lap. The little girl remained hidden behind the sofa. Priscilla continued weaving her rug. The silence overruled even the innocent giggles of the little girl and the incessant sucking of the Coleman lantern.

Norman stared at the envelope several moments, then opened it very carefully, as if he were defusing a bomb. He read it in silence.

"Do you understand why?" Adams asked.

Norman nodded. His face was a blank slate. No anger, no grief, no fear.

Adams wanted to apologize, but he wasn't sure what for. He was about to say something when the little girl's head popped above the sofa like a jack-in-the-box. She giggled and aimed her finger within an inch of Adams's nose. He smiled as best he could and gave her finger a gentle shake. The old woman drifted in from the other room. She looked at Howells, then Adams, and disappeared again. Adams stood up, followed by Howells. They shook hands with Norman, then offered theirs to the little girl who giggled and plunged behind the sofa. Stepping around the wood stove, they held out their hands to Priscilla who paused from her work just long enough to give them each a quick hand touch.

"*Hagoonee*," Adams said.

She looked down and mumbled something in Navajo.

Outside it was dark and moonless. Half the sky was swarming with stars which seemed to be pulsating in rhythm with the crickets chirping in the sagebrush. The other half, above the mesa, was blackened with clouds. A cool wind blew, filling the air with a minty fragrance. Howells inhaled deeply. "Smells like rain. I love that smell."

Adams unlocked the car. "Thanks for coming, Bob."

Howells nodded. "No problem. That's what I'm here for."

As they drove away, the dog pack darted out from under the pickup and began dancing in and out of the headlights, snapping at the tires.

"Rez mutts," Howells muttered.

They drove on in silence, the Datsun vibrating along the bumpy road as night bugs committed suicide on the windshield.

"I still can't figure it," Howells said. "Why they left that nice trailer in town to live up here in a dirty old shack without electricity or running water."

"I don't understand either," Adams said. "I don't even *pretend* to understand anymore. I wonder if Norman even understands."

He shifted into low gear as they started down the steep incline.

"How long have you been out here, Bob?"

"Me? Twelve years."

"That's a long time."

"Yeah. You get used to it." Howells rolled down the window and swallowed a big breath of air. "You've got to learn to say no. Especially out here."

"I suppose."

Adams drove another couple miles in silence before speaking again. "Just wish he'd said something, you know? If he'd yelled at me, called me a *bilagaana* bastard. Anything. But he just sat there—just sat!"

Howells fiddled with his bolo tie. The engine whined as the car angled down the hill.

"How are things at home?" Howells asked. "Between you and Janet?"

"Fine. At home."

"I know sometimes the women have trouble adjusting. It takes time."

"Janet's fine. We are."

More silence.

"You did the right thing, Dave. It took guts."

Adams bore down on the accelerator and the car surged forward, bouncing along the road like a boat on rough waters. Soon he was doing forty, the headlights burrowing through the dust-filled night. He began mumbling to himself.

"What?" Howells said. "What'd you say?"

Adams stared straight ahead, squinting, searching.

"Dave?"

He slowed down to thirty, twenty; the car was crawling. He braked to a stop.

"What's up?" Howells said.

Adams shoved the throttle into reverse and backed up, steering to the left, until the headlights zeroed in on a furry clump no bigger than a handbag. There was a crow, too—a fat black crow jabbing its beak into the clump and tugging out a long red strand of what looked like heavily sauced spaghetti.

Howells started to say something but Adams was already out the door. The fat black bird instantly dropped the spaghetti-looking strand and vanished into the night. Howells strained to see what was going on. Adams was kneeling in front of the clump. His arms and elbows were working rapidly. When he stood up, the clump was gone; a small mound of sand was in its place. Adams was wiping his hands on his slacks as he walked back to the car.

"Sorry about the delay," he said.

"No problem," Howells said.

Adams turned on the ignition. Howells noticed his wrist. A dripping red noodle was wrapped around it like a bracelet and tied with a simple knot.

"You did the right thing," Howells said. "You did what you had to do. God will not be mocked."

Adams pressed down on the accelerator, slowly. The car eased forward. Every so often a red drop splashed on his stay-prest slacks. They rounded the big bend and the lights of town came into view, a small galaxy. Howells turned his hefty body sideways, towards Adams. "Say, what kind of gas mileage do you get?"

"Forty," Adams said. "On the highway."

The Orchard

. . . .

"Did you get a permit?" she asked, looking back without breaking stride.

His white hand patted his shirt pocket. "Right here."

She marched along resolutely, in that fluid, easy style that becomes even the behemoth women of Navajoland, her bare arms swinging freely, her blue-jeaned thighs rubbing brusquely each step, as if striding down a paved boulevard rather than a stone-cluttered trail barely wide enough for a goat. Already winded, Mel wondered how much longer he could keep pace. A bachelor pushing fifty . . . Gene was right: he was too old for this. Much too old.

Picking his way over the talus, he looked for an excuse to turn back—inclement weather maybe. Instant thunderstorms weren't uncommon and the flashfloods could be deadly. In minutes he had seen the innocuous rivulets snaking along the canyon floor grow into a raging river.

Not today. A blue desert overhead, spotless except for a smattering of clouds on the north rim. Although their side of the canyon was submerged in purple shadow, the sun was still well above the mesa. Plenty of daylight.

"How far is it?" he asked.

"Not too far."

Typical of her.

"Does she still live down there? Your grandmother?"

"Sometimes."

He wondered if sometimes meant now. He hoped it did and he hoped it didn't.

The slant of the trail sharpened. Skirting the edge, Mel cautioned himself not to look down but couldn't resist. The cottonwoods along the muddy bottom looked like green and gold clouds, a soft landing, but the thousand foot drop brought to mind haunting recollections of an old Hitchcock movie that sent his stomach spinning up into his head. He finally had to stop and wait until the blue-brown blur became land and sky again.

"This is the worst part," she said. "Are you all right?"

"Fine. Just a little dizzy."

They traversed the near-perpendicular face twice more before the trail widened enough for two goats. Mel relaxed a bit but only for a moment: rounding the first bend, they were confronted by a huge pair of boulders that seemed to have been dumped there to block the way. (By *Yeitsoh* maybe, the people-eating giant of Navajo legend? Mel smiled at the thought.)

As if she had passed this way a thousand times, Dottie turned her lithe body sideways and squeezed between the gap, the sandstone slabs flattening her cone-shaped breasts. When her eyes inadvertently met his, Mel looked away, embarrassed. High overhead a crow was surveilling the scene, not so much flying as floating, drifting on the wind like a black kite. Mel was surprised to still hear the tourists on the overlook. The high fidelity acoustics of the canyon carried their voices so clearly and precisely that they seemed to be chatting right behind him. He felt their curious eyes peering down through binoculars—not at *them*, but at a hogan, a herd of sheep, the water running rippled in the sunlight, like the plated underbelly of a giant snake. Usually crowds gave Mel the shakes, but today the proximity of multiple eyes and voices offered an unusual sense of security—unusual for him.

"Tight squeeze," she said, disappearing through the aperture. "Easy for you."

"We'll see."

Tall and bony, nicknamed *hastiin tsints'osi*, "Stick-Man," by his Navajo co-workers, he couldn't understand why he was having even more difficulty than Dottie slipping through. His work shirt and Levis scraped against the sandy boulders that seemed to press against him like the teasing hands of the giant who had dropped them there. Squeezing through, Mel thought of the Hero Twins— Monster Slayer and Child Born of Water—and their encounter with the deadly Clashing Rocks on their journey to the home of Sun Bearer, whom they would petition for weapons—lightning arrows—to destroy *Yeitsoh*. Recalling the legend aroused in Mel a childlike burst of fantasy. His earlier apprehensions gave way to a swashbuckler spirit as he imagined himself on a similar quest, equally perilous, though in search of what he didn't know. He braced his palms against the facing boulders and shoved as if to divide the two like Samson or Hercules. Too old? He felt fine, now that he was out of the vertigo zone. Now if Gene were only here, the two of them, like the Hero Twins . . . Come on, Mel! You're forty-nine, old buddy. Save it for the kids. Story-time.

Sucking in a deep breath, he slipped through and found himself standing beside Dottie on a ledge that plunged down like an endless elevator shaft. The twisting canyon floor looked like a huge intestine or a long contorted muscle.

"Where's my parachute?" he said.

A quick smile; then, lowering her almond eyes, shyly, in the old way, like her mother and grandmother, not like the Ph.D. from Albuquerque, she was off again, scrambling up and around a smaller boulder. On the other side she picked up a trail so obscured by talus that, from the overlook, it had been no more evident than an erased pencil mark zig-zagging down. "Careful here," she said. Her sneakered foot pressed down on a slab of sandstone that tilted like a tabletop. He waited for her to pass and the slab to settle before stepping cautiously across. The voices above, he noted, were barely audible.

Switch-backing down through the shadows, Mel felt as if he were descending a radical staircase. It seemed so different from the neatly packed, much traveled path to White House Ruins, the only canyon trail open to the public: camera-lugging tourists, candy-wrappers, porta-johns, ice chests, broken bottle glass. The usual, the expected.

When she asked, that warm afternoon he popped the hood on her red coupe, "You've never been down Tunnel Trail?" he had been embarrassed to admit he hadn't. He resented her look of incredulity, this Navajo woman in hose and high-heels who looked about as Indian as he did, bald-headed and hoe in hand. American Gothic.

As he pondered it later, in private, his confession had opened the door to a dozen others that put him on the defensive again. True, he had done very little out here in the way of "things," other than carve himself a comfortable and livable niche, which was more than he could say for most of the *bilagaanas* who came and put in their year or two until something better opened up, then got the hell out. He wasn't too critical, though. He had come with the same objective: fresh out of college, teaching certificate in hand. Alone.

Twenty-seven years later he still had his job teaching fourth grade at the BIA boarding school and his silver trailer, an oversized tin can he kept meticulously clean and for which he paid sixty dollars a month rent; his books, which he read religiously but leisurely, and the vegetable garden he tended passionately. The other church members invited him to all of their socials and family activities, so he wouldn't feel left out; he attended only the annual Christmas party, though he never missed a regular Sunday service. Every three or four months he made the hundred mile pilgrimage into Gallup to stock up on books, eat at a real restaurant, and take in a movie – but mostly to reassure himself he wasn't missing much after all. He had grown fond of the terrain, the country. The austere emptiness that had once appeared so barren and foreboding – "picture the moon with a bad sunburn," he'd written home his first year – now conveyed peace and solitude. Gazing across the valley that seemed without beginning or end, he often imagined himself drifting alone on the South Pacific in search of some uncharted isle.

He cooked his own meals, darned his own socks, washed his own clothes. Each day was perfectly mapped out: Monday through

Friday, up at 5:30 for a light breakfast, then into the garden until a quarter-to-eight when he walked to the school. After putting in his seven hours it was back to the garden until six or six-thirty. After a modest supper he would read until he retired, usually around ten. Saturdays, more time for his garden and reading, a little shopping at the trading post, a few errands here and there. Sundays he had church. On alternate Thursdays he went to Gene's, or vice versa, for dinner and a game of chess—sometimes two, if one of them got lucky with a blitzkrieg win, but that was rare. Stepping carefully, the talus giving underfoot like a pile of ball-bearings, Mel wondered what Gene would do tonight, in lieu of chess and dinner with Mel. Grab a bite at the trading post? Fiddle with his fly rods in front of the TV? A little night fishing? With Gene, it was hard to say. Mel? No question: garden, dinner, books.

He knew that in print his life would read as boring as the Dow Jones, but it wasn't really. All of the small and simple pleasures would be edited out: the fertile smell of the soil after he tilled it each spring and fall and the sun rising out of the mesa like an air balloon on fire. The simple meals. A cool drink of water on a hot summer day. A warm bed on stormy nights when winter howled and banged on the door like the Big Bad Wolf. Sipping hot chocolate as he read about Lord Jim's redemption and Mr. Kurtz's white blindness in the bowels of the Dark Continent and First Woman's infidelity and Abraham on the mountain top for the love of God ready to plunge a knife into his only begotten son.

He also knew that people—high school kids, parents, co-workers, church people, even folks back home, those who still remembered—snickered at or pitied him, his lonely life in which nothing happened. Nothing? Why, in his own backyard he daily witnessed births and deaths, wars, triumphs, tragedies—hundreds of happenings he knew intimately and thoroughly, suffering along with the sufferers, protecting his leafy microcosm from the nibbling evils of the world. Nothing happened! As if a seed swelling to a sweet oval on the end of a vine were any less spectacular than a talking computer or a man on the moon. Nothing? Ha!

He had sailed every ocean and climbed every mountain and fought in every war. He had braved every adventure imaginable and every one was waiting at home on his shelf to be braved again. Except this one.

They had almost reached the bottom when the trail widened again, the talus giving way to red earth. Little puffs of dust powdered the cuffs of Dottie's blue-jeans as she marched untiringly along. Rounding another bend, they passed under a natural bridge that opened to a high-walled corridor of cottonwoods on one side and sandstone on the other, huge, muscle-bound flanks, smooth in parts, knobbed and gnarled in others, bulging at the base.

Mel was disconcerted to see a sign, a splintered square of plywood that seemed to be staring at him like an angry face. Though the flaked and faded lettering looked like Chinese cuneiform, he could sense the spirit of its message, a cryptic paraphrase of the neatly-lettered sign at the trailhead, which in so many words had politely warned him—all white men—to stay out. The massive walls seemed to reinforce this message: a panel of indignant portraits glaring down, twisted and contorted, an Indian Rushmore in the grotesque.

His skin raised goosebumps, but he told himself it was only the breeze which had swept in, a carryover from last night's pre-winter sneak attack which had turned his poor cherry tomatoes into geodes; that, or his joints acting up again. He had suspected arthritis for some time.

Grasses, then flowers, sprang up along the trail. He immediately recognized the orange flame-like petals of the Indian paintbrush and the rabbit weed, but the name of the spotted purple ones escaped him. Dottie pointed to one and said, "Rocky Mountain bee plant."

She stopped beside a small cactus—flat little mittens covered with spikes.

"Prickly pear," he said.

"The fruit looks ripe. Have you ever had any?"

He knew the plant but had never tasted the fruit. She plucked one of the purple bulbs and squeezed the waxy surface until it burst at the top. "Try it." She squeezed some into his palm.

"This part?"

She nodded. "It's like a fig. Some people use it to make jam. Have you ever had cactus jam?"

He confessed he hadn't.

He licked the sticky blob off his palm – bitter, grainy, like eating sweet and slimy sand.

He squeezed the rest of the fruit into his hand and licked it up quickly but neatly, like a cat.

"How is it?" she asked.

He nodded: Good. Very good.

The moment her back was turned, he spit his portion into his hand and stealthily dropped it on the trail, wiping his sticky fingers on his Levis.

She led him a short ways off the trail to a crumbling adobe dwelling, about the size of a bathroom, tucked in a crevice in the canyon wall. Beside it, half-buried in the sand, was a small kiva – round, more like a pit barbecue, he thought, than a sacred ceremonial room.

"Anasazi," she said.

Of course.

He silently identified the masonry as pre-classical. Chiseled into the sandstone bulge above the ruin were tiny figures – spirals, crosses, a row of stick-figure animals lined up like a shooting gallery. From his reading he recognized the supine figure of Cocopelli, the fertility god, and *hache*, the dagger in the ring. He saw potshards from two distinct Anasazi periods, one plain and corrugated, the other smooth and decorated with black zig-zags. He wanted to scoop up a handful to examine and run his palms across the rough adobe walls, but he sensed a breach of propriety. Besides, she had stopped only long enough to look, not touch, and was already hiking on ahead of him. The thought that this place was not much different than it had been a thousand years ago was both comforting and unsettling. He had the strange and awkward feeling he was about to meet an old pen pal face-to-face, except "pal" didn't fit.

Dottie was way ahead of him, marching right on, and he had to run to catch up. Thank God she finally stopped! She must have heard the clumsy clomp-clomping of his boots or the pounding of his heart—he was in no shape for this.

Bending at the waist, hands on his knees, he sucked in air as if it were being metered by the second. Catching his breath, he noticed that the voices from above had faded out completely. He tried to recall exactly when but couldn't. He imagined the people on top now, the old Navajo entrepreneurs packing up their blankets and jewelry for the night, the tourists in shorts taking snapshots. Now was the best time, as the sun barely touched the mesa and every crack and crevice filled with shadow. Too bad their cameras couldn't capture the peace and silence as well: nothing but a slight breeze rustling the leaves, a crow (the same black kite he had seen freeloading on the wind earlier?) caw-cawing far off, their feet marching softly along the padded sand. Mel now spoke in whispers, to preserve the reverence, but even then his voice seemed amplified a hundred times.

"Are we getting close?" He was concerned about the light.

As always, she answered softly, her voice blending with the breeze. "Not too far."

She quickened the pace. Waiting a quarter-mile ahead was a field of tall, autumn grass, shimmering like animal fur in the waning sunlight. Beyond it lay the wash, mud-brown, and beyond that the cottonwoods, a wall of green and gold cumulus. Watching the mesa slowly swallow the sun, Mel wondered why, instead of taking a direct route across the meadow to the water, she was detouring towards a spontaneous path parallel to the canyon wall.

"Lost, Dottie?" he asked with a smile.

She said something, but he couldn't hear it. Only her legs swishing through the waist-deep grass.

He became aware of a strong alkaline smell that brought to mind the ocean—forty years ago, visiting his uncle in Santa Monica—except this raw fragrance was even deeper, older, prehistoric. He breathed in and held it several seconds, as if filling his lungs for an extended period would increase his understanding of it.

Exhaling, he felt a sharp prick on his cheek, then a slight

touch, a pinpoint, on the back of his neck. He slapped but a fraction of a second too slow and took the sting. In seconds they were swarming all over him as he ducked his head and swung at them like a blind prizefighter.

"Mosquitoes?" She had stopped for him again, a white thread between her lips.

"The welcome wagon!" he cried, covering his head with his hands.

She turned back around as if to leave him to his fate but then knelt down and plucked three or four leaves from a small, insignificant-looking plant that vaguely resembled milkweed. These she crushed between her fingers until they were sticky with juice.

"Sit," she said.

He did.

With the crushed leaves she scoured his hands and arms, the back of his neck, his face, all exposed parts. Her touch made him nervous and warm and chilled simultaneously. He put up a calm front, but inside he was feverish, quivering. The feeling was hauntingly similar to when he had first admitted Gene into that small portion of his life: sleepless nights listening to the wind hammer his trailer as if trying to bust in; the ubiquitous dust seeping through the cracks like dirty ghosts, sand spirits. The first time, he couldn't hold his coffee cup steady for Gene to give him a refill.

"You okay?"

"What? I mean, yes, fine. Sure."

"What you need is to get away from that garden for awhile and do some fishing. I'm going up to Wheatfields on Saturday—"

"Saturday? No. No no. I can't. Saturday? No."

Not now. Not so soon.

Gene didn't push it.

"Maybe some other time?"

"Some other time. Yes. Sure."

As her fingers gently worked the juice into his skin, he studied her hands, reddish brown, the color of the soil they were standing on, though much softer, pliant but powerful. The ringed wrinkles around her knuckles looked black and oily, like a mechanic's. Her hands appeared to have never been washed yet they were as soft as a child's. Her nails were long, manicured, painted. Pink. They did not belong in the canyon.

"There," she said, rubbing the last bit into his neck.

"This will do the trick?" He stood up.

"It already has."

"How about you?"

She shrugged.

They hiked on, hordes of mosquitoes buzzing around his head, probing his clothing for openings but never lighting on his juice-protected parts. The taste on his lips was bitter mint. Dottie led the way, immune.

"Don't they go after you?" he asked, more surprised than envious. She glanced back, smiling. "They're Navajo mosquitoes."

Mel wasn't sure how to interpret that. He recalled Gene's warning—albeit jokingly—when he told him in the teacher's lounge he wouldn't be able to make it tonight. Gene, who was five years older but had been on the reservation only half as long as Mel, divorced, no kids, and no true passion other than fly fishing . . . predictably had masked any hurt or disappointment with humor. A sly wink. A nudge. His grinning premonition.

"Oh, come on. She's a former student, that's all. She's a kid."

"How old?" Smiling, the gold-glitter in his teeth. His astute nose, bloated at the tip, inky blue veins.

"I don't know. Twenty-four, twenty-five maybe."

The wink, the nudge. The smile.

"Come on."

He was probably at the trading post now, ordering a Navajo taco. Reading the *Gallup Independent*. Country western, Moe Bandy on the juke box.

The ground grew soft and moist, squish-squashing under foot like a giant sponge. Mel's foot got tangled in a web of blades and branches, tripping him up. He managed to catch his balance before hitting the ground but, untangling himself, he was reminded of the Hero Twins again, their encounter with the deadly eel grass. Using charms, chants, and sacred prayers, they had evaded all dangers. So he was using a Navajo guide and natural bug juice to . . . no no no. Hold your horses, Mel. You're going to her grandmother's orchard to pick fruit, that's all. A few ordinary apples.

For the first time since leaving the overlook, they walked in sunlight. The yellow warmth had a rejuvenating effect. Striding with renewed vigor through the golden grass, behind this Navajo girl–woman? definitely woman–the sunlight dancing on her semi-afro hair, dark, reddish brown, almost blond in spots, Mel felt a surge of joy unlike any he had experienced in . . . well, in a long long time. Not that he was often depressed. Heavens, he was *never* depressed! But this slap-happy childlike bursting-at-the-seams feeling was new to him. Light-footed and heady, walking on air, he grew wings on his heels and was ready to leap, to fly, to soar above the canyon like that carefree crow. He felt talkative, chatty. He wanted to voice his feelings and cry out exultantly, like a kid at the ball park when his team scores the winning run.

But what to say to her? He'd exhausted every topic in that first conversation, outside his trailer, where her car had broken down.

He hadn't recognized her at first. Kneeling in his garden, in overalls, carefully checking his zucchini for dung beetles, a leaf at a time, he had noticed her car–the red Triumph. The polished apple. Hood up. Then her legs: brown, water-smooth. Hose. A skirt to her knees. Unusual out here. He dropped his trowel and walked over.

"Trouble?"

A white girl's smile; a cheerleader. The hair too, a poodle-perm. Madison Avenue Indian. UNM sticker on her windshield. Too old to be a student. A prof maybe? Making a quick visit to mom or grandma. In and out fast. He knew the type. Research-bound.

It was her lips that gave him the first clue–thick, bloated, with a sharp cleft down the middle. And the acne scars. Pitted cheeks. Perforated copper. A premature case, he remembered.

Before she'd even reached junior high. A shame, on such a pretty face.

He monkeyed around under the hood. "Looks new."

"It is."

"Still under warranty?"

"I think so."

Women.

"I think it's just a loose plug wire. Go ahead and start 'er up."

One click and the engine purred. She got back out. "Thanks." He was reluctant but had to. "Do I know you?"

The smile. Rah! Rah! Rah! But sincere. Easy. "Dottie Littlesunday. Fourth grade."

The late-September sun baked his naked head as he thought back through the galleries of student faces, trying to place hers. Judging by her age, it must have been twenty-five years ago, at least. His very first year maybe? This was no college kid.

"Sure," he said. "Dottie Littlesunday."

He made a sweeping gesture, taking in his trailer, a couple of plywood shacks, the rusting shell of an abandoned car, the water tank on the butte. "Hasn't changed much."

Quickly depleting the conversation: What was she doing in town? How was her family? Married? Kids? Her job? He should have saved something, a little. Small talk had never been his strong point. But how could he have known?

"My grandmother, she has an orchard down there. You're welcome to come."

Her English was almost flawless, void even of the usual singsong intonations, but every so often the Navajo slipped through.

"Meet me at the overlook until four o'clock."

He said he would have to see. Maybe.

A shrug. Relaxed. No big deal.

"If you want . . . oh, you'll need a permit. *Bilagaanas* can't go down without a guide and a permit. The Ranger Station . . . just give them my name."

In some ways, a very Navajo way of handling it. So random and noncommittal. Tentative. In other ways, not at all Indian.

. . . . .

But with her protruding lips and dark poodle-perm, she looked more African than Indian and more anglo than either—that whittled body, a jazzercise queen in skirt, hose, and heels. Only her complexion and the high cheekbones. A little Indian blueblood. Grandma wouldn't recognize her—no. She would. They always did. The old ones.

She was humming faintly up ahead. Or was it giggling? He still wondered if this wasn't a big put-on. Part of him—the cynic or the optimist?—was still waiting for Gene and the rest of the staff to burst out of the cottonwoods singing Happy Birthday, surprise! But his birthday was four months away.

So why had she asked? Impulse? A diversion? Pity for this poor teacher growing old alone in the desert? Or maybe she was by nature friendly and outgoing? Surely there was no physical attraction. Tall, lanky, misproportioned, with cornflake-sized freckles patching his bald head and a long, stretched face everyone said needed feeding. His nose was too long, his pale eyes too small, pencil holes in a wooden mask. No, he wasn't handsome—by anyone's standards. The only thing that puzzled him more than why she had asked was why he had accepted.

All right. So he had nothing to say to her now. So what? He was literally bouncing along behind her, walking on springs, his blood bubbling, a celebration. Taking in everything, he marveled at the trees, the flowers, the interplay of light and shadow. His gaze skimmed across the grass like a hockey puck on ice. Then smacked stone. Dropped. And lay there, stunned, where earth met rock: a giant mortar or headstone securely sunken in the ground. He followed it slowly upward, five, six, seven hundred, a thousand feet, tilting his head way way back to take it all in, the smooth and rugged flanks, ax and chisel cuts gleaming purple on vermilion. The shadows seemed to be scaling the wall as quickly as his eyes. He stared at the sunlit rim, dipped in red fluorescence. Though he assured himself it was only an optical illusion, the massive rock seemed to be wavering in the sky, tilting inward, threatening a mighty fall but never quite going over the edge.

The shade line crept higher.

His eyes dropped just as the last patch of Dottie's blue t-shirt disappeared behind a boulder. Still dazed, he ran after her, his boots thudding awkwardly as he muttered mild curses, not so much at her as at the situation.

By the time he reached the wash, she was wading across, knee deep, her sneakers tied together by the laces and dangling around her neck. Her blue jeans were rolled up to her knees, like a tomboy. Whenever the water level dipped a bit, he caught a glimpse of her calves—smooth, brown, inverted cones. Navajo legs.

The main stream was fed by several small, interweaving ones. Skittering with sunlight, the water seemed alive, hopping, an army trotting uniformly along, flashing golden shields. The sour mud smell reminded him of something but he couldn't pinpoint what.

He unlaced his boots and stepped into the stream, the mud giving way then swarming around his feet, thick and cold. The chill of the water surprised him. Goosebumps rose as the pink chill climbed above his ankles. Dottie called from the other side: "Watch out for quicksand!"

He waved to her with a smile, hoping she wasn't serious. Over the years, from the overlook, he had seen trucks and animals get stuck and go under. Something downstream—a sharp-edged cluster of bones or branches—made him wonder.

By the time he reached the other bank the sparkle on the water was gone. The sun had flattened to a small hump on the mesa. It now burned like an oil lamp quickly running out of fuel. The landscape changed color and complexion. Gaping mouths and empty sockets withdrew into the rock.

Viewed from underneath, the cottonwoods weren't nearly as impressive, especially without the highlighting of the sun that heaped on colors like an impressionistic painting. Barefoot, he followed her through the maze of trees, the spiky grass and twigs piercing his tender skin. He toughed it out for several yards before stopping to remove the thorns from his feet and put back on his boots while she waited patiently. He felt like a fool, a dude, a tenderfoot. And he was—sure he was! But she didn't have to go and prove it to him, did she?

"Are your feet made of leather?" he asked, though he really meant her heart. He tugged angrily at his laces. She smiled but not in a teasing way. Her oriental eyes, which seemed to have darkened with the canyon, expressed sympathy. At that point he realized he was not the butt of some colossal joke. His anger quickly subsided.

"It's just a little further," she said.

He mumbled something about hearing an echo again. They crossed another stretch of soggy grass, the smell of dung fresh and ripe, a rustic sweetness. The silence seemed so deep that even the timid titter of a sparrow had the effect of shattering glass. Here there were no trails, no barbed wire fences; nothing clipped or trimmed. Farther ahead a lone appaloosa was grazing in a field of blue and gold flowers, its silver tail swishing lazily back and forth. One look at the two intruders and it galloped off in a panic, as if it had never before crossed eyes with a two-legged creature.

The canyon walls rose before them like a dark barricade. Mel thought it couldn't be too much farther because there was nowhere else to go, but she led him around one more bend which opened into a small box canyon which turned out to be a giant cornfield. Again he was struck by the spontaneity. Seeds seemed to have been tossed down randomly from the sky. Big, healthy stalks, impressive even to a green thumb like Mel, thrust up in uneven rows, sharing the soil with sunflowers taller than he was. Following the black iron streaks running down the canyon walls, he could trace where the water from summer thunderstorms coursed through the fields, gratis irrigation. Not exactly a garden paradise, but everything possible seemed to thrive here—corn, weeds, flowers, grasses of all varieties. A fragrance belonging to none of them pervaded—as strong and ripe as the other but much sweeter; an autumn harvest smell.

They hiked a bit farther and saw it, hidden just below a gentle rise beyond the cornfield: two rows of slightly dwarfed trees decorated with what looked like red and green Christmas ornaments.

Dottie dropped her sneakers and ran.

By the time he arrived, she was sitting in the crotch of one of the trees, munching on an apple. The sweet scent and crispy crunch sparked his appetite. She reached up and plucked four or five more, examining them carefully before dropping them into her little nap sack. Then she climbed down.

"Here," she said, handing him one.

It was small and still a little green. A bit bigger than a golf ball and almost as hard. He bit into it—hard and crispy, a little bitter, too. But he gobbled it up hungrily and then plucked a handful for himself and sat down with her on the rough, spiky grass, their backs leaning against opposite sides of the trunk as if to balance or support it. The sun was a heap of hot coals on the mesa. Thicker than ever, the mosquitoes buzzed around Mel, fit-to-be-tied, hungrily waiting for the repellant to wear off. The sky was changing like a big color wheel, the sundown passion cooling to fuchsia, mauve, black blue.

Darkness filled the canyon a drop at a time.

She broke the silence.

"How are they?"

"Good. Excellent."

"Did you ever marry?"

Her question would have startled him, but she had asked with such innocent candor, as if inquiring about his current address, that he answered with equal frankness. "No. Never."

"I remember you weren't before."

He crunched on his apple.

"Did you ever try?" she asked.

He thought that was an odd way to put it, and perhaps prying a little too deep. "No," he said, but this was a lie.

There had been a girl, a young woman he had met his freshman year at BYU. She was almost as shy and withdrawn but had taken the risk and asked him to the Spring Dance. Ladies' Choice. Clandestine invitations. Curious, he had accepted. They didn't talk much that first night, but they smiled at each other often and went out several times after. Things were going very well, he had thought.

He left on his two-year church mission in June. For thirteen months they wrote each other faithfully. Matrimony had never been discussed explicitly, but when he had boarded the plane for Minnesota she had kissed him full on the mouth, in public, and had whispered in his ear, "I think the Salt Lake Temple would be nice, don't you?" But his second Christmas in Minneapolis he didn't get a card—no card, no letter, no nothing until March; then a token letter, full of drab details: weather, school, her father's hernia operation.

Leaning against the apple tree, the rough and jagged bark slowly digging into his spine, Mel recalled the ugly, snowy day in April, two months before his release, when he received his official Dear John. At first he was hurt, then angry, then bitter. Not just towards her, but women in general. For a year he didn't date at all. Then, partly to placate his fretting mother ("You've been off your mission a year, Mel . . . "), he asked out a few girls, but things rarely warmed beyond the first date. A few times he dropped them, but usually it was vice versa. He wasn't sure if it was his unrealistically high criteria, if his cynicism was showing, or if he was just boring. In the end, he was afraid.

He took a teaching job on the reservation because the market had been so tight, but also to escape—family, friends, the eternal matchmakers. He had planned on staying a year, maybe two.

"Do you ever get lonely?" she asked.

He felt no obligation to answer but did anyway, as a father does an inquiring child. "Sometimes. Not very often."

"Why don't you go home?"

He finished off his apple and tossed the core aside. "This is home," he said, a little irritated.

"I'm sorry," she said. "I'm getting too personal."

"No, no," he said, embarrassed for getting upset. She stood up, brushing off the seat of her pants. "Would you like to see my grandmother's hogan?" The uncalculated innocence. Like a script from a fairy tale.

· · · · ·

He followed her behind the grove. She removed a flashlight from her napsack and switched it on. The narrow funnel of light picked out a domed little dwelling, a giant nipple protruding from a small hill. In the scanty light Mel could barely make out the caulk lines between the logs. Thin grasses sprouted like elephant hairs on the mud roof.

There was no padlock on the door. He followed her in. She passed the light cursorily around the interior. It picked out a wood stove, a scuffed-up stool, a plastic container which read SNOW CAP LARD, and a battered old trunk.

They sat facing one another on the sandy floor, with the flashlight lying between them like a small fire. The hogan smelled cool and damp. She offered him another apple.

"No thanks."

She helped herself.

The dark privacy of the hogan emboldened him. "I read somewhere," he said, clearing his throat, "I read that Navajos have a secret name."

"You mean a Navajo name? Yes. Many do. The traditional ones."

"Do you?"

She looked down at the patch of light dividing them. "Yes."

"Will you tell it to me?" He felt an urgent need to know; to have her divulge this much.

She smiled faintly, more sad than happy.

"It isn't *bahadzid*, is it? Telling someone? A friend?"

She stared at the light, an oval on the sandy floor. In some ways it resembled a gaping mouth; in others, a dim, lopsided sun. Bright in the center, gray around the perimeter. She stared for several minutes before leaning across the light and whispering into his ear.

"That's a war name, isn't it?"

"Most are."

Several minutes passed in silence.

"We'd better go," he said, rising.

"It will be hard to cross in the dark," she said.

He opened the door and looked out. The sun's after-glow

had spread a fluorescent red wash across the horizon, turning the juniper silhouettes to orange sparks. The canyon shadows had fused and deepened throughout; the darkness was complete.

"It's getting cold," she said. "Maybe we should start a fire."

He continued looking out. On the far side, right around where he thought the overlook was, a pair of red taillights lit up like cat-eyes and slowly drifted off. A few tourists, photography nuts, might still be up there, peering down in wonder and mystery and awe. Through binoculars they may have seen the sheer cliffs draped in shadowy colors, the cottonwoods like huge pom-poms, the river, its glitter now gone. But they hadn't felt the water's chill gripping their ankles or the scratch of grass and thistle or smelled the sweet apple scent or the ripe horse dung or the bitter mint repellant rubbed tenderly into their flesh. They hadn't seen this hogan or this orchard or . . . him. They hadn't seen him! Not like this, not now, part of this very exclusive secret.

His tin trailer seemed millenniums away; his entire life, in fact. He wondered if he had ever truly ridden a Schwinn one-speed down the streets of Phoenix or watched Duke Snider club one out of the L.A. Coliseum. Framed in the doorway, a gawky silhouette, he thought about his life, all he had and hadn't done. Along the way he had made decisions, some good, some bad, which had brought him to this place at this moment under these circumstances. He was almost fifty, half a century, but that no longer seemed so terribly old. What was fifty years in the bowels of this canyon which had been sculptured over the course of ten million? Or those stars which had been burning for fifty times ten million? Only a handful sprinkled the desert sky, but soon it would be packed, jammed, sparkling with possibilities. He imagined this hogan, a campfire, the head-banded grandfather telling stories of Coyote the trickster and the Hero Twins and the Navajo creation story, of First Man and First Woman, of beginnings and endings and re-beginnings.

A muffled crunch fractured the silence. He glanced back. Hands locked around bent knees, she was gazing thoughtfully at the small oval of light on the sand, munching slowly. His thoughts raced through the many stories and legends he had read.

. . . . .

"There are some blankets in the chest, I think," she said.

He turned back around. Watching the stars multiplying over-head, he felt naked in the cool night air. He waited for one of the stars to drop and dissolve into the night, but they remained firm in their places. He stepped outside. "I'll get some wood," he said. "For the fire."